THE HARVEST MURDER
BY
JOHN RHODE

CONTENTS:

CHAPTER I

UNDER ordinary circumstances Sergeant Wragge would have greatly resented being disturbed at the untimely hour of nine o'clock on Sunday morning. But past experience had taught him that hop-picking time was altogether exceptional. Almost anything might be expected to happen while it continued. And on this particular morning, September 1st, hop-picking had been in progress for about a week.

The effect of the hop-picking season upon a little place like Culverden must be emphasised at the outset. For a period of three or four weeks every year the normal quietude of the countryside is completely shattered. An influx of townsfolk, far outnumbering the regular inhabitants, descends upon it. The fact that one farm alone is in the habit of employing three thousand workers, drawn almost without exception from the East End of London, may convey some idea of the extent of this invasion. Nor are the hop-pickers alone the only invaders which have to be reckoned with. For during the week-end all their friends and relations come down in a solid phalanx to visit them.

As may be supposed, then, the usual routine of things at Culverden is apt to be disorganised during hop-picking time. The inhabitants regard hop-picking very much as they would some recurrent natural phenomenon. It is an essential point in their calendar. People say that such and such a thing happened just before last hop-picking, or that somebody's wedding took place a couple of months after hop-picking five years ago. So powerfully does the upheaval of hop-picking impress itself upon their imaginations and memories.

When the telephone call came through Sergeant Wragge had already finished his breakfast. He had just put on his uniform and was ready to start off on a morning round of inspection. He left his cottage without any undue haste, took his bicycle from the shed from the back door and rode off.

His route took him through the main street of the little town of Culverden, and even at this hour the symptoms of hop-picking were unmistakable. Normally the street would have been practically deserted. But on this particular Sunday morning, which happened to be brilliantly fine, it was full of life. Groups of girls, in the most surprising finery, stood about laughing and chattering with extraordinary animation. The male element was less predominant. There was, as yet, nothing to bring the men from their belated sleep in the shelter of the hop houses. Only a few resigned figures leaned against the walls of the public houses, which would not open for another three hours. Some of these showed symptoms of alertness as the Sergeant passed on his bicycle. It was just possible that, the coast being thus clear, the landlord might be induced to open his window, if only for a moment. It needs so short a moment for a thirsty man to imbibe a pint of beer!

Sergeant Wragge smiled slightly to himself. Experience had taught him that it was folly to be unreasonable. He knew very well that during hop-picking the licensing laws were not observed to the letter. Mere drinking, in his eyes, was not a crime, at whatever hour of the day it might be indulged. And this morning, according to the telephone message which he had received, a really serious matter was awaiting his attention. He glanced at the thirsty loungers, at the ostentatiously closed doors and windows of the public houses, and passed on.

Once clear of the town the road ran between a long succession of hop gardens on either side. The hops, dependent from their tall poles, hung in fragrant bunches. Here and there among the gardens lay a green meadow upon which the long row of hopper huts were erected. These were often no more than mere sheds, but they seemed capable of accommodating an astounding number of people. Each group of hopper huts had its own cook-house, and around these a dense crowd of men, women and children were assembled. Cheerful crowds they were too, thoroughly enjoying the experience of a fine morning in the country. Sergeant Wragge eyed them benevolently. They were all right, these queer London folk, when you knew how to treat them. It was rarely that the hop-pickers themselves gave any trouble. But some of the friends who came down to visit them at the week-ends were pretty tough customers, and among so many thousands there was no possibility of keeping proper track of them.

For a mile and a half the almost unbroken succession of hop gardens continued. All this way, dotted at intervals along the road-side, rose the conical shapes of the oast houses, sometimes singly, sometimes in groups of three or more. The faint scented vapour floating from their cowls was the only indication of the fire burning beneath the layers of hops. The expert hop driers, local men all, who tended those fires remained invisible. The Sergeant glanced at the passers-by he met. But their faces were all strange to him, hop-pickers from the various farms strolling aimlessly towards Culverden.

As he proceeded along the road he reached a point where the hop gardens ended abruptly. There was no apparent reason why they should do so. Probably it was because of some change in the nature of the soil. Beyond this point the aspect of the landscape began to change. The hop gardens gave place to orchards and woods, and the road, leaving the comparatively flat plain, began to ascend gently. Standing on the rising ground ahead of him, Sergeant Wragge could discern a cluster of houses.

This was the village of Matling, and just beyond it was his destination, a house known as Paddock Croft.

He pedalled along the now practically deserted road. He was thinking not so much of the immediate business on hand as of the loin of roast pork which awaited him for dinner. Mrs. Wragge had been a cook in a gentleman's house before he married her, and her roast pork was a thing to dream of. The crackling just caught so that its delicious crispness crumbled in the mouth. The potatoes baked with the joint to a golden brown. The apple sauce not too liquid and free from any suggestion of core or pip. And finally the sage and onions, both grown in the sergeant's own garden. With such a meal in prospect even an uphill bicycle ride had its compensations.

It was merely by chance soon after he had passed the Chequers that he noticed something bright lying half-hidden by the wayside. The sun happened to catch it, and that attracted his attention. He glanced at it without any particular interest and then deliberately stopped his bicycle and dismounted. He walked to the edge of the road, bent down and inspected the object more closely. It was a curious thing to find lying in such a place. A heavy butcher's knife with a wooden handle and a blade at least twelve inches long. Sergeant Wragge wondered how on earth it could have got there. He bent down and picked it up. It was sharp enough, although the blade was spotted with something that looked like rust. Wragge decided that he had better take charge of it. He couldn't leave a thing like that lying by the wayside. Somebody might come along and tread on it. Very likely they'd get a nasty cut. He took a length of string from his pocket and with this carefully tied the knife to the cross-bar of his bicycle. Then he mounted once more and proceeded on his way.

He reached Paddock Croft about half an hour after he had started from Culverden. The house was squarely built and of medium size. It stood some little distance back from the road and was approached by a short drive. As Wragge rode up the drive the front door of the house opened and its owner, Mr. Speight, came out to meet him.

Speight was a man of middle-age who had retired early from a lucrative position of some sort in the City. He had been settled at Paddock Croft for a matter of five years or so, and had by now become a member of local societies. He and Mrs. Speight entertained freely and were correspondingly entertained in return. Sergeant Wragge, as he once expressed himself confidentially, had no particular use for him. It wasn't that he had anything definite against him, but in Wragge's opinion a man of Speight's position and means might do a little more for his poorer neighbours than he did. He was reputed to be a hard man and was not over-popular in the village of Matling.

"Good-morning, Sergeant," said Speight in reply to Wragge's rather perfunctory salute. "I'm glad you've come along so promptly. I've been on the look-out for you ever since I telephoned just now. It's a most annoying affair. One of those confounded hop-pickers is at the bottom of it, I'll be bound. Come along in and I'll tell you the story."

He led the way into the hall. "I'll take you upstairs and show you where it happened in a moment," he continued. "I expect you'd like to hear first why it wasn't discovered until this morning. You see, my wife and I went out to dinner and bridge last night with Colonel Cranby, who lives on the other side of Culverden. We left here in the car at half-past seven and weren't back till after midnight. My wife had a shocking bad headache all the evening. It was terribly hot and close at the Cranbys'. So when she came back she undressed and went to bed at once. She never thought of looking in her jewel case until this morning and when she did she found that it was empty."

"Who remained in the house during your absence, Mr Speight?" Wragge asked.

"Oh, the servants. Three of them, you know. Their quarters are at the other side of the house and they wouldn't have heard anything. The jewel case was standing on my wife's dressing-table where it always is. I've told her more than once that she ought to keep it locked up, but women are so careless in those matters, you know. And the fellow got in by the window, there's no doubt of that. There's some soil from the garden on the carpet just inside it. But come along, I expect you'd like to see for yourself."

He led the way upstairs into a luxuriously-equipped dressing-room. Wragge, glancing round, saw that it had two casement windows, both of which were now tightly shut. Speight pointed to the carpet in front of one of these. "There you are," he exclaimed triumphantly.

Wragge followed the direction of his pointing finger. On the light blue carpet there was a dark smudge which upon inspection proved to consist of several grains of earth. "This window was left open while you were out, Mr. Speight?" the Sergeant asked.

"Yes, it was wide open. Wide as it could be, and hooked back. Both Mrs. Speight and myself like as much fresh air as we can get. And the jewel box was standing exactly where you see it now. I wouldn't let anybody touch it until you came. That's it on the corner of the dressing-table."

Speight pointed out a silver casket about the size of a small biscuit tin. "My wife keeps nearly all her jewellery in that," he continued. "It was given to her as a wedding present by her godmother and she's very much attached to it. It wouldn't have happened if she'd kept her things locked up in a safe as I've always advised her. Last night, when she was dressing before we went out, she opened the box to take out a couple of emerald ear-rings. And when she next looked at the box before she came down to breakfast this morning it was empty. Absolutely cleaned out. Not a thing left in it."

"Can you give me a list of the articles that are missing, Mr. Speight?" Wragge asked.

Speight shrugged his shoulders. "I'll do my best," he replied. "I asked my wife as soon as she told me of the loss if she knew what had been taken. She wrote down all she could remember on a piece of paper, but we can't be certain that she's thought of everything. I've got the paper in my pocket. Here it is."

Wragge took the slip of note-paper which Speight handed him and glanced over it. About a dozen articles of jewellery were enumerated. Diamond rings, a pearl necklace, a pair of platinum bracelets, various pendants set with precious stones and so forth. A collection, Wragge imagined, of some considerable value.

Speight's theory was probably correct. The garden mould upon the carpet certainly suggested that the thief entered by the window. The Sergeant opened the window and glanced out. He saw that the sill was no more than ten feet above the ground level. Directly beneath the window was a narrow flower bed and beyond that a grass plot. Wragge shut the window and turned to Speight.

"I think I should like to go down and look about outside," he said.

Speight led the way downstairs through a side door into the garden. "That's the window of my wife's dressing-room," he said, pointing towards the house.

They walked to the flower bed immediately beneath it. There had been no rain for some days and the ground was fairly hard. But in spite of this, at the outer edge of the flower bed two rounded depressions were plainly to be seen. These were about fifteen inches apart and perhaps a couple of inches deep. The Sergeant looked at them and nodded wisely. "Have you got a ladder about the place, Mr. Speight?" he asked.

"Why yes, there's a ladder hanging up against the garden wall not more than a few yards from here," Speight replied.

"I should like to see it, if you don't mind, Mr. Speight," said Wragge.

Speight took him across the grass plot to a wall upon which were trained a number of fruit trees. They passed through a gate set in this wall which led them into the kitchen garden. On the farther side of the wall were a couple of iron hooks and on these was hung a twenty-rung ladder.

The Sergeant looked at it for a few seconds, then picked it up and carried it to the window. There he raised it against the wall of the house with the lower ends resting in the depressions he had already noticed. The ends of the ladder fitted these depressions exactly. Further, with the ladder resting against the wall in this position, it would be a perfectly simple matter for any one to climb up it and so step into the dressing-room through the window.

"Yes, that's the way the thief got in, no doubt," said Speight. "Very smart of you to tumble at once to the ladder like that, Sergeant. Now the point is, who was it, and what's become of the jewellery? I can't tell you how upset my wife is by this affair. She went straight back to bed as soon as she discovered what had happened."

The Sergeant made no reply, for at present these questions were unanswerable. He walked slowly up and down the grass plot looking about him. "The servants' quarters are on the other side of the house, you say, Mr. Speight?" he said.

"Yes, that's right. And the only windows on the ground floor looking out this way are those of the drawing-room and the dining-room. Since we were out there would be nobody in either of those rooms, of course. The fellow, whoever he was, could have put the ladder up against the wall without anybody being a penny the wiser. What I can't understand is why he left the jewel box behind him. It's of considerable value, as you can see for yourself."

"Too bulky to carry," the Sergeant replied tersely. "Just cleaned it out and emptied the contents into his pocket. Well, I'll do my best for you, Mr. Speight. You don't mind if I potter round here for a bit, do you?"

"You must take any steps you think fit," Speight replied. "I think I'll go in now and tell my wife you're here. I'm sure she'll be relieved to know that something is being done about it."

The Sergeant was rather relieved to be rid of him. He began to explore minutely the outside of the premises. There was just a possibility that the thief had left some sort of clue behind him, but on the hard and unyielding ground this seemed rather a faint hope. It did not take him long to discover that there was no need for any one wishing to reach that side of the house to approach it from the road. The garden sloped toward an open meadow from which it was separated merely by a four-foot iron railing. Across this meadow was a public pathway. It would be the simplest thing in the world for any one to leave this pathway, cross the meadow, climb the iron fence and so find themselves in the garden. Another point which Wragge ascertained was this. Although only the first floor of the house was visible from the pathway, the wall upon which the ladder had hung was plainly to be seen. In fact, from one point of the path the ladder itself could be discerned without difficulty. The path from its appearance seemed to be frequently used. Indeed, during his inspection of it, two or three straggling hop-pickers passed him, wending their way towards Matling.

It was on his way back to the house from this path that Wragge made his first discovery. It had occurred to him that an intruder wishing to reach the house would not risk walking openly across the grass plot. He would instinctively seek some cover for his approach. And, as it happened, this was readily available. A gravel path skirted the grass plot, and this was overhung by the branches of a line of ornamental trees. Wragge followed this route with his eyes upon the ground, seeking some unlikely clue. He happened to look up and saw in the branches of the trees above him a patch of scarlet. Closer investigation showed a suspended paper cap, bright green with a red cockade upon it.

Such an object in such a place might well have puzzled any one unacquainted with the neighbourhood. But it did not puzzle Sergeant Wragge. His experience of the etiquette of the hop-picking fraternity was profound. It was considered the thing for visitors to the hop fields to assume a holiday appearance. This was usually done by the wearing of paper caps of divers hues and shapes. It was not likely that Mr. Speight or any of his household were in the habit of wearing paper caps in the garden. This cap, then, had almost certainly been the property of one of the hop-pickers or their friends.

He detached it carefully from the thorn which had pierced it and turned it over in his hands. It was very slightly damp and had lost some of its original stiffness. But the colours seemed as bright as ever, and the paper was untorn. It could not have been exposed to the dew and the weather for more than one night. This seemed to the Sergeant to prove conclusively that the cap had belonged to the thief. This find was an unexpected piece of luck. Surely somebody would remember the man or woman who had been wearing this cap on the previous day. And then Wragge smiled rather ruefully. Remember, yes. They might remember all right, but whether they would confide their memories to the police was quite another question.

Despite a minute examination of the exterior of the premises, the Sergeant found no further clue. He folded up the cap and put it in his pocket. Then he re-entered the house, where he found Speight awaiting him. "Any luck, Sergeant?" the latter asked.

Wragge did not feel disposed to disclose the discovery of the cap. "As good as can be expected, Mr. Speight," he replied. "I shall have to go away now and make certain inquiries in the neighbourhood. And I shall be very grateful if you will allow me to take the jewel box with me."

"The jewel box!" Speight exclaimed. "Why, whatever for? It's quite empty, as you've seen for yourself."

The Sergeant certainly had seen this for himself. But he had also noticed that the jewel box was of silver and brightly polished. If the thief had removed its contents he must first have opened it to do so. He must therefore have touched it, and polished silver was an almost ideal surface for recording fingerprints. However, he had no wish to explain all this to Speight. "It is possible that it might assist in the investigation," he replied.

Speight looked doubtful. "Well, you'll have to take it away if you want to, I suppose," he said. "I think I won't say anything about it to my wife, though. She wouldn't like it at all, I'm sure. She values that box very highly, you know. She was very fond of her god-mother, who has been dead for several years."

"I assure you that the greatest care shall be taken of it, Mr. Speight," said the sergeant. "I wonder if you could let me have a cardboard box and a few sheets of newspaper?"

Speight produced these without difficulty. The sergeant fetched the jewel box, being careful to hold it at one point only. Then he placed it in the cardboard box, packing it round very carefully with newspaper. He tied the package to the handlebars of his bicycle and rode away, promising Mr. Speight he would hear again from him very shortly.

As he left the house Wragge looked at the clock in the hall-it was barely half-past eleven. Plenty of time for him to do what he had to do and then enjoy his dinner. He would enjoy it with the greater zest because he felt distinctly pleased with himself. That paper cap had indeed been a lucky find.

CHAPTER II

IMMEDIATELY upon his return to Culverden, Sergeant Wragge communicated with his superior, the Superintendent of the district. As a result of their conversation, Mrs. Speight's jewel box was despatched that afternoon by a trusty messenger to Scotland Yard. Since Inspector Waghorn of the Criminal Investigation Department was on duty, the package was delivered to him.

Inspector Waghorn was a young man with a university education who had entered the police force by the medium of the Police College at Hendon. At this time he was acting as assistant to Superintendent Hanslet, well known as one of the leading lights of the Yard. To his friends in the force, who were many, the Inspector was popularly known as Jimmy. He was already beginning to gain something of a reputation as a smart officer.

The arrival of the silver box with its accompanying request for examination by the fingerprint department was to Jimmy no more than a matter of routine. Finding himself with nothing particular to do that afternoon, he took the box to the fingerprint department himself. The officer in charge of that department, with whom Jimmy was on excellent terms, eyed the box critically.

"What's this, Jimmy?" he asked. "It looks expensive, whatever it is. I can't bring myself to believe that you're bringing me the freedom of the city in a silver casket."

"Fine bit of plate, isn't it?" Jimmy replied. "It's been sent up from a place called Culverden for your inspection. From what I can gather something has been stolen from it, and the local people believe that you may be able to find the fingermarks of the thief."

The officer in charge of the department took the box and held it up to the light. "It's been polished fairly recently," he remarked. "If there are any fingermarks on it we ought to be able to find them. As it is, I can see some faint smudges which may or may not turn out to be prints. It's a matter for a little dusting powder, I fancy."

The expert carried out the necessary dusting with grey powder. "Fingermarks all right," he exclaimed immediately. "Two sets of them, by the look of it. We can only hope one set hasn't confused the other. Wait a minute, till I get my magnifying glass to work upon them."

For a couple of minutes he examined the surface of the box intently and in silence. "Half a dozen really fine specimens," he said at last. "The complete fingermarks, four fingers and thumbs, both hands of two separate people. I rather fancy that one of these people is a woman, but I can't be sure. And the other fingermarks I've seen before, I'm certain of that. I wouldn't mind betting you that we've already got them in our records."

"Wonderful how easy detection is to chaps like you!" Jimmy murmured.

"Easy!" exclaimed the other. "Why, it's as simple as falling off a log. If you'd been working at fingerprints as long as I have, my lad, you'd learn to recognise them at a glance. I'm not going to pretend that I remember to whom each set of prints belongs, but if I've seen them before I know them again. Wait a minute."

He glanced fixedly once more at the fingerprints which his operations had disclosed, then went to one of the set of cupboards that occupied the sides of the rooms. From this he extracted a file which he consulted, turning over the leaves slowly one by one. In a few moments he extracted a leaf and held it out for Jimmy's inspection. "There you are," he said, "the very identical prints. You'll want the prints on this box photographed, of course. I'll see to that for you, and send the lot up to your room as soon as I've finished."

"Thanks," Jimmy replied. "You're a bit of a wizard in your way, aren't you? But one trifling detail seems to have escaped you."

"What's that?" the expert asked suspiciously.

Jimmy laughed. "You haven't told me who the prints belong to."

"Oh, that!" said the expert with a sudden lack of interest. "You don't suppose we attach the life history of our subjects to these files, do you? You'll have to go next door for that. The man's name is Christopher Elver, and the number of his record is 17534. Now run along and leave me to get on with those photographs."

Armed with this information Jimmy went to the Criminal Record office where he obtained the file numbered 17534 and marked with the name of Christopher Elver. This he took up to his own room for perusal. By the time he had read through the various documents contained in the file, he was fully conversant with the history of Christopher Elver.

Some nine years previously the police had become aware that a fairly extensive system of drug distribution was at work in London. At last, as a result of long and patient work on the part of the C.I.D., the focus of this system was traced to a small shop in Lambeth kept by a woman who gave her name as Mrs. Hawkins. Mrs. Hawkins was arrested and search of her shop resulted in the discovery of considerable quantities of cocaine. Mrs. Hawkins refused to give any explanation of how she came to be in possession of the stuff, but various indications made it seem extremely probable that the drug had been imported to this country from Germany. Further, it was ascertained by inquiry that a young man known in the neighbourhood as Sea Joe was a regular visitor to the shop.

At this stage the conduct of the investigation had devolved upon Superintendent, then Inspector, Hanslet. Mrs. Hawkins had proved unexpectedly obstinate; it was impossible to obtain from her any information regarding this man Joe. However, the nickname had seemed significant to Hanslet. It suggested to him that some seaman frequenting the Port of London was the agent who was importing the drug. He arranged for a strict watch to be kept throughout the port and, within ten days of the raid upon Mrs. Hawkins' shop, he detained a ship's steward as he was in the act of stepping ashore at Butler's wharf. This man was taken to the police station and searched. To Hanslet's intense satisfaction he was found to be carrying a supply of cocaine.

In the face of this discovery the man attempted no sort of defence. He admitted that the cocaine was intended for Mrs. Hawkins, with whom he had done business for many years. He stated that his name was Christopher Elver, that he was known to his intimates as Sea Joe, and that he was employed as steward on the steamship Etrurian, trading between London and the Elbe. He gave his age as thirty-one and declared that nobody but himself and Mrs. Hawkins knew of his criminal activities.

Mrs. Hawkins, on being told that Elver had been arrested and had mentioned her name, became more communicative. She was quite prepared to tell the police everything she knew about him. But her statement, though long and vituperative, amounted in the end to very little. It appeared that Christopher Elver was his real name, and that he had posed as her nephew, though actually they were not related in any way. She added mysteriously that there was a girl who might be able to tell the police even more than she could. But the only information she could give concerning this girl was that Elver had brought her to the shop more than once to have a cup of tea. Elver, upon being pressed for information on this point, had strenuously denied the existence of any such girl. He had said, with some show of heat, that the old woman was telling a pack of lies as was her usual habit.

And Hanslet, who by this time had had considerable experience of Mrs. Hawkins' powers of imagination, was inclined to credit this. Nobody on board the Etrurian knew anything of the girl, and since it seemed that she could have played at most only a minor part in the conspiracy, Hanslet let the matter drop. Elver had been sentenced to seven years' imprisonment and had been released two years ago. A final note, dated the current year, was attached to the file. "Elver now under observation of M Division."

Wonderful how simple a thing detection can be sometimes, Jimmy thought. The sequence of events appealed to his imagination. Not a link was missing, and each was perfect in itself. The silver box with its surface so perfectly adapted to the reception of fingerprints. The instant recognition of those prints by the expert, and the immediate identification of the person to whom they belonged. The previous history of that person neatly recorded and filed. The fact that, as a time-expired convict, he was still under the observation of the police. It only remained to arrest the man and to find in his pockets the proceeds of his burglary.

But this most desirable conclusion was not Jimmy's job. He picked up his telephone and put a call through to Sergeant Wragge at Culverden. He gave the Sergeant a resume of his discoveries and tactfully asked him what steps he proposed to take.

"Of course if I can do anything to help you, you've only got to say the word," he concluded.

"That's very good of you sir," replied Wragge, gratefully. "You see, at hop-picking time like this it's very difficult for us chaps to get away for more than an hour at a time. If it wouldn't be troubling you too much, sir, I would be very grateful if you could get in touch with M Division and ask them to detain the man and then let me know."

"Right, I'll do that straight away," said Jimmy. "I'll send you back that silver box as soon as the fingerprint people have done with it. Perhaps we may have the pleasure of meeting some day, Sergeant. Good-evening."

Jimmy glanced at the clock. It was now after six o'clock and his turn of duty at the Yard had expired. He had nothing special to do that evening and it occurred to him that the simplest way of rounding off the matter would be to pay a personal visit to Southwark Police Station, the headquarters of M Division. He left the Yard, walked over Waterloo Bridge, and took a bus to his destination.

At the police station he had no difficulty in finding a sergeant who knew all about Elver.

"He's the chap who did seven years for cocaine smuggling, sir. He was luckier than some after he'd been let out of goal. He got a job almost at once, and kept it for a year or more. No more than a labourer's job, but still that's something these days. Then the firm he was working for closed down and he went out of a job for a bit. However, he got taken on as a casual labourer at the Surrey Commercial Docks and he's at that still. He lodges with a man called Pilbeam and his wife at 85 Halibut Street. Close to his work and not so very far from here. Perhaps you'd like me to go along and make inquiries, sir?"

"It wouldn't be a bad idea," Jimmy replied. "And if you've no objection I'll come along with you."

"I'd be very glad to show you where the man lives, sir," said the sergeant.

They took a bus which deposited them at the end of Halibut Street, a narrow, rather unsavoury thoroughfare in the wilderness of Bermondsey. Upon knocking at the door of No. 85, this was opened by a slatternly woman. In reply to the Sergeant's inquiry, she said that her name was Mrs. Pilbeam, and that she had a lodger by name Chris Elver. Her lodger, however, was away, and she did not expect him back until late that night.

"Where has he gone to, Mrs. Pilbeam?" the Sergeant asked.

"Couldn't say," replied the woman surlily. "T'aint none of my business. He's not gone far, that I'll warrant."

"How do you know he hasn't gone far?" asked the sergeant sharply.

"Because he hasn't got no money, that's why. I took all the wages what he drew on Friday evening for the board and lodging that was coming to me."

"Does your husband know where he's gone to?"

"Couldn't say, I'm sure. You'd better ask him. You'll find him along at the Tanners' Arms around the corner."

"When did you last see Elver?"

"Haven't seen him since he went to work on Saturday morning," replied the woman shortly. And that ended the conversation.

Jimmy and the Sergeant went to the Tanners' Arms where they discovered Mr. Pilbeam ensconced in the public bar. But that worthy, a heavy broad-shouldered man of somewhat ferocious aspect, wouldn't or couldn't give them any information. He hadn't seen Elver since early on Saturday morning when they both left Halibut Street on their way to work. Elver had tried to borrow five bob from him, on the pretext that he wanted to go and get some money from somebody who lived in the country, but the attempt had been unsuccessful. Anyhow, Elver was cleaned out, and there didn't seem any prospect of his pockets being replenished before next pay day. As to where he had gone or why, Mr. Pilbeam professed a profane indifference.

"He can stop in my house as long as he pays his way," he said. "But when he's out of it he can go to hell or − −" Mr. Pilbeam indicated an unmentionable and wholly fabulous region.

"Well, that's about all we can do for this evening," said Jimmy as they left the Tanners' Arms. "You might have a watch kept on that house in Halibut Street, and if Elver returns to-night you can have a chat with him. If he hasn't come back by the morning you might let me know, and we'll try the place where he works. One or other of his pals may be able to tell us where to find him."

Jimmy went home, his mind occupied by Elver and his wanderings. He was not in the least perturbed by his failure to lay his hands upon him immediately. Elver could not evade justice for more than a day or two at most. In the first place he had no money and that would strictly limit his sphere of action. He would probably try to raise money by the sale of the proceeds of his burglary but that would only accelerate his arrest. Fences whom he would approach for the purpose were probably as well known to the police as they were to him. Owing to Elver having already been in prison, the Yard was in possession of the fullest possible description of him illustrated with an imposing array of photographs. It was one of those fortunate occasions when everything was in favour of the police and everything against the criminal.

It seemed to Jimmy that the motive of the crime was obvious enough. Elver, finding himself penniless, had decided to recoup his finances during the week-end. A comparatively safe way of doing so had occurred to him. He would have known that the neighbourhood of Culverden would be thronged with hop-pickers and that he could easily conceal himself in the crowd. He had gone down there and had kept his eyes open. Jimmy knew nothing of the details of the burglary at Paddock's Croft, but he assumed that Elver had no definite objective. He had seen his opportunity and taken it. And, but for his carelessness in the matter of the fingerprints, his crime would probably never have been detected. Just another example of the otherwise thoughtful criminal omitting the most obvious precautions. Well, Elver with his previous record against him would get it in the neck, that was pretty certain.

When Jimmy reached the Yard the following morning he found a message from the Sergeant of M Division. Elver had not turned up at Halibut Street during the night and the Sergeant, following Jimmy's suggestion, proposed to make inquiries at the place where he worked. Did the Inspector wish to accompany him?

"Yes, I'll come," Jimmy replied. "Wait for me at the police station and I'll be there as soon as I can."

So Jimmy and the Sergeant set off on a second expedition. This time their destination was a warehouse on the outskirts of Surrey Dock. Here the Sergeant interrogated the foreman of a gang of labourers, of which Elver was a member.

"Chris Elver," replied the foreman. "I've been wondering what's become of him. He hasn't turned up to work this morning."

"We are wondering, too," remarked the Sergeant grimly. "When did you last see him?"

"Why, when we knocked off work at twelve o'clock on Saturday. He didn't say anything to me then about not coming to work this morning. But as it happens it doesn't signify much. Got his notice last Friday when he was paid up."

"Got his notice?" inquired the Sergeant. "You mean he was given the sack?"

"Well, if you like to put it that way," the foreman replied. "It wasn't his own fault, if you understand me. I'd had orders to stand off half a dozen men at the end of this week and I had to choose who should go and who should stay; naturally I kept the men who had been on the job longest and Elver wasn't one of them. So they gave him the usual week's notice at the office when he drew his pay on Friday. He's a steady enough chap and I wish I could have kept him on. But there, orders is orders, as you know as well as I do, Sergeant."

"He didn't say anything to you about going out of London for a week-end?"

"No, he didn't say anything to me. As it happened I hadn't more than a couple of words with him on Saturday. There's his pal Joe Fuller over there. He may be able to tell you more than I can."

Joe Fuller, a middle-aged man with a prominent, somewhat highly-coloured nose, was approached. Upon being questioned he appeared resentful. "Know where Chris Elver is," he replied. "That's what I've been asking myself this last hour or more. I want to see him just as badly as you do, I dare say."

"What do you want to see him about?" the Sergeant asked.

"I want to see him about that five bob I lent him on Saturday morning."

"Oh, you lent him five bob, did you? Did he tell you what he wanted it for?"

"Oh, yes, he told me all right. And I was fool enough to believe it. I'd never have thought it of a chap like Chris. All the time I've known him, and that's getting on for a year, I've never known him play a trick like that. And now he's cleared out and my five bob with him."

"Why, he said he was broke and hadn't a penny in his pocket. And that's likely enough, for Mrs. Pilbeam what he lodges with squeezes every bit of his wages out of him. But he said that if I'd lend him five bob he'd be able to pay me back this very morning. I asked him how that was since he wouldn't get no more pay till next Friday, and he said that he knew somebody who wouldn't see him down and out."

"Did he tell you who this somebody was?" asked the Sergeant quickly.

"No, he didn't tell me that. What he said was that he knew somebody who'd hand him over a quid or two. But he said that the trouble was that the person was down in the hop-fields, and he hadn't the money to pay his fare to get there. Talk a hind leg off a donkey, can Chris, and in the end I let him have the money. More fool me, that's all I've got to say."

There was no further information to be obtained from the warehouse. Jimmy parted from the sergeant after arranging for the watch for Elver to be continued, and returned to Scotland Yard. He rang up Sergeant Wragge and discussed the question of Elver's whereabouts with him.

"It's quite likely that Elver hasn't come back to London yet," he said. "He may still be lurking about in your part of the world, looking out for another opportunity of digging up something of value. Fortunately we've got his description and photographs. I'll have a few copies of these made and sent down to you at once. There's this in your favour. It seems to be pretty well established that he's got very little money, if any. He may try to dispose of some of the jewellery locally, though I shouldn't think he was such a fool as all that. I expect you'll circulate a description of him as widely as possible, and I'll do the same. I'll have it put round among the fences. Meanwhile I've got M Division keeping an eye open. It oughtn't to be very long before we get hold of him."

Jimmy was fully convinced that his optimism was justified. And when the man was caught there would be no difficulty in proving him to have been the burglar. The fingermarks themselves were decisive proofs of that. But juries, even in these days, were sometimes a bit sceptical of fingerprints, unsupported by any other evidence. And here Joe Fuller's statement would come in very useful. Elver had told him that he wanted to get down to the hop country. In order to provide a suitable pretext he invented this mythical person from whom he could extract funds. It was ridiculous to suppose that any such person really existed. Hop-pickers, though as a rule perfectly respectable people, were not usually in possession of surplus funds. They usually drew from the farmer for whom they worked sufficient to meet their needs week by week. They were not finally paid up until the end of the hop-picking period, and, even then, the amount earned by an industrious worker was not excessive. Most of them regarded hop-picking as a holiday rather than as a means of augmenting their incomes. So long as the holiday paid its way they were content. On the whole, it was extremely unlikely that Elver knew of a generous hop-picker who could be persuaded to hand over to him such a sum as a pound or two.

Jimmy was convinced that Elver's journey to Culverden had been entirely speculative. If he were lucky it would prove profitable. If not, he would merely have to come back again with a confession of failure duly prepared. Probably he thought that he would be able to pick up something or other which could be readily turned into money. Jewellery which could be identified was really of very little use to him. No doubt he had realised this for himself. In which case he would probably hang about the neighbourhood for a day or two longer, hoping for a second and more favourable chance. Meanwhile, what was he likely to have done with Mrs. Speight's jewellery? He would hardly risk wandering about the countryside with the stuff in his pocket. Nor, in all probability, would he risk trying to dispose of it locally. The only alternative would be to deposit it somewhere until his return to London. Well, that was up to Sergeant Wragge. It was certainly no business of the Yard's till that organisation was definitely called in to search for it.

CHAPTER III

AT this time of the year Mr. Raymond, of the Matling Chequers, was wont to proclaim to anybody who could be found to listen to him that nothing would induce him to remain in the house for another hop-picking.

"I'll give the brewers notice this very month, blest if I won't," he used to say at the end of each day's work. "They can find a tenant who doesn't mind his home being turned upside down. I've had enough of it, and so has the missus, to say nothing of the boys and girls."

But this was merely the expression of Mr. Raymond's annual exasperation. Neither he nor his wife had the least intention of leaving the Chequers. They had been there twenty years and more and the place suited them admirably. It was a sturdily built, commodious house, with an acre of garden which was Mr. Raymond's special pride. The Raymonds were very comfortable there, and there was plenty of room for them to put up their children and grandchildren on the frequent occasions of their visits. Certainly the trade was not very extensive. Matling was quite a small place of not more than two or three hundred inhabitants. Agricultural wages were not so good that their recipients could afford to spend much of their time in public houses. However, the village provided a few regular customers, especially on Saturday evenings and Sunday mornings. Passing motorists and cyclists would not infrequently drop in, and in summer time people would sometimes walk over from Culverden and the neighbouring villages. Taking it all round, the business kept Mr and Mrs. Raymond just comfortably busy. They were fortunate that their livelihood did not entirely depend upon it. They had a little money of their own, carefully invested, which augmented the receipts of the till.

In normal times the Chequers was a very pleasant place in which to spend half an hour or so. It stood a little way back from the road, with an aged and very much decayed elm tree in front of it. You walked under the branches of this tree up to the front door. Passing through this doorway you found yourself in a very pleasant, rather low-pitched bar-room. Mr. Raymond hated the cold, and at the first touch of winter a blazing fire was lighted in the capacious fireplace. This fire was never allowed to go out until the following spring. Facing you, as you entered the room, was the counter, behind which you were pretty certain to find Mr or Mrs. Raymond polishing glasses. Round the fireplace were arranged a form and a few chairs. On the opposite wall was a dartboard showing signs of much use. What space remained was occupied by a heavy deal table scrubbed to snowy whiteness by the vigorous arm of Mrs. Raymond.

Next the bar parlour, but not communicating directly with it, was a second, rather smaller room. This could be entered from the outside by a smaller doorway set in the same wall of the house as the front door. In it was a fireplace, a long table covered with an old-fashioned tablecloth and several chairs. This room had no definite appellation. It was always referred to by the Raymonds as the "other room." In theory, it was supposed to accommodate such superior-minded customers as did not care to use the bar parlour. But in this matter local opinion was severely democratic. The local farmers and gentry when they frequented the Chequers much preferred the comfort of the bar parlour to the rather arid selectness of the other room. The consequence was that it was very rarely occupied. Had you by chance wandered into it you would have detected the peculiar aroma which is associated with uninhabited rooms.

Next to this room was the extensive stone-paved cellar. The floor of this was slightly below ground level and the room had two entrances. The first was from outside, being the third doorway set in the front of the house, and through which the barrels of beer were rolled when the brewers' dray delivered them. For obvious reasons it was only on these occasions that the door was unlocked. The second means of entrance was from the interior of the house, down a couple of steps. Round the walls of the cellar were set a series of massive low stands, on which rested the barrels and the cases of bottles. The shelves above these held jugs, glasses and mugs. In the centre of the room was a marble-topped table, used mainly for standing glasses on when beer was being drawn. At the Chequers every drop of liquor was drawn straight from the wood, and thus the position of the cellar had its disadvantages. It was a matter of several yards from the counter to the barrels, along the passage which ran behind the three rooms already mentioned. Since during the greater part of the year there was never a rush of customers, this hardly mattered. The Raymonds used to say that going to the cellar to draw beer was as good a way of taking exercise as any other.

On the other side of the passage was the Raymonds' sitting-room and their kitchen and scullery. From the centre of the passage a staircase ascended. On the first floor were four bright, airy bedrooms, one of which was occupied by the Raymonds. Above this again were two large rooms, partly furnished and very useful for storage purposes. Standing close to the main building was a large outhouse, which had once been an oasthouse, and was now known as the lodge. Besides this there was stabling, now disused and consisting of a coach-house and two stalls.

From this description it will be gathered that the Raymonds were very comfortable. "Plenty of room to move around," as Mrs. Raymond expressed it. Four of their surviving children, two sons, and two daughters, had married and lived away from home. But they frequently contrived to pay brief visits to their parents, usually bringing their families with them. The fifth, a son, was unmarried, but his work lay in a town about ten miles away, and he found it more convenient to lodge there than to live at home. Besides, he was courting a girl in the same town and that probably had something to do with it. When, as sometimes happened, all the sons and daughters and their respective families arrived together, the accommodation at the Chequers was fairly heavily taxed. But the house always seemed sufficiently elastic for the demands made upon it.

It was the disturbance to his domestic comfort by hop-picking which made Mr. Raymond dread that period. Although there were not actually many acres of hop gardens in the parish of Matling, the Chequers was a favourite place of resort for the pickers from round about. Obviously the arrangements of the Chequers, though perfectly satisfactory for the service of a couple of dozen of customers or so, would have broken down completely if called upon by several hundreds. At the approach of hop-picking time, therefore, the place had to be reorganised. And this reorganisation was a very strenuous matter.

The first sign of the approaching upheaval was the arrival at the Chequers of the Raymonds' eldest daughter, whom they regarded as their right hand. Mary Raymond had married a fruit farmer, who was in a small but prosperous way of business. It was a standing joke in Matling that she had only accepted him under one condition. This was that she would always be free to leave her husband and family in order to help her parents over hop-picking. She was a jolly, energetic woman of thirty-five or so, with a manner calculated to charm even the most truculent customer. Mary, immediately upon her arrival, rolled up her sleeves, and she and her parents set to work.

The principal problem was to organise a system of serving beer to thirsty crowds with the least possible delay. This problem had been solved in rather an ingenious way. It would have been folly to admit the hop-pickers to the bar parlour and hope to serve them over the counter, owing to the distance between that and the cellar. This room was therefore closed entirely, the furniture removed and the front door locked. On either side of the front door was an extensive window. Inside these windows were fixed wide shelves. Tables were set on either side of these shelves to accommodate glasses and mugs. The remainder of the room was almost entirely filled with barrels of beer, ready tapped, leaving only sufficient room for the servers to move between the barrels and the windows. At opening time the windows were flung wide open, and the hop-pickers standing outside the house could be served with the minimum of delay.

The main problem was thus solved. But there was a secondary one also, almost equally important. The local inhabitants, distinguished from the invading hop-pickers by the appellation of "home-dwellers", could not be thus excluded from their favourite pub. The other room was therefore brought into use for their benefit. Home-dwellers alone were allowed to enter the house, and in order to separate the sheep from the goats during the busy week-ends, a gatekeeper was employed by Mr. Raymond. He knowing all the home-dwellers by sight would admit them to the other room. But, as Gabriel at the gates of Paradise, he rigidly excluded the pickers. The specially privileged were allowed to use the cellar. If you were one of these, you had to follow a devious route. Round the back of the house, in by the back door and so along the passage into the cellar. Here you might sit on a case of bottles, drawing your beer yourself and laying the money for it on the marble table. If you liked watching the crowds from a secure retreat in the very heart of them, you could enjoy a lot of quiet amusement while you drank your pint.

The house having been thus rearranged, the next thing was to organise an adequate supply of drinking vessels. Mary as a rule took charge of this. She brought down the hundreds of glasses not used during normal times from the upper rooms, where they had been carefully packed away in the wooden boxes. And upon the bottom of each of these, after having washed and polished them, she proceeded to put a dab of black paint.

A stranger to the neighbourhood might well have inquired the purpose of these dabs of paint. It was a dodge invented by Mr. Raymond, and he was very proud of it. It has already been explained that the hop-pickers were not admitted to the house, but were served through the windows of the bar parlour. Now when this experiment had first been tried it had somewhat unexpected results. Some of the hop-pickers, when they had finished their drinks, instead of returning their glasses through the window, absent-mindedly carried them off. No doubt they came in very useful in their hopper huts. But Mr. Raymond, on counting his glasses at the end of the season, found that he was several dozen short. And, being of an economical turn of mind, he realised that this shortage made a serious inroad upon the takings. So he adopted the plan of charging a deposit of threepence upon each glass handed through the window. This deposit returned to the customer when he brought back the glass.

But, again distinctions had to be drawn between hop-pickers and home-dwellers. The latter could not be subjected to the indignity of paying a deposit on their glasses. Consequently nothing was charged on glasses served in the other room; But it sometimes happened, in spite of all precautions, that a wily hop-picker gained access to the precincts sacred to the home-dwellers. Having done so he could smuggle out his glass, take it round to the window of the bar parlour, and draw threepence upon it. Now that was where the dabs of paint came in. The glasses so marked were only used at the windows, and solely upon these was a deposit refunded. The designing alien was therefore foiled. He might contrive to penetrate the inner sanctuary and remove a glass. But if he innocently tendered it at the window and demanded a refund of threepence upon it he was doomed to disappointment. Whoever took it from him looked at the bottom, saw that it was unmarked with paint and shook his head. "You've got to be as cunning as a basketful of monkeys to get even with some of these folk," as Mr. Raymond remarked.

It sometimes happened that even all these dispositions were inadequate to cope with the crowds which besieged the Chequers. During the week-ends, when the hop-pickers' friends came to visit them, the resources of the house were taxed to their utmost. And if it happened to be wet on these occasions, extraordinary measures had to be taken. You couldn't expect even hop-pickers to enjoy their drinks in the rain, so that they had to be admitted to what shelter was available. The lodge, the stabling, and even on some occasions even the Raymonds' private sitting-room, were pressed into service. The state of the Chequers after a wet hop-picking week-end can better be imagined than described. No wonder that Mr. Raymond's patience sometimes yielded to the strain.

As he himself was the first to admit, he could never have carried on without the help of the family. Their response to the call of parental duty was really admirable. Each and severally they gave up the week-ends for the strenuous task of serving beer. John, the eldest son, a constable in the Metropolitan Police, always managed to wangle week-end leave, and brought his wife with him. Henry, the second son, a driver in one of the local transport services, contrived to get the necessary time off, and also brought his wife. Walter, the unmarried one, found no difficulty. Having no wife he brought his girl with him, and exceedingly useful she made herself. Mary's husband, the fruit farmer, abandoned his apple trees and came to bear a hand. Ethel and her husband, who kept a general shop in a village not many miles away, arrived in their little delivery van. From noon on Saturday till late on Sunday night, the Chequers was the scene of a reunion of the whole of the Raymond family.

By Monday morning things had quietened down. The temporary helpers, with the exception of Mary, had gone, and an interval of comparative quiet ensued. Only comparative, however, for there was much to be done. The empty barrels in the bar parlour had to be removed, and full ones put in their place. Enormous batches of dirty glasses, which had accumulated from the Sunday evening, had to be washed and put in order. And all the time, long before the Chequers opened, there was a piteous stream of applicants. Thirst, especially on a bright September morning, is no respecter of the licensing laws. Every few minutes there would come a tap at the closed windows. And then an appealing voice, "Give us a drink, guv'nor. I'm parched right up and there ain't no cops anywhere about." It is no part of this story to disclose the success or otherwise of these appeals.

At eight o'clock on the morning of Monday, September 2nd, Mr. Raymond, his wife and Mary, were all busy with their separate duties. Mr. Raymond, with the assistance of a local old-aged pensioner, was trundling barrels between the cellar and the bar parlour. Mrs. Raymond had carried a tub of boiling water into the other room, and was busy washing glasses. Mary was in the bar parlour, sweeping up and generally putting things straight. A few thirst-stricken souls had already pestered her, but the flow of these suddenly ceased. Then came a vigorous tap on the window. She looked up to see the familiar face of Sergeant Wragge.

She opened the window at once and smiled at her visitor. "Good-morning, Sergeant," she said cheerfully. "Bit early for you to be riding round these parts, isn't it?"

"Good-morning, Miss Mary," Wragge replied. She was always known locally as Miss Mary although she had been married now eight years or more. "Is your dad about anywhere? You might tell him that I've ridden over to have a word with him."

"Here's the Sergeant to see you, dad," shouted Mary. Mr. Raymond appeared, carrying a crate of beer bottles in each muscular hand.

"Glad to see you, Sergeant," he exclaimed. "Do you want a word with me? Drat it, there isn't a room in the house a man can call his own these days. Just step round to the cellar door, will you? I'll have it unlocked in half a shake and let you in."

Wragge entered the cellar, taking off his cap as he did so. "I know you're busy, Mr. Raymond," he said apologetically. "But I won't keep you more than a minute or two. You've heard about that affair up at Paddock Croft, I expect?"

"Jim, the gardener up there, was in here last night," Mr. Raymond replied. "I heard him talking about it to some of the chaps, but I didn't stop to listen. Too busy. Some one broke in and pinched some jewellery, didn't they?"

As he spoke he picked up two glasses and approached the barrel containing old ale. "No harm in my giving you a drink if I don't charge you for it," he continued. "Here you are, Sergeant. It's a drop of the best. Good health."

They raised their glasses simultaneously, then set them down. The Sergeant took an envelope from his pocket and drew out of it the paper cap he had found in the garden at Paddock Croft. He laid it on the table and looked at it critically. "You don't happen to have seen that before, do you, Mr. Raymond?" he asked.

"Seen it before!" exclaimed Mr. Raymond. "I won't swear to having seen this particular one; I reckon I must have seen some hundreds of paper caps yesterday and the day before. Nearly all these folks that come down to visit the hop-pickers wear them, as you know as well as I do."

"I was wondering whether you might have seen anybody wearing this cap," said Wragge impressively.

24

"Likely enough I did, but you can't expect me to distinguish one paper cap from another. Wait a minute, I'll call my daughter. She was serving at the window most of the week-end and she's got a wonderful memory. We'll ask her."

But Mary, upon being summoned, could give no information. Although she had been at the window she had no time to observe her customers closely. She had been kept far too busy serving beer and taking money for it. Wragge thanked her and she returned to her duties.

"It's like this, Mr. Raymond," said Wragge confidentially. "The chap who was wearing that cap is the one who broke in at Paddock Croft. And that's not all we know about him, by a long chalk. Left his fingermarks on a silver box there. We sent the box up to Scotland Yard, and a smart young chap up there found out his name for us in no time."

"Wonderful!" exclaimed Mr. Raymond, deeply impressed. "But if you know his name, Sergeant, all you've got to do is to arrest him, surely."

"It's not quite as easy as all that," Wragge replied. "You see, although we know his name we don't know where he is, to go and lay our hands on him. That smart young chap up at the Yard thinks he'll be hanging round here still. I won't say that he mayn't be right. Anyway he's got this chap's photograph and is going to send it down to me. I'll let you have a look at it as soon as I get it."

"Wonderful!" exclaimed Mr. Raymond for the second time. "You've got his name and his photograph. My eldest boy always says the police know a thing or two. There's no doubt about that."

"Yes, we do know a thing or two," replied Wragge in a tone of professional pride. He picked up the cap and, having put it in its envelope, replaced it in his pocket. "All fairly quiet here on Saturday night, Mr. Raymond?" he asked.

"We hadn't any trouble to speak of," Mr. Raymond replied. "What with me and my three sons about the place folks think twice before they kick up a disturbance here. There was a bit of a bust, though, just after closing time in the road outside. That fellow Lavis, that lodges with his sister over by Park Gate, was at the bottom of it, I fancy. A perfect nuisance, that chap. Comes in here, has a couple of drinks and then gets quarrelsome. Many's the time I've told him that I wouldn't have him in the house again, if he didn't mend his ways. He was shouting and hollering with a lot of others outside on Saturday night so I just went out and told them to clear off. I will say this, that they went off quite quietly."

"Who were the rest of them? Local folks?" Wragge asked.

"Well, there was Tom Adcorn," Mr. Raymond replied. "I don't know what can have upset him, for he's usually quiet enough. And of course his brother Fred. You never see one of those two without the other. The rest of them were strangers. What they were all arguing about is more than I can say. I didn't trouble to ask. I just told them to get along home and sleep it off."

Wragge finished his beer and rose from the case on which he had been sitting. "Well, I must be getting along," he said. "That Paddock Croft affair has given me a lot of work, besides all the things I have to see to at hop-picking. Good-morning, Mr. Raymond. I'll bring that photograph along and let you have a look at it."

Mr. Raymond resumed his labours with beer barrels. The burglary at Paddock Croft was no affair of his he felt. Nasty thing to happen in the neighbourhood, of course. Never for a moment did it occur to him that any of the inhabitants could have been guilty of such a thing. Nor surely any of the regular hop-pickers. The same people came down year after year and all undesirables had long ago been weeded out by the farmers. It could only have been one of those hooligans who came down from London during the week-end. You never knew what folk like that might be up to. Why, they had even stooped to pinching his glasses.

Mr. Raymond had no sympathy for the annoyance caused to the Speights. He didn't like them, and made no pretence of doing so. In spite of their five years' residence at Paddock Croft, they were still strangers in Matling. They had never made any attempt to interest themselves in the village, and seemed to make a point of spending as little money in it as they could. Soon after their arrival, Mr. Raymond had put on his best clothes as a mark of respect and walked to Paddock Croft to call on Mr. Speight. He had informed that gentleman that he would be happy to supply him with alcoholic liquors, mineral waters, cigarettes and anything else the Chequers provided. Mr. Speight had replied disdainfully that he was not in the habit of dealing at village pubs.

The memory of this incident still rankled. An incipient frown over-shadowed Mr. Raymond's face whenever Paddock Croft or its occupants were mentioned. Fortunately, they very rarely were mentioned in the bar parlour of the Chequers. If the Speights betrayed a lack of interest in the villagers, the latter retaliated by a complete unconcern in their affairs.

Such were Mr. Raymond's meditations during the few minutes which followed the departure of Sergeant Wragge. And then the rumbling on the road outside announced the arrival of the brewers' drays. In that instant the burglary was forgotten. Mr. Raymond's mind was occupied with far more important things.

CHAPTER IV

THAT same Monday Superintendent Hanslet and Jimmy had been invited to dinner by Dr. Priestley at his house in Westbourne Terrace. Dr. Priestley was a retired professor whose ostensible occupation was the writing of scientific treatises. His more or less secret hobby, however, was the solution of criminal problems. This hobby had led, some years before, to his making the acquaintance of the Superintendent. Since then the two had become fast friends and had collaborated in many puzzling cases. Jimmy, as Hanslet's assistant, had since been admitted to the friendship. It should be added that Dr. Priestley was a man of means, and kept an extremely well-appointed table. Dinner at Westbourne Terrace was la luxury which Hanslet never refused if he could help it.

On this occasion there were two other members of the party: Harold Merefield, Dr. Priestley's secretary, who lived in the house, and Dr. Oldland, a very old friend of his host, and now a physician with an extensive practice in Kensington.

It was in Dr. Priestley's study, to which they had retired for coffee and conversation after dinner, that mention was first made of Christopher Elver. It was Hanslet who first broached the subject. Not that he had the slightest interest in the Paddock Croft burglary. That was a matter entirely beneath his notice. Even should the Yard be called in, which seemed extremely unlikely, Jimmy could be trusted to deal with the job. Hanslet's interest in Elver was purely reminiscent.

"I think I remember you saying some time ago, Professor, that a criminal was usually a specialist," he said. "You meant, I suppose, that a burglar doesn't usually indulge in arson, or a murderer go in for forgery in his spare time."

"I remember suggesting something of the kind," Dr. Priestley replied. "My limited knowledge of criminology appears to support that view."

"As a general rule you're quite right," said Hanslet. "But every rule has its exception. I happened to come across an exception to this very rule to-day. Jimmy told me that one of my old acquaintances, who was jugged for cocaine smuggling

27

some years back, broke into a private house on Sunday night and stole some jewellery. By the way, Jimmy, have you had any further news of the fellow?"

"Nothing had been heard of him at the time I left the Yard this evening," Jimmy replied.

"Do I gather that this man has not yet been apprehended for the burglary?" Dr. Priestley asked quietly.

"Not yet, but his arrest can only be a matter of hours," Hanslet replied.

"Then, since he is still at large, how can you be certain that he committed the burglary?" Dr. Priestley asked.

Hanslet laughed. "There is no room for a shadow of doubt," he replied. "Tell the Professor about the fingerprints on the silver box, Jimmy."

Jimmy complied with this demand and Dr. Priestley listened attentively to his story.

"I will admit that appearances are very much against this man, Christopher Elver," he remarked. "Your theory is, I suppose, that want drove him to commit the burglary."

"That's about it, Professor," Hanslet replied. "But somehow, I shouldn't have expected it of a man like Elver. Not that he's a man of respectable character. He's anything but that, in fact he's a thorough-paced crook. But he knew perfectly well that his fingerprints were recorded at the Yard, and I should have thought that he would have had more sense than to leave them about like that. In fact, it's a ridiculously clumsy crime for a man of Elver's ability."

"Clumsy crimes are usually the result of sudden temptation," said Oldland from the depths of his arm-chair. "That's my experience, anyway. You haven't seen Elver since he's been released from gaol, I suppose? Well, I can imagine that seven years in prison, followed by two years' work as a labourer, has changed his character entirely. According to what Jimmy has told us, the man found himself without a penny in his pocket and the prospect of losing his job at the end of the week. He may have felt that there was nothing left for him but to return to his criminal activities. And, rather foolishly as it turns out, he took the first opportunity which presented itself to him."

"You may be right, doctor," Hanslet agreed. "Still, it's rather curious that he should have turned his hand to burglary, I should have thought his natural inclination would have been to pick up the old threads. I don't mind confessing in the privacy of this room that we haven't succeeded in suppressing the drug traffic altogether. Elver, if he found himself out of a job, could easily have got in touch with some of his old associates. They would have found him lucrative employment, I haven't a doubt of that."

Oldland shook his head. "I think you under-rate the respect in which the force is held by the criminal classes," he said. "Jimmy has told us that since his release Elver has been under observation by M Division. You may be quite sure that he was well aware of that fact. And I suppose that he imagined that his every movement was watched -- which in point of fact it was. He would be far too much afraid to resume his criminal activities in London. If he made a permanent move to any other district, the fact of his having done so would be notified to the police there. He was intelligent enough to make his attempt during a short visit to the country."

"Oh, he's intelligent enough," Hanslet exclaimed. "At least that was the impression I formed of him after his arrest. He managed that drug-smuggling business very cleverly. We found out quite a lot about him, one way and another. He first went to sea as a pantry boy and worked himself up to the position of steward by sheer efficiency. The owners and captain of the Etrurian gave him the highest possible character. In fact for a long time they wouldn't believe that he was a crook. I've always had a theory that he somehow got into the clutches of that confounded old woman, Mrs. Hawkins, and that it was she who induced him to bring the stuff over. It's another proof of his intelligence that he covered his tracks so well that we never discovered where he managed to procure the drug."

"Who is or was Mrs. Hawkins?" Oldland asked.

"She was the woman who distributed the stuff in London. Clever in her way, but not quite clever enough, since we managed to unearth her. She posed as Elver's fond and affectionate aunt. He never stopped on shore when the Etrurian was in London. He used to go back to the ship every night. However, as soon as the ship came in, the dutiful nephew used to pay a visit to his aunt, and that was when the drugs were conveyed to her."

"Did her benevolent attitude towards Elver continue after his arrest?" Oldland asked.

"Up to a point. She denied all knowledge of him until she heard that he had mentioned her name after his own arrest. Then she turned right round. It almost seemed as if she couldn't think of anything bad enough to say of him. However, she couldn't tell us much that we didn't know already. When Elver was arrested he had a quantity of cocaine in his possession and that was good enough for us."

"Do you suppose that the two have met since Elver's release?" queried Oldland.

Hanslet shook his head. "She was taken seriously ill two years after her sentence and died in hospital," he replied. "She hardly came into the picture so far as Elver's case was concerned. I mean that she in no way contributed to his arrest."

"I should like to hear the process of deduction that led to your success in this case, Superintendent," Dr. Priestley remarked.

Hanslet seemed much gratified by this request. "It was before I was lucky enough to meet you, Professor," he replied. "I expect you'd have tumbled to it very much quicker than I did. I'll tell you the whole story if you'd like to hear it."

"It would interest me exceedingly," said Dr. Priestley.

"Well, I won't bore you with the preliminaries. It will be sufficient to say that sheer accident led us to Mrs. Hawkins' shop in Lambeth. There we found ample evidence for her arrest. But that wasn't quite enough. We wanted to trace the source of the drug. We soon discovered that Mrs. Hawkins rarely or never left the shop. Hence we deduced that she didn't herself fetch the stuff but that somebody brought it to her.

"Naturally, for the next few days that shop was under constant observation. Everybody who entered it was detained and questioned. Very few of these people turned out to be genuine purchasers. The great majority of them were poor devils of addicts who came to fetch their supplies of the drug. But not one of them had any drugs in their possession when they entered the place.

"Then we came to hear that Mrs. Hawkins had a nephew who visited her regularly. Even drug traffickers may have perfectly genuine nephews, so there didn't seem to be anything in that. It wasn't until I heard this nephew referred to as Sea Joe that I sat up and took notice. He wouldn't have had a nickname like that if he hadn't been connected with the sea. And as a seaman trading with foreign ports he would be a very suitable agent for the smuggling of the drug into the country.

"Still, that wasn't very much to go upon. And I didn't dare wait for Sea Joe's next appearance at the shop. I had found out that his visits were extraordinarily regular, that they occurred almost without exception on alternate Mondays. Mrs. Hawkins had been arrested on a Wednesday, and her nephew had visited her on the previous Monday. That meant that he wasn't likely to turn up again for another twelve days. The affair had got into the papers and Sea Joe would probably hear of it before he had been two minutes ashore. That being so, he wasn't likely to risk another visit to the shop. I had to get hold of him and of the evidence to incriminate him, before he got wind of what had happened.

"That meant that I had to arrest him on board his ship or immediately he left it. Of course, there was always the chance that he would hear the news before the ship got back to London, but I was prepared to risk that. My difficulty was to discover which was the ship, and which of her complement was the man I wanted. It was one of those cases in which I had to make a devil of a lot of inquiries, and in a field with which I was not in the least familiar.

"I had one thing to go upon, and one only. The regularity of those visits by her nephew to Mrs. Hawkins. They had always occurred on alternate Mondays, and it was reasonable to suppose that the ship was in the habit of returning to port on those days. That London was the port seemed highly probable, for a seaman could not regularly absent himself from his ship for any length of time. He couldn't, for instance, be so attentive to his aunt if his ship docked in Liverpool or Bristol. So I began by making inquiries about vessels which regularly docked in London on alternate Mondays.

"It sounds simple enough, but it wasn't, I can assure you. I started with the Port of London Authority and then went round every shipping agency in the town. One way and another I compiled a list as long as my arm. By the time I'd finished I was convinced that every vessel afloat engaged in the continental trade docked in the Port of London on alternate Mondays. There were dozens of them, and they seemed to come in from every port in northern Europe. Norway, Sweden, Denmark, the Baltic ports, Germany, Holland, France and even northern Spain. And which of them was the floating home of Sea Joe was more than I could be expected to guess.

"There was just this. At that time, it was known to us that Hamburg was a likely place in which to procure drugs. So I concentrated on the vessels which traded from that port. You mustn't suppose that I neglected the others. I didn't. I had an officer told off to each vessel on my list. Now there were no fewer than six vessels from Hamburg expected on the date when Sea Joe should have paid his next visit to his aunt. Two of these were English, two German, one was a Norwegian and the sixth a Swede. Which of these was the most promising? I had men enough at my disposal to watch them all, but naturally I wanted to arrest Sea Joe myself if I could. So I had to try to watch for his ship myself.

"Now, by this time, I was beginning to learn quite a lot about seafaring ways. I had discovered, for instance, that although we as a nation don't mind foreigners serving under our flag, most foreigners have a rooted aversion to Englishmen sailing in their ships. Sea Joe was almost certainly an Englishman. If he had been a foreigner Mrs. Hawkins' neighbours would almost certainly have spotted the fact at once. Therefore, the probability was that he was to be found on one of the two English ships.

"These two were the Etrurian and another whose name I have forgotten now. It seemed to me that I might just as well toss up for which I should choose. Heads the Etrurian, tails the other. In fact, I was taking a coin out of my pocket for that very purpose when another idea occurred to me. As I said just now, if Sea Joe had already heard the news of Mrs. Hawkins' arrest my chance was gone. He would have chucked overboard any drugs he might have, and, even though I spotted him, there would be no evidence against him. It was most unlikely that the news had found its way into the Hamburg papers. Sea Joe could only have heard it if his ship was fitted with wireless. So once more I started worrying the agents of the two vessels. I found that although the other one was fitted with wireless the Etrurian wasn't.

"That decided me. From that moment my money was on the Etrurian. I had plenty of time before she was expected, and I spent a couple of hours of it chatting with a retired sea captain, who happened to be a neighbour of mine. From him I got what seemed to be a pretty useful hint. A most likely person to be able to get away regularly from a ship immediately upon her arrival in port was the steward. He would have to see the ship's chandler to arrange for stores for the next voyage and so forth. Of course, as my friend explained, this was only an off-chance. Any member of the ship's company might wangle it somehow. But still, as a result of all this, I got it fixed in my head that it was the steward of the Etrurian I wanted.

"It's all very fine to get a thing fixed in your head. But, once you've decided on a definite move it always seems to be the wrong one while you're waiting for it to come off. It does to me, anyhow. That November afternoon, when I got news that the Etrurian had passed Gravesend and was coming up the river, I felt that my chances of making an arrest were about one in a thousand. I went to one of those wharfs -- just below Tower Bridge on the Surrey side -- and stood about in a most infernally cold drizzle, cursing myself for a fool.

"Well, the Etrurian came in at last. She was a drab-looking tramp steamer of about fifteen hundred tons, and I wondered what power in the world could ever induce men to go to sea in a thing like that. She came alongside with much throwing of ropes and blowing of whistles, then the customs people went on board her. I let them do that. I didn't want Joe to see any stranger come aboard yet. It was dark by then and the drizzle was falling in front of the electric lamps of the wharf in long, straight lines. I was cold, wet and irritable, but still I waited. The customs men came ashore again and nothing more happened. I had somehow expected the people on that ship to jump ashore like rats as soon as she was tied up. It seemed to me that even the London river-side was preferable to that dingy steel tank in which they were cooped up. But they didn't seem in any hurry. Not they. They disappeared one by one into their lairs, till not a soul remained on deck. Having their tea, I suppose. I fancy I detected a smell of kippers coming from the galley. I bet I stood in the rain an hour or more watching that confounded ship. Nobody on shore but me seemed even faintly interested in her, and nobody on board her seemed faintly interested in any one else. And I didn't want to go on board of her. I was afraid that the minute I stepped on the gangway Sea Joe might take alarm.

"By that time my hopes of coming face to face with that elusive individual were at zero. What chance was there, in heaven's name, that he was more likely to be found on this ship than on any other? I had almost made up my mind to go away and get myself something stiff to drink when one or two folks began to appear on deck. Among them was a youngish man with a brown rain-coat and a slouch hat. He seemed so well-dressed that at first I thought that he must be the captain. He certainly seemed to be coming ashore. And then one of the other chaps called out to him, 'Hallo, Joe, are you going ashore?'

"Joe! That made me straighten up pretty suddenly, I can tell you. Of course, as I told myself it was just a chance. I suppose if you went aboard any British ship and called out 'Joe', somebody would answer you. But it seemed a good omen. And anyhow this man couldn't be the captain or he wouldn't have been spoken to like that. So I decided to risk it.

"He came up the gangway like a man who knew exactly where he was going and why. I'd been keeping in the shadows as much as I could, which meant that I was round the corner of a shed where there wasn't any shelter. And as the man stepped on to the wharf I walked up to him. 'Excuse me,' I said, 'but are you the steward of the Etrurian?'

"'Got it in one,' he replied jauntily. 'But I'm afraid I can't do anything for you, old cock, for we've got our regular ship's chandlers. And it's not a bit of good going aboard to see the old man, for he always leaves these things to me.'

"'I'm not worrying about ship's chandlers just now,' I said to him. ' Do you happen to have an aunt who lives down Lambeth way?'

"We were standing just under one of those electric lamps. I could see his face clearly and the moment I spoke I knew I'd found my man. His hand made a movement towards his pocket but I'd been watching for that and I was too quick for him. I caught hold of him by the wrist and after the first moment or two he didn't make any resistance. It wouldn't have been much good if he had, for he was a slight, thin sort of chap, and I could have picked him up and thrown him into the river. 'It's no good,' I said to him as soothingly as I could. 'I want you on a charge of cocaine smuggling. If you take my advice you'll come along to the station quietly.'

"I found a taxi outside the wharf and bundled him into it. I didn't let go of his hands, you may be sure of that. He never said a word all the way to the police station, and I didn't ask him any questions. I was much too intent upon what would happen when I got him there. And then it all came out much more convincingly than I had dared hope. We searched him and found a lot of little packets of drugs sewn into the lining of his waistcoat. He didn't tell us that his tailor had put them there or any yarn like that. He just said, 'Well, it's a fair cop. What's become of the old lady?'

"I told him that Mrs. Hawkins was at present provided with free board and lodgings. Then I began to question him. I always believe in striking while the iron's hot. I got him to cough up the whole story without much trouble. He'd been smuggling cocaine over in this way for years and delivering it at the shop in Lambeth. He must have done pretty well out of it, by all appearances. But he didn't seem to have anything put away. I learnt later that he indulged in pretty expensive habits when his ship was in Hamburg. Hamburg, I'm told, is an easy place to spend money in.

"He told us among other things that his name was Christopher Elver, and we were able to verify that from his discharge papers. But he'd been called Joe ever since he went to sea as a boy. He gave his age as thirty-one and said that he was unmarried. His parents were dead and so far as he knew he had no relations in the world. Mrs. Hawkins wasn't really his aunt, that was only an excuse for his visits to the shop. I asked him if he had any friends in London, and he told me pretty sharply that he hadn't. He said that when a man was in port for only two or three days on end he hadn't much chance of making friends. I don't know whether he was telling the truth or not. But when I went and had a little chat with Mrs. Hawkins next day, she told me that he'd got a girl.

'I wasn't disposed to place any implicit credit in what Mrs. Hawkins said. I'd already caught her lying too often for that. But I felt bound to ask her more about this girl of his. Mrs. Hawkins had been quite positive about her; she said he had brought her to the shop more than once. However Elver flatly denied that any such person existed. And I think on the whole I'd rather believe him than Mrs. Hawkins. Anyway, the girl never materialised, and we heard no more of her."

"All this happened nine years ago," said Oldland reflectively. "Did you at that time attach any particular interest to the possible existence of this girl?"

"I can't say that I attached much significance to her, once I had satisfied myself that she had played no part in the drug organisation. You see, we satisfied ourselves that Mrs. Hawkins and Elver were the only two who had a hand in that, unless you include the unfortunate addicts who came to the shop to buy the stuff. Against them we had all the evidence we wanted. It didn't seem worth while to waste time and money looking up their innocent associates."

"So that the existence of this girl was never really disproved," Dr. Priestley suggested.

"Well, if you like to put it that way, I suppose it wasn't, Professor," Hanslet replied. "I dare say that Elver had a girl friend in London, possibly several. But it wasn't that sort of casual acquaintanceship Mrs. Hawkins implied. According to her, a girl existed with whom Elver was particularly infatuated. She declared that she had seen her more than once. She even gave some sort of a description of her. She said that Elver called her Kitty, but swore she didn't know her surname. But as I say, Elver flatly denied her story. He insisted that he had never taken a girl to Mrs. Hawkins' shop and that none of the girls he knew answered to Kitty. On the whole, as I say, I prefer to believe him rather than Mrs. Hawkins."

"As being apparently the more truthful of the two?" suggested Oldland.

"Yes, to some extent. And the facts then and later appeared to be in Elver's favour. If he had been on any sort of intimate terms with a girl we should have been bound to hear of her. She would surely have made some sign when she read of his arrest in the papers. She would have asked permission to see him when he was in gaol or something like that. But nothing of the kind happened. Now I don't mind admitting that I had formed some sort of a sneaking regard for Elver. I can't explain it. The fact remains that we fellows do take an interest in one or two of the poor devils who fall into our hands. I can't begin to explain why I took an interest in Elver. Perhaps because he never whined. He took all that came to him like a man and didn't try to throw the blame on to anybody else. Anyhow, I took the trouble to look him up when he was released a couple of years ago."

Jimmy looked at his superior with sudden interest. This was the first time that Hanslet had mentioned anything of the kind.

"It sometimes happens that we can do a discharged prisoner some good," the Superintendent continued. "Elver looked a good deal older than when I last seen him, but otherwise he seemed much the same. He didn't seem to bear me any grudge for having arrested him; in fact, I think he was genuinely pleased that I had turned up. But he made it quite clear to me that he didn't want any assistance. He said that he reckoned that he could find himself a job provided that his past wasn't always dragged up against him. And, as I took the trouble to inform myself, he did find a job very shortly. Indeed, I believe that he's very rarely been out of a job from then till now. Isn't that so, Jimmy? You know more about his recent history than I do."

"He certainly seems to have been able to find work," Jimmy replied. "And from what one can gather his work was satisfactory. The foreman whom I saw this morning said he was loth to part with him."

"No doubt the fellow would have been able to get on all right if only he had kept straight," said Hanslet. "By the way, there's another thing I asked him when I saw him that time. I suddenly remembered the girl whom Mrs. Hawkins had insisted upon. I didn't mention her directly, but I asked him if there was any one with whom he would like to get in touch. He told me that there was absolutely nobody. He wasn't going to apply to his old employers or anybody like that. He wanted to make a fresh start and see if he couldn't put the past behind him. And as for friends, he hadn't any who would care to remember him. I rather liked the fellow for that. And I must admit that I'm downright sorry that he's made such a fool of himself."

"There's no chance of his getting away with it, I suppose?" Oldland asked.

The Superintendent shrugged his shoulders. "He can't remain at large very much longer," he replied. "A man with no money in his pockets, or at most a shilling or two, is hopelessly limited in his movements. The only way that he can raise any more is to realise some of the proceeds of the burglary, and he won't venture to do that just yet. I won't say that a man with plenty of means can't give the police a run for their money, but if he's destitute he must rely upon his own legs to get him about, and even then he's got to procure food somehow. Besides, Elver is handicapped by the fact that we've got photographs and an accurate description of him. Jimmy has already seen to it that these have been circulated. He daren't return to his old haunts, and he can't wander about the country indefinitely. No, he's bound to be caught, and then I'm afraid he'll get a stiffish sentence. Well, it serves him right, I suppose. I'm afraid, Professor, that there aren't even the elements of a problem about Elver's case."

CHAPTER V

A S Hanslet had remarked, Jimmy had sent copies of Elver's description and photograph to Sergeant Wragge at Culverden. The latter received them later that afternoon, and, having studied them, set to work to consider what use he could best make of them.

In his heart of hearts the Sergeant was not very much in love with the idea that Elver might still be in the neighbourhood. He knew from experience that the instinct of the criminal is to get away from the scene of his crime as early as possible. Even assuming that Elver's capital had been no more than five shillings, he could with this sum have bought an excursion ticket from London Bridge to Culverden. He also knew that excursion trains for the benefit of the friends of hop-pickers ran between the two places at frequent intervals during Saturday and Sunday. So crowded were these trains that it would have been sheer waste of time to take the photographs to the railway officials for recognition. There was nothing particularly striking about Elver's appearance, and he would have passed unnoticed among the thousands who used the trains. If indeed he had returned to London, there was little chance of his being recognised during his short visit to the country.

On the other hand Wragge realised that there was a possibility that he might be still hanging about somewhere. He might be hoping to cadge a shilling or two from the hop-pickers by spinning some pitiful yarn. The pickers as a class were open-hearted folk, and they were always ready to listen to a tale of woe if it was skilfully enough pitched. And their hearts were most easily touched when their throats were moistened. If that were Elver's game, he would certainly hang round one or other of the pubs.

But, the Sergeant asked himself, would he venture to do so? On the whole, he decided, he might. He probably didn't realise that the identity of the burglar was already known through the medium of the fingerprints on the silver box. He would feel convinced that nobody in the neighbourhood of Culverden or Matling could possibly recognise him. That being so, he would see no immediate reason for hiding himself. That he had selected Paddock Croft as the scene of his depredations, suggested that he was making Matling his headquarters in the country. The Sergeant got out his bicycle and rode to the Chequers, where he arrived shortly before six o'clock.

There, everything was in readiness for opening time. Mr and Mrs. Raymond and their daughter were already in the bar parlour, ready to throw open the windows and serve the throng assembled outside. Of course, on an ordinary week-day evening, nothing like the hordes of the week-ends were to be expected. Still, there were fifty or sixty customers already waiting, mostly women, but with a fair sprinkling of their men friends.

The Sergeant explained what he wanted, and Mr. Raymond, always anxious to keep in with the police, raised no objections to his plan. Mr. Raymond took him upstairs and installed him in a chair beside the window of the best bedroom. From this point of vantage he was able to inspect all those who came to the window of the bar parlour below. And Mr. Raymond thoughtfully left a jug of beer and a glass beside the chair.

With the photographs spread out on his knees, Wragge began to watch for the possible appearance of his man. He soon satisfied himself that he was not in the crowd already collected. This crowd was good-tempered and orderly enough. Mr. Raymond, acutely conscious of the presence of a policeman in the house, waited until the stroke of six to open the window. Then the crowd surged forward, automatically forming itself into a queue. As each in turn was served with his or her drink, the recipient moved away to what was locally known as the arbour. This was a row of tables with benches set on either side of them, over which a wooden framework had been erected. A tarpaulin could be drawn across this framework in case of wet weather.

The stream of customers was constantly replenished. And very soon the open space in front of the Chequers assumed the aspect of a minor market place. Matling boasted no more than a single village shop, and this was a fairly primitive affair. It was, on the whole, adequate to deal with the needs of the home-dwellers. Upon its counters were disclosed a miscellaneous collection of articles, ranging from ready-made suits of clothes to halfpenny bars of chocolate. If you wanted anything in reason you would probably get it. In any case, the obliging proprietor would procure it for you the next time the carrier called. But since not more than half a dozen people could crowd into it at a time, it was obviously unsuited to the invading army of hop-pickers. Other arrangements had therefore to be made to provide for them.

The comparison of the hop-pickers to an invading army is not altogether inapt. For like an old-time army of invasion, it was accompanied by a horde of sutlers. Where these sutlers came from, and how they earned a living in other times, is something of a mystery. But they appeared as if by magic at suitable centres throughout the hop-picking districts.

So while Sergeant Wragge kept his vigil at the upper window, the scene outside the Chequers was gradually transformed. The open space round the elm tree became covered with stalls, upon which were displayed goods of every kind. The stall-holders arrived in various ways. Some, accompanied by their wives and families, came trundling barrows and perambulators. From these they extracted pieces of wood, erected a rickety bench, and displayed their wares upon it. Others, more enterprising, or perhaps more prosperous, employed the services of a horse and cart. The aristocracy arrived in cars and lorries, drawing these up in such space as they could find.

The goods displayed upon these improvised stalls comprised the whole extent of the hop-pickers' needs. One, for instance, sold bread and sticky confectionery which attracted all the flies in the neighbourhood. Another bore the legend "Proger's Perfect Pork Pies". Next to this was an appetising display of jellied eels and whelks. Conspicuous under the branches of the elm tree was a lorry laden with boxes of kippers and bloaters.

Round these stalls and round the windows of the bar parlour an ever-changing crowd eddied and swirled. The technique of shopping was in nearly every case the same. A family of hop-pickers would appear from somewhere down the road, possibly a mother, two grown-up daughters and a couple of small boys. They would walk first round the stalls in solemn conference. The meals for the following day required the most careful consideration. Breakfast was easy. There would be enough bread and butter left over from to-day for that. Possibly an egg or two, purchased locally, could be afforded. The dinner was a more momentous question. This usually involved a visit to the lorry which bore a huge placard "Come here for the best joints". Bargaining for the scrag-end of a neck of mutton was an exciting business. The mother, ably seconded by her two daughters, conducted this campaign. Eventually the joint would be secured and placed at the bottom of an enormous black American cloth bag. Vegetables were a simple matter, for every home-dweller who possessed a garden or an allotment sold these. You could, for instance, ask Mrs. Raymond for two-pennyworth of pot herbs and be sure of getting a generous supply of carrots, turnips and greens. Then there was tea to be considered. A loaf of bread and two or three pairs of kippers or bloaters. The black bag carried by mother became bulkier and heavier at each step.

By this time the small boys would become clamorous. Household shopping was all very well in its way, but it provided no delicacies for the youthful appetite. With much vocal resentment of their importunity mother would buy each a large and an incredibly viscous jam tart. Then came the real problem of the evening.

This problem was what was to be done with the remainder of the money allotted to the day's expenditure. And it was an acute one. Expenditure had to be limited. You couldn't always be going subbing to the farm bailiff. If you did there would be nothing left at the end of the week when your tally came to be checked. And when father and Uncle Dick came down on Saturday and found the family spent out there would be ructions. So mother and her two daughters put their heads together over the change remaining in the battered purse. Eighteen pence exactly, not so bad considering. And then ensued a loud argument as to ways and means.

The two daughters were as usual united in their opinions. Jellied eels were above all things desirable, but they were disappointingly unsatisfying. Whelks were far better value. Besides, there was the thrill of extricating them skilfully from their retreat. Mother had a craving for cockles, still unsatisfied in spite of long indulgence. But she allowed herself to be over-ruled and four-pennyworth of whelks were purchased. Quite a nice taste between the three of them. The three of them, because whelks were not suitable for the puerile digestion. Besides, the kids already had a jam tart. What more could they expect?

The rest was simple, for it is notorious that whelks are insipid unless you have something good to wash them down with. So the eldest girl paid a visit to the window of the bar parlour. Half a pint of stout for mother, half a pint of mild each for the two daughters. Finally a fizzy lemonade to be shared between the two small boys. Armed with these refreshments the family retired to the arbour, and somehow squeezed themselves into the only couple of seats which still remained.

Sergeant Wragge watched all this with a tolerant eye. He became reminiscent, and recalled how different things were when he was a young constable. Then, hop-picking had meant the invasion of a crowd of rowdies, and sometimes pitched battles between them and the police. Now everything was changed. The hop-pickers seemed to be of a different class altogether. They were a happy, good-natured set of people, who meant no harm to anybody. The same families came down to the same farms year after year. He never had what you might call serious trouble with any of them. They got a bit noisy sometimes, certainly. They couldn't understand why the law forbade them to have a drink except during certain restricted hours. Well, he hardly blamed them. They were in a sense out on holiday and it seemed very hard that they shouldn't be allowed to do what they liked within reasonable bounds. He fancied that he recognised some of the faces from previous years. He even wondered vaguely what law of nature ordained that all the more elderly women should run to such preposterous behinds. The girls were slim enough, good-looking too, most of them. But their mothers! You'd have a devil of a job to seat them five in a row in a railway carriage.

Not many men came hop-picking these days. The occupation did not seem to appeal to the unemployed Londoner. The few who did come seemed to be men in

39

jobs from which they could afford to take three weeks' holiday, and to bring their wives and families with them. They had a way of segregating by themselves. The wives and families were left to do the shopping and to them would have been assigned a bench in the arbour.

The men, for the most part, sat on the grass under the elm tree, exchanging talk in a dialect foreign to the country ear of Sergeant Wragge. Every now and then one of the men would rise and lurch across to the window of the bar parlour. Having got there, he glanced anxiously towards his family assembled in the arbour. Fair's fair. Besides, it doesn't look well to leave your family out of it when you fetch another pint for yourself. The family, watching him, was as well aware of his feeling as he was himself. They hastily emptied their glasses and looked at him expectantly. With a sigh he strolled to the arbour and collected their glasses. There was at least threepence to be collected on each of them. Then he gave his order and carried it away from the window on a tray. With his own pint he returned to his previous seat beneath the tree.

Wragge scanned each of these men carefully as they came into his field of vision. Not for the first time he realised how extremely difficult it is to recognise an unknown person from his description and photograph. More than once he leant forward eagerly. Something in the shape of the nose or the curve of a chin seemed to correspond with the photograph. But each time on closer inspection he shook his head. The object of his scrutiny had a mole on his face, or his eyes were set too widely apart, or his ears were the wrong shape, or his cheeks didn't seem to fit in with that queer phrase in the description, "sanguine" complexion. What was a sanguine complexion, anyhow?

It began to grow dark. At last Mr. Raymond, bursting out of his house like an enraged fury, lighted the gas lamp which was set above the front door of the Chequers. This immediately changed the aspect of the scene. The gas lamp in spite of its two incandescent mantles, shed its light only over the restricted area in front of the window. The stall holders, by way of attracting custom, produced hurricane lanterns which they hung up to produce the best light possible in the circumstances. But these, seen from the window where the Sergeant sat, gave little more light than so many glow-worms. The upper branches of the elm tree remained outlined against the fading sky. Beneath it appeared a constellation of faint stars, the lighted cigarettes of the men assembled there. The arbour became shrouded in darkness. Not until a figure moved into the rays of the gas lamp did it become anything more than a vague shadow.

But the darkness utterly failed to depress the spirits of the hop-pickers. Somebody unseen, probably one of the men beneath the elm tree, produced a mouth organ. He played the first few bars of a popular tune, and from a dozen quarters more or less harmonious whistlers joined in. It seemed almost as though this had

The Sergeant thought it time to put in a word. "The Matling folk would never let you go, Mr. Raymond," he said. "Nor would the brewers, either. They know how to appreciate a tenant that runs his house properly. By the way, did you hear the chaps this evening say anything about that Paddock Croft affair?"

"I didn't see any of the chaps to speak to," Mr. Raymond replied. "Mary and I were kept busy in the bar parlour all the time. You'd better ask mother, she was in and out of the other room serving the home-dwellers."

"Old Daddy Wright's nephew was talking about it," said Mrs. Raymond. "It's a bad business, Sergeant. The first time I've ever known anything of the kind happen in the parish. But you'll catch the man sure enough, won't you Mr. Wragge?"

"Oh, we'll catch him right enough," replied Wragge confidently. "There must be folk round about here who've got a pretty good idea who did it. Some of the pickers or their friends must know him. What did Wright's nephew say about it?"

"Only what he heard," Mrs. Raymond answered. "It seems that Mr and Mrs. Speight are terribly upset. You couldn't expect anything else with all that valuable jewellery taken. And Wright's nephew says that Lizzie, the parlourmaid down there, told him that it wasn't insured. You'd never think that anybody would take a ladder and climb in through the window like that."

"You never know what desperate things some of these chaps will do, Mrs. Raymond," said Wragge solemnly. "There's some bad characters in the world, there's no mistake about that. Wright's nephew didn't drop a hint that he suspected anybody by any chance, did he?"

Mrs. Raymond looked suddenly uncomfortable. She glanced half-apprehensively, first at the Sergeant and then at her husband.

"Well, he did mention a name, and that's a fact," she said hesitatingly, "but you know what the chaps are. They get together and talk a lot of nonsense. I never take any notice of what they say, myself."

"They do get some queer ideas into their heads sometimes, I'll allow," said the Sergeant. "So a name was mentioned, was it? Do you happen to remember what it was, Mrs. Raymond?"

Again Mrs. Raymond glanced at her husband. "Well, I overheard them talking about that chap Lavis," she replied.

"Lavis!" exclaimed Mr. Raymond. "Why, that chap's a perfect nuisance, as I was telling the Sergeant only this morning. What were they saying about him to-night, I'd like to know?"

"What's Lavis doing now?" the Sergeant asked, "He had a job travelling for one of the hop-manure companies, I know that, but somebody was telling me the other day in Culverden that he'd lost it."

"Of course he's lost it," replied Mr. Raymond scornfully. "It isn't the first job that he's lost and it won't be the last. You know what it is, Sergeant. He and his sister have a pound or two a week coming in. Money left them by their father, they say. They can't touch the capital, I'm told, or it would all have gone long ago. Lavis had got the idea that he needn't work unless he wants to. Employers won't put up with that sort of thing these days, and I don't blame them. He's got another job now, I hear. But I'm willing to bet a gallon of beer that he won't keep it long."

"I'm sorry for that sister of his," said Mrs. Raymond. "She's steady enough, from the little I know of her, and she must have a terrible time of it keeping house for that man Lavis. If I was her I'd tell him to find lodgings somewhere else, to be rid of him."

The Sergeant knew well enough that any direct approach to the subject would be useless. "What job has Lavis got now?" he asked.

Both Mr and Mrs. Raymond shook their heads. "Couldn't say," the former replied. "Selling something or other on commission, I believe. That's what he's been doing ever since I've known him. Sometimes it's hop-manure, sometimes it's sewing machines. What it might be this time I really couldn't say. What was Wright's nephew saying about him to-night, mother?"

"Oh, nothing very much," said Mrs. Raymond off-handedly. "Only that he'd fallen off his bicycle last Saturday night and used a lot of swear words about it."

"He knows better than to cuss in my house," said Mr. Raymond. "Fallen off his bicycle, had he? Well, it wouldn't be the first time. A couple of pints of cider's enough to upset him, and then there's no telling what he might do."

"Did Wright's nephew see him fall off his bicycle?" the Sergeant asked.

"Not exactly, so far as I can make out," Mrs. Raymond replied. "He lives with his uncle, you know, in that cottage to the right between here and Paddock Croft. He'd been in here with his uncle that evening, I heard him say, and they'd both gone home about half-past nine. Not long after ten he was thinking of going up to bed when he heard a crash in the road outside. Terrible clatter it was, he was saying, just as if somebody had thrown down a lot of pots and pans. He waited a minute or two but didn't hear anything more. Then he thought that there might have been an accident and that he'd better go out and see. And then he found that it was only Lavis fallen off his bicycle. He'd got a big bag which had dropped off, and when Wright's nephew saw him he was just strapping in on to the bicycle again. When Wright's nephew asked him if he was all right, he only swore at him."

"He's like that when he gets a bit of drink in him," said Mr. Raymond philosophically.

"He'd better not let me catch him swearing on the public highway," said the Sergeant. "If I'd been Wright's nephew I'd have answered him back properly."

"Oh, he didn't do that," said Mrs. Raymond hastily. "Everybody around here knows Lavis. They don't take any notice of him when he's in drink. Wright's nephew just watched him as he got on his bicycle again and rode off. But it was the way he went that made him wonder."

"Why which way would he go but straight along the road until he got to Park Gate?" Mr. Raymond demanded.

"Well, he didn't go that way, or so at least Wright's nephew was saying. He turned off to the right along the path which runs through the meadow and comes out at Hobb's corner."

"Why, whatever possessed him to go along there at that time of night, I wonder?" exclaimed Mr. Raymond.

Mrs. Raymond shook her head. "That's just what Wright's nephew was asking the chaps this evening," she replied. "He couldn't have any business that way. And likely enough, he was up to no good."

An idea seemed suddenly to strike Mr. Raymond, but he didn't put it directly into words. "You know that path and the way it runs, I daresay, Sergeant," he said significantly.

"Yes, I know it well enough," Wragge replied. "I was there on Sunday morning. It runs across the meadow below Paddock Croft."

"That's just what Wright's nephew was saying in the other room," said Mrs. Raymond.

Her remark was received in silence. It was, of course, well known locally that Paddock Croft could be approached without any difficulty from the path. Quite clearly the story of Wright's nephew would be sufficient to arouse suspicion that Lavis was the burglar.

Of course the Sergeant knew better. The fingerprints proved beyond all possibility of doubt the guilt of the mysterious Christopher Elver. Elver and Lavis could not be one and the same person, since the latter had been a familiar figure in Matling while the former had been in prison. It was possible, even probable, that Lavis had been up to no good on Saturday night. But certainly he had had nothing to do with the burglary at Paddock Croft. Unless... .

The Sergeant laid down the tankard which he had been raising to his lips. It sounded wildly improbable, but still there was just a chance. Supposing that at some time Lavis and Elver had become acquainted? There was nothing impossible in that. Suppose that they had met sometime on Saturday afternoon and had a little chat? Suppose that in the course of their conversation Lavis had mentioned the open window at Paddock Croft and the ladder so conveniently disposed? He might even have heard that the Speights would be out to dinner that night. And perhaps the two had arranged the affair between them. Lavis to act as guide and Elver to carry out the operation.

"I'll make it my business to have a talk with Lavis," said the Sergeant. "Well, it's time I was getting home, or the missus'll wonder whatever's become of me. I'm sure

I'm very much obliged to both of you. It was real kind of you to think of offering me a bite of supper. I dare say I'll be along this way some time to-morrow and, if so, I'll look in. Good-night, all."

CHAPTER VI

WRAGGE'S first care on the following morning was to ring up Scotland Yard. He fully expected to learn that Elver had been arrested and that his presence would be required to give the necessary evidence before the magistrate. But to his astonishment he was told that nothing had been heard of the wanted man. M Division had not been idle. They had been making inquiries in Halibut Street and its neighbourhood, but up to the present had obtained no information. Nobody had been found who had seen Elver more recently than noon on Saturday. They were firmly of the opinion that he had not returned to London. The obvious conclusion was that he was still lurking in the neighbourhood of Matling.

The Sergeant scratched his head over it. It was now Tuesday. Two whole days had elapsed since the burglary. Elver could not have subsisted all that time in solitude. He had not stolen food, or the matter would certainly have come to the Sergeant's ears. Therefore, he must have a confederate in the district who was supporting him.

This offered the choice of two theories. The first was that Elver was being sheltered among the pickers in one of the hopper huts. This was not improbable. Cases were not unknown of vagrants having excited the pity of the pickers and been given temporary accommodation by them. Elver might have pitched some tale about being penniless and out of work and of having no roof under which to lay his head. If this was actually the case, there was only one thing to be done. The Sergeant would have to make a tour of the hop fields, description and photograph in hand. This, in addition to being a more tiresome procedure, would involve the expenditure of a considerable deal of time.

The second theory was suggested by what Wragge had been told at the Chequers on the previous evening. If Lavis had been Elver's confederate on Saturday night their partnership might not yet be at an end. Perhaps Lavis had undertaken to dispose of the stolen goods. In that case Elver would be anxious to keep his eye on him until the proceeds were divided. Lavis, with his local knowledge, could easily conceal him in some place, and there attend to his bodily wants. Nobody but Lavis need know of this place of concealment. This theory began to appeal to the Sergeant, perhaps because it involved less labour on his part. He breakfasted rather less leisurely than usual, mounted his bicycle and rode off to Park Gate.

It was not yet ten o'clock when he reached the house occupied by Lavis's sister, Mrs. Creach. But, early as it was, the bird had flown and Mrs. Creach could give the Sergeant no information as to his whereabouts. She was a middle-aged widow, slight and rather nervous looking. This visit from the police clearly upset her.

"I'm sorry, I'm sure, Mr. Wragge," she said. "My brother isn't at home. He went away to work on his bicycle the best part of an hour ago."

"That's very unfortunate, Mrs. Creach," said the Sergeant tersely. "I particularly want to speak to him. He's gone to work, you say. Where has he gone to?"

"I'm sure I couldn't tell you, Mr. Wragge," she replied. "My brother never says where he's going or what time he'll be home. But he did say this morning that he wouldn't be home to dinner. He told me to have some supper waiting for him when he got back. I put him up some cold beef and bread and cheese sandwiches to take with him."

Cold beef and bread and cheese? This would suffice for a hidden man's daily ration. Lavis could very easily secure a meal for himself in an inn. It almost seemed that the theory which at first had sounded so improbable was about to prove correct.

"What work is your brother doing now, Mrs. Creach?" the Sergeant asked.

"Well, it isn't exactly regular work," she replied. "He's only doing it to oblige a friend of his who's in business. He goes round the country on his bicycle selling things for him, if you understand me."

"Yes, I understand well enough," said the Sergeant, rather impatiently. "What sort of things is he selling?"

"Knives and things like that for butchers and fishmongers," Mrs. Creach replied. "He carries samples with him in a bag on his bicycle. When he gets an order he sends it off to his friend who delivers the goods direct."

"I see," said the Sergeant. "And what time did your brother get home on Saturday night, Mrs. Creach?"

At the mention of Saturday night she started perceptibly. "I couldn't tell you that, Mr. Wragge," she replied. "I had a bad headache that night, and went to bed early. I took some aspirin for it and I was asleep before nine o'clock. My brother wasn't back then and I didn't hear him come in. But he was in bed and asleep when I took him in a cup of tea at eight o'clock on Sunday morning."

"What time do you expect your brother home this evening?"

"It might be any time, but it's usually round about six that he comes home. He likes to have supper then and go round to the Chequers and have a pint of cider later on."

Wragge left the house and started to ride back to Culverden. He was not anxious to press his questioning of Mrs. Creach too far. She had probably told him the truth about her brother's absence and expected return. On the other hand it was not impossible that she knew something about the affair at Paddock Croft. She had certainly shown concern when Saturday night had been mentioned. It might be worth while to keep an unostentatious watch upon the house at Park Gate.

Sergeant Wragge had two young constables under his immediate direction. Upon his return to Culverden he sent for one of these and gave him his instructions.

"I've got a job for you, Frank," he said. "You know Lavis and his sister Mrs. Creach that live over at Park Gate, I dare say? Well, slip over to their place and stay there till I come and see you this evening. Don't show yourself if you can help it, but just keep an eye on things. If Mrs. Creach goes out, follow her and find out where she goes to. Of course, if you should happen to fall in with this chap Elver that we're looking for, arrest him on the spot. Otherwise, don't interfere with Mrs. Creach. Her brother may come home during the day. If he does don't let him go out again. Tell him that he's to stay where he is until I've been over to see him. That's clear enough, isn't it?"

The constable replied that it was perfectly clear, and went off immediately. Since it was getting on for dinner time, Sergeant Wragge went home. He sat down in his favourite chair and lighted a pipe. It would be a very pleasant feather in his cap if he was able to lay the burglar by the heels. There was just a chance that he would kill two birds with one stone. Not only Elver himself but Lavis, his accomplice.

So Lavis was travelling in butchers' knives just to oblige a friend, was he? Butchers' knives! The words sent a sudden flow of recollection through the Sergeant's mind. He'd never thought of again since that moment. The Paddock Croft affair must have put it clean out of his head. The knife he had picked up on Sunday morning as he was cycling to the scene of the burglary! On his return to Culverden he had untied it from his bicycle and locked it up in a cupboard. He had intended to put a notice up on the board stating that it had been found, but what with one thing and another he had entirely forgotten to do so. He rose from his chair, unlocked the cupboard and laid the knife upon the table.

Yes, it was a butcher's knife, right enough. And now that he looked at it closely the Sergeant saw that it was comparatively new. It had been sharpened, but the shape of the blade showed that it had not been much used. Lying in the dew by the roadside had dulled its brightness, and the spots he had remarked upon it had turned a dull brown. One could do a lot of damage with a knife like that, the Sergeant reflected. Was Lavis altogether a suitable person to be carrying things like that about the country? Only the previous evening Mr. Raymond had said that there was no telling what he might do when he got a bit of liquor inside him.

Wragge frowned as he recalled the spot where he had found the knife. He had passed the Chequers and had reached a spot nearly half-way between there and Paddock Croft. Not very far, in fact from old Daddy Wright's cottage. Was this the spot where Lavis had fallen off his bicycle? Wright's nephew had spoken of his having a bag with him. If this knife had been in the bag he might well have dropped it and failed to recover it in the darkness. That was an explanation and an obvious one.

On the other hand, why should Lavis have been carrying his samples about with him at that time of night? And why should he have gone along the path which led to Hobb's Corner? However drunk he might have been he could hardly have expected to secure an order under those particular conditions. Or had the knife been intended as a weapon should the burglar be disturbed in his operations? Certainly Lavis's movements on Saturday night required looking into. Meanwhile the Sergeant supposed that he would have to spend his afternoon making inquiries in the hop fields. An unsatisfactory job whichever way you looked at it. Good-natured as they might be, the hop-pickers were not fond of giving information to the police.

It was a fine, warm afternoon when the Sergeant began his tour of the hop gardens. He started on the farm nearest his own house, intending to work farther afield should it be necessary. Work was in full swing. Around each bin was assembled a group of hoppers, chattering merrily while they plucked the ripe fruit from the vine. Wragge approached each in turn, to be greeted with a storm of good-natured chaff. Was there nothing better for the police to do than to go round the gardens? Entering into the spirit of the game he answered them in their own coin, but as soon as he produced the photographs of Christopher Elver, and began to recite his description which by now he almost knew by heart, he was conscious of an immediate coolness.

Some of the hoppers, after the merest glance at the photographs, declared fervently that they had never seen anybody like him. Nor did the description shake their convictions. No, never in their lives had they met anybody who in any way answered to it. Others took a more cautious line. They had seen faces like that, but they couldn't remember where. Certainly never in this neighbourhood. It must have been a long time ago, and if they had ever known the name they had forgotten it. As for the description, well it might apply to almost anybody. Others again were immediately struck by the resemblance of the photographs to somebody they had known. But upon patient questioning it always turned out that that somebody was dead long ago, or was living in some impossibly remote place. And all with one accord affected a stupidity in surprising contrast to the usual sharp alertness of the East-End Londoner.

By the end of the afternoon Wragge had had enough of it. He saw the utter fruitlessness of pursuing his quest by these methods. It was not that the pickers were in any way antagonistic to his efforts. They were not deliberately trying to shield a criminal. It was simply that their native caution bid them be very wary of their dealings with the police. Those of them who lived in Stepney where the Thames Police Court is situated had learned the local rendering of the Lord's Prayer, "Lead us not into Thames Station". Even if one's conscience were perfectly clear the police would be a terrible worry. They had a way of asking indiscreet questions about one's neighbours, for instance, answers which might lead to endless trouble. And, beyond it all, there was always the prospect of an appearance in the witness-box, to be bullied by magistrates and impertinent people in wigs and gowns. They might be as rude as they pleased to you, but if you answered back it was contempt of court. No, the law was like the snakes sometimes to be found in the hop gardens, better left alone.

This being their attitude, Elver might remain concealed among them until the end of hop-picking. They had a code of justice of their own. They would try the case for themselves. And their sentence would depend upon the heinousness of the crime in their own eyes. Murder, the betrayal of a pal, the pinching of a poor man's savings - - all these would meet with their instant condemnation. They would have no hesitation in handing the perpetrator over to the police, and serve him right. But undoubtedly they would view the burglary at Paddock Croft with considerable lenience. After all, it was the toff's fault. He had simply asked for trouble. The open window, the ladder so conveniently placed for entering it. Could a poor chap be blamed if he climbed in and helped himself? After all, what did he take? A few bits of jewellery! The toff and his wife would be no worse off for that. If they didn't like doing without the trinkets, they could buy some more. If the police found the chap, well and good. But not one of the pickers would raise a hand to give them active assistance.

Wragge, being an extremely tolerant man, did not blame the pickers for their point of view. He knew well enough that the policeman, by virtue of his office, must fight his battles single-handed. If Elver was to be found it would be by subtler methods than broadcast inquiries. So, having had his tea, the Sergeant cycled out to relieve his subordinate who was keeping watch at Park Gate.

The constable's report was satisfactory, so far as it went. Shortly before noon, Mrs. Creach had gone out. The constable had followed her and found out that her goal was the village shop. Here she made a few purchases. She had then returned home and had not left the house since. The baker had called at the house during the afternoon and delivered a loaf. Mrs. Creach had had no other visitors. Nor had anybody else appeared from the house. Finally, the Sergeant learnt that Lavis had returned home shortly before his arrival. He had been riding a bicycle to which a large bag had been strapped.

"All right," said the Sergeant, "you cut along home and leave the rest to me." He walked up to the house and hammered on the front door, which was opened by Mrs. Creach.

"Oh, here you are back again, Sergeant," she said without enthusiasm. "My brother's just come back. He's in the kitchen if you want to see him."

Wragge entered the kitchen, to find Lavis seated at the table with a plate of cold meat in front of him. He was a short stocky man, with red hair and a scowling expression. He looked as though he might be an ugly customer to deal with if it came to trouble. But he seemed in no way disturbed by Wragge's entry.

"What's your business, Sergeant?" he asked truculently. "My sister says you've been here once before to-day to see me. What's it all about?"

"That's soon told," replied Wragge shortly. "I've been hearing complaints about you using abusive language on the public highways."

Lavis laid down his knife and fork and glared savagely. "Who's been complaining about me, I'd like to know?" he asked.

"That's no business of yours. I've warned you, and that's enough. Next time it won't stop at a warning. You were at the Chequers on Saturday evening, I hear."

"Well, what if I was? A man can go into a pub and have a drink if he likes, can't he?"

"So long as he behaves himself decently," replied the Sergeant swiftly. "The trouble is you didn't. You were involved in a row outside after you'd been turned out."

"Well, that takes the cake, that does," exclaimed Lavis indignantly. "There was a bit of a row going on, I remember that, but I had nothing to do with it. It was those two Adcorn chaps that started it. They wanted to set about a stranger who was there, from what I could make out. However, it didn't come to anything. I just jumped on my bicycle and rode home."

"You rode straight home?" asked the Sergeant innocently.

"Why, yes of course I did. Where else could I go when the pub was closed?"

The sergeant looked at him severely. "Lavis, you're a liar," he said. "Or else it is that you were too drunk to remember what happened that night. How many glasses of cider did you have at the Chequers?"

As soon as he had spoken the Sergeant saw that he had made a slip. He had offered Lavis a means of escape which he was not slow to take. A look of cunning crept into his eyes.

"Well, sergeant, I'm bound to say that I had a drop more than I usually do," he replied. "You know what Raymond's cider is. Feeds it up with sugar and raisins until it's nigh as strong as whisky. Couple of pints is enough for anybody. But I was terribly thirsty that evening, and I dare say I had three, with perhaps another half to top if up with. When I got outside into the air it came over me all queer. I'm bound to say I don't remember anything very clearly until I found myself back here, sitting in this very chair."

"You don't remember falling off your bicycle, for instance?"

Lavis's eyes widened as though a dim recollection had returned to him. "Why yes, now I come to think of it, I did have a bit of a tumble," he replied. "You know what that road from the Chequers is like. Terrible slippery when there's a bit of dew on the ground. And I must have got too near the edge of the road and my bike skidded."

"That's no excuse for using bad language when you were offered help. And perhaps you'll explain why, after that, instead of coming straight home you took the path which leads to Hobb's Corner."

A look of complete innocence over-spread Lavis's countenance. "Why I never did that, did I?" he exclaimed. "Just shows the tricks that cider will play with a chap. I do mind now that it seemed a long time before I got back here. Fancy that, now! All the way round by Hobb's Corner! Why, it would be a mile or more out of my way."

The Sergeant disregarded this. "Who did you meet on your way home?" he asked suddenly.

Lavis's eyes flickered, but he allowed no other sign of discomfiture to escape him. "Who did I meet?" he replied. "Why, nobody that I can remember. Wait a minute, though. There was a chap that came up to me when I'd that skid, but who he was or what he said I can't rightly say. There wasn't anybody else that I'm sure of."

The Sergeant decided on a bold stroke. He knew by experience that sudden accusations often startled a man into betraying himself. Lavis was still seated at the table. His sister was standing beside him, glancing anxiously from one to the other as the conversation between her brother and the Sergeant proceeded. Wragge suddenly produced one of Elver's photographs from his pocket and laid it on the table in full view of both of them. "That's the portrait of the man you met on Saturday night," he exclaimed triumphantly.

The reaction was instantaneous. Lavis looked at the photograph incredulously, then in a flash his expression changed to one of amazement. "It's Joe!" he exclaimed.

Meanwhile Mrs. Creach had bent down to view the photograph more closely. Her recognition of it was as immediate as her brother's. "Why, that's the man who came here asking for you on Saturday afternoon," she said. "I told you about him next morning, if you remember."

Lavis turned upon her savagely. "Came here asking for me!" he exclaimed. "Why, you're out of your senses, woman! How should he come asking for me when he didn't know I lived here?"

"Perhaps it wasn't him," replied Mrs. Creach picking up the photograph and looking at it more closely. "Why of course it wasn't. How silly of me. The man who came here on Saturday was a good deal older than this. I can see it wasn't him now. There's just a sort of likeness that made me think for the moment that it was him."

"You say that a man called here on Saturday afternoon and asked for your brother?" queried the Sergeant.

"Yes, that's right. I told him that my brother wasn't in and he seemed very disappointed. He asked if there was any chance of seeing him later in the evening, and I told him I thought not. You see, my brother told me that he wouldn't be back for tea, and I knew that he'd stop at the Chequers until ten o'clock like he always does on Saturdays. And that's what I told to the man."

"Better for your brother if he stayed away from the pub," the sergeant remarked sagely. "What did the man say when you told him that?"

"He said that he'd come back on Sunday morning. But he never did. And he's never been here since. I supposed that he had to go back to London."

"How do you know that he came from London?" the Sergeant remarked quickly.

"Why, I don't know for sure. But I took him to be a friend of one of the hop-pickers who'd come down for the day. You see, he was wearing one of those paper caps like Londoners do when they go on holiday."

Wragge felt a thrill of triumph. "Do you remember what the colour of the cap was?" he asked.

Mrs. Creach considered this for a moment. "So far as I recollect it was green with a touch of red on it," she replied.

Ever since Sunday morning Wragge had kept the cap which he had found at Paddock Croft in his pocket. He now produced it and showed it to her. "Anything like that?" he asked quietly.

Mrs. Creach glanced at her brother doubtfully. She was evidently not at all sure that he approved of her disclosure. But he made no sign and after a moment's hesitation she replied. "If that isn't the one it's very like it."

"Had you ever seen the man before, Mrs. Creach?"

She shook her head. "No he was a perfect stranger to me," she replied.

The sergeant turned sharply to her brother. "Not to you, Lavis," he said. "What business had Sea Joe with you on Saturday afternoon?"

"Don't you let yourself be led astray by any woman's tales," Lavis replied. "It can't have been Sea Joe that came to see me. How could he have known where I lived?"

The Sergeant shrugged his shoulders. "Because you told him, I suppose. Now let's get to the bottom of this, Lavis. What do you know about Sea Joe?"

"I don't know anything, and that's the truth," Lavis replied emphatically. "I used to meet him years ago when I was working for a ship's chandlers in London. He was a steward on board a ship then -- I've forgotten her name. It was my job to call on ships when they got into dock and see if I could get any orders. That's how I came to meet Sea Joe."

"I see, and you've kept up the acquaintanceship ever since?"

"Nay, that I haven't," replied Lavis virtuously. "Sea Joe isn't the sort of chap I took him for. He got himself into trouble with the police and was sentenced to seven years hard. I haven't seen him since."

"Come now, Lavis, that won't wash," said the Sergeant. "What was Sea Joe's right name to begin with?"

Lavis looked up craftily. "You ought to know that, Sergeant, since he's been in prison," he replied.

"Never mind about that. I asked you if you knew what his right name was."

Lavis hesitated for a moment. "Chris Elver," he replied sulkily. "At least that's what he used to sign himself."

"Oh, you were familiar with his signature, were you? You used to do business together, I suppose?"

"I used to get his orders and pass them on to the firm."

"And of course he got in touch with you again when he was released from prison?"

"No, that he didn't I'll swear," exclaimed Lavis emphatically. "How could he do that when he didn't know where I was? It was like this you see. I left the firm a few months after he'd been put in gaol. They hadn't treated me properly, and I wasn't going to work for anybody who didn't appreciate my services. That would be eight or nine years ago now, and I came down here to live with my sister. That's right, isn't it, Flo?"

Mrs. Creach nodded. "Yes, it's as long ago as that," she said wearily.

"Well, if he didn't get in touch with you, you got in touch with him," the Sergeant insisted. "How else do you account for his coming here and asking for you?"

"Can't have seen him," replied Lavis promptly. "You don't think I'd have anything to do with a chap that had served time, do you?"

"I'm not so sure," replied the Sergeant. Then abruptly he changed his tone. "Tell me where Elver is at this moment, and I won't ask too many questions about his associations with you."

"How should I know where he is at this moment?" Lavis exclaimed indignantly. "I've never set eyes on the chap since I took my last order from him all those years ago."

"You'll find it will pay you better to tell the truth, Lavis," said the Sergeant sternly. "We have reason to believe that you met Elver on Saturday night for an illegal purpose. You understand that when he is arrested, as he will be before very long, your position will become pretty serious. Perhaps you will pretend that you don't know it's a crime to shelter anybody who is wanted by the police? It's a very serious offence, let me tell you. I'd recommend you to think about that pretty hard. What were you carrying on Saturday night in that bag strapped to your bicycle?"

This sudden change of subject seemed to puzzle Lavis. "What should I be carrying?" he replied. "My samples to be sure. Yes, and that reminds me. Somebody stole one of my samples that night. You'd be better employed in finding that than in asking me questions about Elver, whom I haven't so much as heard of for years."

"I know how I'm best employed," said Wragge shortly. "But let's hear a little more about this theft. What was it that was stolen?"

"Why, one of my knives to be sure. It was in my bag when I went to the Chequers on Saturday evening. It wasn't there when I came to look inside on Sunday morning."

"How did you come to take your bag with you when you went to the Chequers?"

"Because I hadn't been home first, see? I'd been on my rounds down Bathdown way, calling on a few likely customers, and I didn't get back to Matling until seven o'clock or later. I'd had my tea with some friends of mine that I'd called upon, so I just called into the Chequers for a drop of cider as I passed."

"Where did you leave your bag while you were in the Chequers?"

"Why, strapped to the bike, where it had been all day. I didn't leave the bike outside the house, for you never know, with all those pickers and their friends about, what tricks they may be up to. So I just pushed it in behind the lodge where nobody would be likely to see it. It was there all safe when I came out and got it again."

"When did you look inside the bag next?"

"Well, I didn't exactly look inside it until Sunday morning. But I mind when I had that skid the old bag fell off and the knives and things tumbled on the road. I reckoned that I'd got them all picked up, but I see now what must have happened."

"And what do you think happened?"

"Why, that chap that came up and spoke to me must have sneaked one of them."

"Oh, that's when you must have cut yourself," exclaimed Mrs. Creach suddenly.

"What's that to do with you whether I cut myself or not?" replied her brother savagely.

"It's got nothing to do with me. But you'll remember that I found the leg of your trousers all covered with blood on Sunday morning."

"Well, that may have been it," replied Lavis sullenly. "Knives are nasty things to pick up in the dark, and maybe one slipped and gave me a jag in the arm. But there, I'm bound to confess that what with the cider I'd drunk I don't remember much about what happened that night."

"I'd try to remember a little more, if I were you," said the Sergeant. "You might recall, for instance, your meeting with Elver and what happened in consequence. I'm only trying to advise you for your own good. Surely you can see for yourself what's bound to happen? Elver will be arrested and then he'll have his own story to tell. Whereas if you tell your story first, you may manage to get into the witness-box instead of the dock. And, as I don't mind telling you, you'll be a lot better off that way. Now just you sit and think it over for a bit." Without any further farewell the sergeant left the house.

He called in at the Chequers on his way home. The Raymonds had lived in the district for many more years than he had, and he was anxious to verify whatever he could of Lavis's statement. Mrs. Raymond, who was a walking directory of the countryside, was able to supply him with the information he required. Mrs. Creach's husband, who had been a small farmer, had died some ten years before. Mrs. Creach had then sold the farm, retaining for her use only the house in which she now lived. A year or so after this event -- Mrs. Raymond could not be more accurate than that -- Lavis had come to live with his sister. Since then he had travelled for various firms and had never been able to hold his job for long.

"Do you happen to know what he was doing before he came down here?" the Sergeant asked.

"I can't say for certain," Mrs. Raymond replied. "I have heard that he had something to do with ships in London. But you can't rely on things folks say."

Wragge returned home very well pleased with his excursion. He had very little doubt that before long Lavis would make a clean breast of it. He wasn't the sort of man who would endanger his own liberty to secure the safety of a friend. When he had had time to think it over he would see on which side his bread was buttered.

He had been cunning enough to weave a weft of lies upon a warp of truth. He had not guessed that the Sergeant was already aware of the identity of the burglar, or he would not have admitted a previous acquaintanceship with Elver. It had been a slip on his part to admit that he recognised the photograph, but he had countered by admitting his previous acquaintanceship with Elver.

One point, indeed, had been satisfactorily cleared up. The Sergeant was aware of the financial transactions between Elver and Joe Fuller. The former, as an excuse for borrowing five shillings, had said that he knew some one in the country who would supply him with money. Until now that had sounded like a fairy tale. But in the light of Mrs. Creach's statement it assumed an appearance of possibility. Elver might have been telling the truth. Lavis was the friend whom he proposed to visit. And he had reason to believe that he could extract money from him.

That opened up a very interesting line of conjecture. Why was Elver confident that he could extract money from Lavis? On the strength of their previous friendship? Hardly. It was more likely that their association had been confined to ordinary business transactions. They probably shared some guilty secret between them.

If that were the case, Elver's actions were understandable. He had kept Lavis up his sleeve, so to speak, until necessity should arise. When this occurred he resolved to visit him, assuming the disguise of the friend of one of the hop-pickers.

That paper cap had turned out a useful clue after all. Mrs. Creach had recognised it as the one worn by her visitor of Saturday afternoon. The Sergeant was no logician, but his arguments seemed to him unassailable. The cap had been worn by Mrs. Creach's visitor. The cap must have been left in the garden at Paddock Croft by the burglar. It was proved conclusively by the fingerprints that Elver had been the burglar. Elver therefore must have been Mrs. Creach's visitor. Surely that would be obvious enough to anybody. Elver had failed to find Lavis at home, but Mrs. Creach had told him when and where he might be expected. No doubt the two had met during the course of the evening. It was not difficult to guess what had passed between them. Elver had endeavoured to blackmail Lavis by a threat of revealing the secret, whatever it was, Lavis, then, no doubt thoroughly scared, had protested that he had no money to spare. But, spurred into activity by Elver's threat, his fertile brain had discovered an alternative. He had suggested an attempt upon Paddock Croft, offering himself as a guide for the purpose. Elver had accepted the offer, on condition that Lavis should shelter him until the proceeds could be realised.

As for the knife, its discovery by the roadside was easily explained. When Lavis had fallen off his bicycle it had slipped out of his bag together with the rest of his samples. Lavis, fumbling about in his fuddled condition in the darkness, had failed to recover it. It had lain where it had fallen until the Sergeant picked it up.

Everything, in fact, was capable of a perfectly simple explanation. It only remained for the Sergeant to arrest Elver and the case would be complete. And, in his own mind, Wragge was convinced that the arrest would be affected within the next few hours.

CHAPTER VII

HOBB'S corner was a cross-road, at which there was a cluster of buildings about a mile from the Matling Chequers. It derived its name from Hobb's Farm, of which the hop gardens surrounded the cross-roads on all sides. The path which has already been mentioned ran from a point not far from the Chequers to the cross-roads. But this path was available only for pedestrians and cyclists. Vehicles proceeding from Matling to Hobb's Corner followed the road which ran through Park Gate. The Matling end of the path, Hobb's Corner and Park Gate, were situated at the extremities of an almost equilateral triangle, each side of which was rather more than three-quarters of a mile.

Of the buildings at the cross-roads, the most conspicuous were a range of two oasthouses. Facing these was a pair of tumbledown cottages, now uninhabited and used as a store. About fifty yards away from these in the direction of Park Gate was a modern bungalow.

This bungalow had been built some five or six years previously by Mr. Pershore, the head of the firm Pershore and Huggins, artificial manure manufacturers. Mr. Pershore had bought the land upon which the bungalow stood from Mr. Velley, the owner of Hobb's Farm, or rather, as it was said locally, he had taken it in exchange for a large consignment of the hop manure which was one of his firm's products. The bungalow was small but well and attractively built. Mr. Pershore, who was a lover of antiques, had furnished it at considerable expense. But he did not live there permanently. He had a house in London which was also full of beautiful things. The bungalow was occupied only at the week-ends, when either Mr. Pershore himself or one of his family usually came down from Saturday till Monday. During the remainder of the week, the bungalow was unoccupied. It was looked after by Mrs. Adcorn, who lived with her two sons, Tom and Fred, in one of the cottages belonging to Hobb's Farm. She came in daily and aired the place.

In Mr. Pershore's eyes the bungalow had only one disadvantage. Within a few hundred yards of it were the hopper huts belonging to Hobb's Farm. These were, of course, unoccupied for the greater part of the year. But during hop-picking they were inhabited by a clamorous crowd whose favourite diet appeared to be bloaters. Mr. Pershore, after one experience, refused to come down to the bungalow during hop-picking. He said that he might just as well stay in London, where the crowd was no denser and the culinary odours more diversified. His last visit during the current year, upon which Mrs. Pershore had accompanied him, had been from August 17th to 18th, the last week-end before hop-picking had begun.

Sergeant Wragge had just reached the comforting conclusion that the arrest of Elver could not be long delayed. He was unlacing his boots preparatory to the enjoyment of a quiet evening when his telephone rang. With a muttered objurgation he rose and answered the call. An excited voice at the other end of the wire greeted him.

"Hallo, is that you, Sergeant? This is Velley of Hobb's Farm speaking. Mr. Pershore's bungalow's on fire. I've rung up the brigade and they'll be along as soon as they can. I've plenty of water in my pond, fortunately, and I've got everybody I can collect carrying buckets."

"Right, I'll be along in a couple of shakes, Mr. Velley," Wragge replied. He hurriedly relaced his boots and ran out of the house. This was surely an emergency which warranted abnormal expenditure. A few doors away was the local garage which always had a car available for hire. The Sergeant engaged this, and a few minutes later, he was being driven towards Matling at breakneck speed.

The rising ground, upon which the village of Matling stood, screened the fire from his sight until he was well past the Chequers. Then, as the car reached the summit, he could see it plainly enough. In the twilight it appeared like a huge bonfire, round which an interested circle of figures appeared to be dancing. As he approached them they turned out to be men and women running between the pond and the fire with buckets and shouting at the tops of their voices. The car pulled up and Wragge jumped out.

The bungalow was blazing fiercely, there was no doubt about that. It was built of brick with a tiled roof, but its internal fittings consisted mainly of wood. By the time the Sergeant arrived, the fire had got a good hold. Flames were bursting out through the front windows and also through the centre of the roof. He saw at a glance that the place was doomed unless the fire brigade arrived without much further delay. But the nearest brigade was stationed nearly ten miles away, and it must traverse country roads where excessive speed would be dangerous.

The crowd assembled outside the bungalow was doing all it could. It consisted mainly of the temporary occupants of the hopper huts, though the Sergeant could distinguish a few familiar faces directing their efforts. Among these were Mr. Velley and his wife and the two Adcorn brothers. A chain had been organised between the pond and the bungalow, a matter of three or four hundred yards. Every bucket or similar utensil which could be found had been pressed into service. The two Adcorns were superintending the filling of these at the pond, while Mr. Velley in person directed the efforts of those grouped round the bungalow. The buckets left the pond full to the brim. But as they passed from one excited hand to another much of their contents was spilt. By the time they reached the seat of the fire, they were, as a rule, barely half-full. And however eager those who poured them into the flames might be, the task was no easy one. It was impossible to get close to the burning building because of the intense heat. Each man had to run in as near as he could, fling the contents of his bucket, and retire hastily. Very little of the water that left the pond actually reached the scene of the fire. Such water that did reach it evaporated almost at once in a cloud of steam.

The Sergeant shook his head. There was really nothing that he could do. But while he stood there wondering what in the world Mr. Pershore would say when he heard about it, the sound of a motor-horn rang out above the clamour. A pair of headlights flashed into view and above them the glint of the fire on the firemen's helmets. The engine came to a standstill with much grinding of brakes and the men jumped off.

Mr Velley ran to meet the captain. "Plenty of water in my pond," he said. "You can run your hoses --"

"We'll see to that," replied the captain shortly, "show us where the pond is, there's a good fellow."

On the arrival of the fire engine, the helpers desisted from their work and clustered round it. It gave an opening for the Sergeant's activity. He marched up to them with dignified rapidity.

"Now then, stand back, stand back, please," he ordered. "It's no good getting in the firemen's way, you know. A little farther back, please. You'll be able to see just as well."

He shepherded them gently to a point a few yards down the road, where he stood barring the way. Meanwhile the firemen had run a hose to the pond and the pumps began to throb violently. A steady crackling stream of water emerged from the nozzles, to be directed through one of the broken windows into the heart of the fire. A huge cloud of steam arose into the air, its underside tinged pink by the flames. Very soon it became evident that the fire brigade had arrived just in time to save the bungalow. The flames died down gradually and Wragge found himself at leisure to investigate to origin of the conflagration.

Mr. Velley, a big stout man, was standing by the engine. He was perspiring freely and mopping his face with an enormous crimson handkerchief. Mr. Wragge went up to him.

"Good-evening, Mr. Velley, this is a bad business." he said. "Have you any idea how it started?"

"Haven't had time to think about it," replied Velley. "All I know is that Fred Adcorn ran up to the house hollering that the place was afire. He's my drier you know, and was working down at the oast. I got on to the brigade by telephone, and then I told Fred to turn out his brother and lay hands on all the buckets he could find and give them to the pickers from the huts. Then I rang you up and since then I've been trying to do what I could. You'd better ask Fred about it. He's over there yonder, collecting the buckets."

The Sergeant approached Fred Adcorn, who was a tall, powerful, pleasant-faced man of about thirty-five or so.

"Good-evening, Adcorn," he said. "How did you come to see the bungalow burning?"

"Why I was working down at the oast," Fred replied. "Tending the fires and that, you understand. We'd got a load of hops in but they wasn't dried yet, so after I had a look at them I came out for a breath of fresh air. Then I caught a queer smell like as if something was burning. It wasn't my hops, I knew that well enough. And I couldn't make out at first what it was. Then I happened to look over towards the bungalow and saw a sort of twinkling light in the windows. I thought that was queer, for I knew that Mr. Pershore wasn't there and mother was at home cooking the supper."

"What did you do about it?" Wragge asked.

"Why, I went over to have a look. And when I looked in at the window I saw the place was properly afire. The flames had got hold of the floor and some of the furniture. So I hopped it up to the farm and told Mr. Velley."

"Which room was it that you looked into?"

"The big room in the front. The lounge, I think they call it. It was all alight properly, and no mistake. Then Mr. Velley told me to get out the buckets and call the pickers. But it wouldn't have been much good if the brigade hadn't come along when they did."

"Could you see if any of the other rooms besides the lounge were on fire?"

Fred Adcorn shook his head. "I couldn't swear to it, of course, Sergeant," he replied. "Naturally I didn't waste time going round the house looking in at all the windows. But it seemed to me that the only room that was alight was the lounge. The wall farthest from the window that I looked through seemed to be all afire. And if you don't mind, Sergeant, I'll be getting back to my oast. I don't want that lot of hops spoilt, and I've been away from them long enough already."

He hurried off and the Sergeant strolled back to the scene of the fire. Fred Adcorn, he knew, was a steady, reliable chap, not in the least likely to imagine things. And yet if his observation was to be trusted, the fire seemed to have started on one of the inner walls of the lounge.

Now the Sergeant was more or less familiar with the bungalow and its arrangements. He knew, for instance, that although it was equipped with central heating, it was not fitted with electric light. How then had the fire originated? There was no fireplace in the lounge in which ashes might have been left smouldering. Nor could the familiar explanation of an electrical short circuit be given in this case. He would have to see Mrs. Adcorn and hear any suggestions she might have.

He had not far to go in search of her. She was standing in front of the smouldering bungalow, a horrified expression on her face, watching the efforts of the firemen to extinguish the last remnants of the fire. When the Sergeant accosted her she started as though she expected him to arrest her on the spot. Her first words expressed the underlying current of her thoughts.

"Oh, Sergeant, whatever will Mr. Pershore say when he hears of this?"

"He'll want to know how it happened, I expect," the Sergeant replied quietly. "And that's what we've got to try and find out between us, Mrs. Adcorn. You're taking care of the bungalow for him, aren't you?"

"That's right," she replied, with the tears starting to her eyes. "And I know he will think it was all my fault. But it wasn't, Sergeant, I'll take my oath upon that."

"When were you last inside the bungalow, Mrs. Adcorn?"

"Just before six o'clock this evening. It was like this, you see, Sergeant. When there's nobody living there, I go in every morning and sweep round a bit. If it's fine like it was to-day, I open the windows then. And then sometime between five and six in the afternoon I come round again, shut the windows and make all safe for the night."

"You leave the windows open all day? Isn't that a bit risky?"

"It's Mr. Pershore's particular orders. More than once I've said to him that I didn't like leaving the windows open like that. But he only laughed and said that nobody round about here would take anything. Then I asked him what about the hop-pickers, and he said that not even they would dare to go inside the house in broad daylight. There's too many of us folk passing to and fro for that. Still, I never liked it, but Mr. Pershore said that it would be all right."

"You were in the house at six o'clock, you say, Mrs. Adcorn? Did you think that any one could have been hidden in it while you were there?"

Mrs. Adcorn shook her head vigorously. "I'll take my oath that nobody was there, Sergeant," she replied. "You see, I've always got those windows on my mind when the pickers are about. I wouldn't say anything against any one of them -- they're all steady respectable folks and most of them have been coming to this farm for years. But it's those Londoners that come down and hang about the hopper huts that I don't trust. I wouldn't put it beyond some of them to slip in through a window and doss down for the night. So I always look round everywhere before I lock up of an evening. And there was nobody in the house this evening when I left it, I'll swear to that."

"Not hidden under a bed, or in a cupboard or anything like that?" suggested the Sergeant.

"There's not a place like that I didn't poke into," Mrs. Adcorn replied firmly. "I looked under all the beds and in all the cupboards. I even looked into the garage and into the shed where the central heating furnace is. And there wasn't a soul on the place anywhere."

"You went into the lounge this afternoon, of course?"

"Yes, I went in there, shut the windows and looked all round, and everything was right, just the same as it always is."

"From what your son Fred tells me, the fire seems to have started in the lounge. He says that when he looked in at the window, the opposite wall was burning. What was standing against the wall?"

Mrs. Adcorn made an effort of memory. "Let me see, now," she replied. "There are no doors or windows in that wall. At one end there was a big sofa thing, which Mrs. Pershore called a divan, or some such name. That was covered with a whole lot of cushions. Bright looking things they were, but they'll be all spoilt now, more's the pity. Then there was an old grandfather clock in an oak case. I never thought it was very much to look at, but Mr. Pershore told me it was worth a lot of money. He says that nothing does a clock more harm than to be stopped and that I was to be sure to wind it up to the full every Saturday morning. I wasn't to alter the hands or anything like that, you'll understand, Sergeant, but just to keep it wound. And on the other side of the clock was a bureau, with a glass-fronted bookcase above it. I think that was all. Oh, no, there was a little old-fashioned chair which stood between the clock and the bureau."

The Sergeant was struck with a bright idea. He produced a packet of cigarettes from his pocket, opened it and offered it to Mrs. Adcorn. "I expect you're a bit upset," he said. "Have a cigarette. It might do you good."

Mrs. Adcorn raised her hands in protest. "I'm sure it's kind of you, Sergeant, but I never smoke," she replied. "Nearly everybody does now, I know, but somehow I've never taken to it. You may laugh at me, but I've never had a cigarette between my lips in my life."

That disposed of the matter, then. It had occurred to the Sergeant that Mrs. Adcorn might have thrown a cigarette down somewhere. This might have set fire to some fabric which had smouldered and burst into flames. But since Mrs. Adcorn did not smoke, that theory must be discarded.

At this moment the captain of the fire brigade came up. "Good-evening, Sergeant," he said. "We've pretty nearly finished our job now, I think. There's no sign of any fire now that I can see. But I'll leave a man here overnight in case of accident. I'm afraid there's been a lot of damage done, what with the fire and water. An almost perfect place for a bonfire with those panelled walls and old dry furniture. It's a mercy that we've been able to save as much as we have."

"Have you any idea what started the fire?" the Sergeant asked.

"Somebody must have an idea, if I haven't," replied the captain significantly. "There's nothing to account for it that I can see. No flues with old oak beams running across them, no electric light wires or anything like that. The occupants are away, I understand? Who was looking after the place?"

"Mrs. Adcorn here," said the Sergeant. "She's the caretaker and has been ever since the place was built. She's just been telling me that everything was all right at six o'clock this evening."

The captain turned to Mrs. Adcorn. "Six o'clock," he repeated thoughtfully. "We got the call at five and twenty minutes past eight, and according to Mr. Velley the fire had only just been discovered then. You're sure that nobody could have got into the house after you left it?"

"Not unless they broke in, sir," Mrs. Adcorn replied. "I shut and fastened all the windows and locked both doors behind me."

The captain nodded. "That's so. We had to break open the back door to get in. Well, it's not my business, but it seems pretty queer. How was the house lighted, by the way? There's no gas or electricity laid on?"

"With Aladdin lamps and candles, sir," Mrs. Adcorn replied. "The lamps are all kept on a shelf in the scullery and I fill them up when they want it. I last filled them on the day when Mr and Mrs. Pershore went away, a fortnight ago yesterday. And they haven't been used since, as there's been no occasion for it."

"What did you fill them from?"

"There's a five-gallon drum of paraffin in the scullery, sir, with a tap on it. Mr. Pershore has it filled up again whenever it runs out."

"When was the central heating furnace last in use?"

"It hasn't been lighted since last winter, sir. I couldn't say exactly when it was let out. I think it was sometime in April."

"Was there anything inflammable about the house besides the drum of paraffin? Matches, petrol or anything like that?"

"There are a few dozen boxes of matches kept in the cupboard in the pantry, sir. And a packet of candles in case anything went wrong with any of the lamps. But there was no petrol in the house, or even in the garage. The garage is only used when any of the family have driven down in a car."

"The scullery is the room with the concrete flooring on to which the back door opens, I suppose?"

"Yes, that's right, sir."

"I noticed that drum of paraffin when we broke in. How much oil was there in it when you last filled the lamps?"

"It must have been more than three parts full, sir. The oilman had been round and filled it the Saturday before."

"Well, the fire didn't reach the scullery, and everything there should be pretty much as you left it. Suppose we go round and have a look at that drum. You've got an electric torch, I expect, Sergeant? It's too dark now to see anything without a light of some kind."

"Yes, I've got my torch," Wragge replied. The three of them went round the house and entered it through the broken down back door. Mrs. Adcorn pointed out the five-gallon drum standing on a wooden packing-case. The Sergeant picked it up and shook it. Then he put it down again and turned on the tap without results. "Well, it may have been three parts full when last you used it, Mrs. Adcorn," he said. "But as you can see for yourself, it's pretty nearly bone dry now."

Mrs. Adcorn seemed incredulous. She lifted the drum for herself, then put it down again with a helpless gesture. "It's one of them dratted London folk, I'll be bound," she exclaimed. "They must have got through one of the windows when nobody was looking and drawn off the oil. I was always telling Mr. Pershore that something like that would happen."

The captain shrugged his shoulders. "Well, I must be getting along," he said. "My chaps have been waiting for me this last ten minutes. Good-night."

He went off and a minute or two later the Sergeant heard the sound of the engine driving away. He turned to Mrs. Adcorn. "You've got Mr. Pershore's address, I dare say," he said.

"Yes, I've got that and his telephone number," she replied. "I spoke to Mr. Velley and he said he'd ring him up from the farm. I don't know what he'll say when he hears about this, I'm sure."

"Well, Mrs. Adcorn, you can't do anything to-night," said Wragge. "If I were you I'd go to bed and try to get a little sleep. You've been terribly upset, I can see that."

"I'll go to bed, but not a wink of sleep shall I get, Sergeant," she replied dolefully.

Wragge paid a visit to the farm, but he learnt that Mr. Velley had already telephoned to Mr. Pershore, who seemed very much disturbed by the message. He promised to come down and inspect the matter by the first train in the morning,

Seeing that there was nothing more to be done for the moment, the Sergeant decided to return home. But the question arose, how was he going to get there. He had sent the car back to Culverden, not knowing how long he might be detained. It was hardly worth while having it out again, and besides, the authorities might grumble at the expense. And then an idea struck him. Mr. Raymond had a bicycle that he could borrow. It wouldn't hurt him to walk as far as the Chequers, and he could ride home from there.

It was now past ten o'clock, and the crowd which had assembled to watch the burning bungalow had dispersed. The pickers had returned to their huts. Here and there through an open door Wragge could see the flickering glow of a candle. The monotonous sound of a shovel told him that somebody, Fred Adcorn probably, was working in the oast house. But as soon as he left Hobb's Corner, the countryside seemed deserted. A solitary dog barking somewhere, and he could hear the rumble of a train in the distance. But he met nobody the whole length of the path which led to Matling.

By the time he reached the Chequers the house was shut up for the night, and the doors in the front securely locked. Wragge went round to the back and tapped at the kitchen window, through which a light shone. The door was opened by Mr. Raymond.

"Hallo, Sergeant, back again!" he exclaimed. "Come in. You've been over to the fire, I have no doubt. Is there much damage done?"

"More than Mr. Pershore will care about, I'm afraid," the Sergeant replied. "He's coming down in the morning, and we'll hear what he has to say."

"Well, I'm awfully sorry about it. Mr. Pershore's a very pleasant gentleman, as you know as well as I do. It'll hit him hard to have his nice things burnt up like that. Not that he can't afford to buy plenty more, that's one comfort. It's an ill wind that blows nobody any good, as they say, but a fire benefits no one. It hasn't benefited me. I've scarcely had a soul in since half-past eight. As soon as the news of the fire spread everybody ran off to have a look at it."

"Folk will do that," said Wragge philosophically. "But two or three of them must have stayed behind, surely."

"I don't think I've served a dozen at the window since the fire started. And the only other customer I had I should have been pleased to do without."

"Who was that?" the Sergeant asked.

"Why that blinking chap, Lavis," replied Mr. Raymond in a tone of intense disgust. "He came in here not two or three minutes after you'd gone, and ordered half a pint of cider. He seemed quiet enough when he came in. He sat down in the other room all by himself, just as though he'd got something on his mind. He didn't say a word to any of the other chaps who were in there then. I hoped he'd drink up and clear off, but he sat on and on over that half pint of his and there was no getting rid of him. And then somebody or other opened the door and shouted out that Mr. Pershore's bungalow was on fire, and all the chaps in the other room ran out. But Lavis just laughed and said serve him right, for I heard him."

"What made him say that?" asked the Sergeant quickly.

"Why, he always had a grudge against Mr. Pershore," Raymond replied. "He worked for Pershore and Huggins for a time, taking orders for their manure from the farmers. But he never did his job properly, always skulking about instead of getting to work. So in the end he got the sack. It was always a wonder to me that they kept him on so long."

"Did he stop on here after the others had gone this evening?"

"Yes, he stopped until closing time all by himself in the other room. And he had more than was good for him, I'm sorry to say. Three pints in all, and that's more than any man can properly stand."

"You should have refused to serve him," said Wragge with a hint of severity in his tone.

"That's all very well, Sergeant," replied Raymond sharply. "I can't refuse to serve any one so long as they keep sober and behave themselves. And Lavis was quite quiet while he was in the other room. Just sat there with his arms on the table and his mug in front of him. It wasn't until he got up that anybody could see that he'd had too much. Then he fell down twice before I got him to the door. In the end he went off towards Park Gate hollering at the top of his voice. He hadn't got his bicycle with him this evening. He would never have been able to ride it if he had."

"Lavis and I shall quarrel before long," said Wragge sharply. "By the way, talking of bicycles, that's what I dropped in here for. I was wondering if you'd lend me yours to get home to Culverden on?"

"Surely," replied Raymond. "It's in the lodge. I'll come out and get if for you. And you needn't be in a hurry to bring it back. I never have a chance of getting outside the house during hop-picking time."

Wragge rode home and sat down to a late supper. Mrs. Wragge was eager for news of the fire, but her husband proved unduly taciturn. His mind was full of the events of the evening and he wanted to arrange these in some sort of order. As if he hadn't enough perplexities already without this fire coming on top of them!

He had seen and heard enough to convince him that the fire had not been accidental. Somebody must have started it, which suggested that yet another crime had been committed in his district. And the only person who could do such a thing must have had a grudge against Mr. Pershore.

The identity of that person was obvious. According to Raymond, Lavis had received the news of the fire with unconcerned pleasure. But the trouble was that Lavis couldn't possibly have started it. Mrs. Adcorn had declared that everything was all right at six o'clock, and her statement could be accepted without question. She was a thoroughly reliable woman, in whom the Pershores had every confidence. Therefore, the fire must have been started some time after six.

Lavis's alibi was unimpeachable. Shortly before six, Wragge himself had arrived at his house and found him at home. Their conversation had lasted for perhaps twenty minutes. Wragge had then ridden straight to the Chequers, where he had remained for ten minutes, not more. According to Raymond, Lavis had arrived at the Chequers a very few minutes after Wragge's departure. He had still been there when news of the fire had reached the house. He had walked to the Chequers from Park Gate; in order to arrive there when he did, he must have left home immediately after Wragge's departure. He must have taken the direct road and not made the detour through Hobb's Corner. Besides, between six and seven Hobb's Corner must have been alive with people, pickers and others. Lavis could not have entered the bungalow without being seen. He seemed to be exonerated in spite of his prejudice against Mr. Pershore. The incendiary must be sought elsewhere.

But again the same difficulty arose. Wragge found it impossible to imagine how anybody could have entered the bungalow at that time of the evening unobserved.

Yet somebody must have done so. Somebody must have got into the house at some time after all the windows were fastened and the doors locked, and made the necessary preparations. Probably the contents of the drum of paraffin had been sprinkled on the floor and furniture of the lounge, and a match applied. Then the criminal must have escaped again without being observed, even by the vigilant Fred Adcorn.

Could any of the Adcorn family be implicated? It seemed to Wragge the most unlikely thing in the world. They were a highly respectable family who had worked on Hobb's Farm before Mr. Velley had bought it, and that was many years ago. The father, who was now dead, had been the carter. The two sons were quiet, steady, hard-working fellows. Fred was a trusted hop-drier, and hop drying is a science which takes a good deal of application. Tom, during hop-picking time, was employed as a weigher, which is very definitely a position of trust, and Mr. Velley, as Wragge knew, had the highest opinion of both of them. The Pershores had always treated Mrs. Adcorn rather as a friend of the family than as a mere caretaker. And even if it were possible to imagine any of the Adcorns stooping to arson, what possible motive could they have had? They had nothing whatever to gain by the destruction of the bungalow or its contents. In fact, if it had been destroyed and was not rebuilt, Mrs. Adcorn would have lost the few shillings weekly which were derived from her job.

Every irregularity which occurred during hop-picking time was attributed locally to the pickers, or rather to their casual friends. The theft of a stray chicken or the damaging of an apple tree could thus be explained. But surely not the deliberate burning of the bungalow. Even the most depraved would hardly set fire to a house for an evening's entertainment. And no casual stranger could in any way derive profit from the blaze.

It was perhaps natural that at this point the shadow of Elver should fall across Wragge's mind. He was already convinced that Elver and Lavis were linked in some unholy league. Was this latest crime yet another evidence of their malevolence? Lavis had a grudge against Mr. Pershore as the result of his dismissal. Elver had committed the burglary at Paddock Croft probably at Lavis's instigation. Lavis was sheltering Elver from the keen eye of justice. Was it possible that as a return of his kind offices. Elver had consented to set fire to Mr. Pershore's bungalow? But then, again, how could Elver contrive to enter and leave the place unobserved? Would a man in hiding attempt such an audacious action?

While he was still on the scene of the fire it had occurred to Wragge that somebody might have appropriated the bungalow as a temporary residence and had set fire to it not by design but by carelessness. Hence his questioning of Mrs. Adcorn. But her statement had seemed to dispose of any such theory. The same idea had occurred to her, and she had searched the place thoroughly every day. Elver, for instance, could not have been concealed there since the previous Saturday evening.

Wragge, as he reached this conclusion, began to feel righteously indignant. A criminal, possibly a gang of criminals, had been let loose in his district. How could anybody expect a Sergeant of police and two constables to prevent crime in an area of several square miles, over-run as it was by a horde of strangers? The first thing in the morning he would call the Superintendent up and lay the case before him. Additional police should be drafted into the district at once. Or, as a last resource, the Yard should be called in.

Wragge, though in many respects a typical policeman of the old school, had no feelings of antipathy towards Scotland Yard. He was not ambitious. He had no desire to achieve renown by the capture of some desperate criminal. One might get hurt in the process. Besides, renown had no attractions for him. At his age he could scarcely hope for promotion. He was anxious to complete his term of service with as little inconvenience to himself as possible. He had never been heard to make any plans as to what he would do after his retirement. But more than once he had remarked to Mrs. Wragge that the Raymonds were very comfortable at the Matling Chequers. And if one day Raymond should carry out his reiterated threats of giving up the house, well, one never knew.

By the time he went to bed the Sergeant had convinced himself that Scotland Yard were the people to deal with the situation. He anticipated very little difficulty in persuading his superiors to agree to this. They would communicate with the Yard, and some clever young chap would come down and take the responsibility off his shoulders. He couldn't be expected to go round chasing burglars and incendiaries at his time of life. He and his two constables had enough to do in minding the normal affairs of the district. So, with a clear conscience, Sergeant Wragge went to bed and was very soon fast asleep.

CHAPTER VIII

MR. Pershore was a tall thin man of sixty or so with an ascetic face. He wore powerful glasses, and, on the whole, looked far more like a student than the shrewd man of business he was. As he stepped out of the train at Culverden station on the Wednesday morning, Wragge, who had been waiting on the platform, came forward and saluted.

Mr. Pershore peered at him in the short-sighted way habitual to him. "Ah, good-morning, Sergeant," he said. "My bungalow has been burnt down, I hear. It's really most annoying. Has everything been destroyed?"

"Not quite so bad as that, sir," replied Wragge comfortingly. "But I'm afraid a lot of damage has been done. The fire had got a good hold before the brigade came and then the water they pumped on it made a terrible mess of things. You will be going to see it, I expect, sir?"

"Yes, I've ordered a car to meet me," Mr. Pershore replied. "It'll be waiting outside the station now. If you happen to be going that way I could give you a lift."

"Thank you, sir. I should like to talk to you about the matter."

They entered the waiting car, which was the same that Wragge had hired on the previous evening, and were driven rapidly to Hobb's Corner. The bungalow presented a desolate sight enough. All the windows in the front were broken and their frames charred. The walls and roof were blackened, and in one place the tiles had fallen in, leaving a yawning gap through which could be seen the half-burnt rafters. The appearance of the house inside was even more depressing. The floors of every room were covered with a couple of inches or more of black mud, the product of ashes and water. No part of the bungalow had escaped this defilement, but the principal damage was confined to the lounge and the dining-room next to it. In these rooms little but the bare brick of the walls remained intact. The wood floors and the panelling had almost entirely disappeared, and to add to the confusion the ceilings had fallen in. Most of the furniture was unrecognisable, all that remained of it being shapeless pieces of charred wood.

Mr. Pershore surveyed the wreckage in silence. At last he shook his head disconsolately.

"This is a bitter blow, Sergeant," he said. "It isn't the financial aspect of the damage that worries me. That's covered by insurance. But there were some things in this house that money won't replace. They were almost unique survivals of the past, and the only other specimens of their kind are in museums. I'd rather have lost a thousand pounds than have had this happen. But I must be thankful, I suppose, that some of my possessions have been saved."

"The furniture was of great value then, sir?" said Wragge commiseratingly.

"It depends upon what you mean by value. You could, I suppose, go to Tottenham Court Road and buy things which would serve the purpose equally well. That wouldn't cost you a lot of money. But the things that have been burnt were made by craftsmen many years ago, and for that reason had what I suppose is a sentimental value. The bureau that used to stand in the lounge, for instance. I don't suppose there are a couple of others like it in England. To say nothing of the clock, which was the only example I know of the work of a celebrated clockmaker. And the dining-room chairs too. A complete set of a very rare pattern and date. I find it very difficult to be philosophical about our loss. What I can't understand is how the fire started."

Wragge looked suddenly mysterious. "We have reason to believe sir, that the fire started maliciously," he said.

Mr. Pershore turned upon him sharply. "We!" he exclaimed. "And who are we, I'd like to know?"

"The police, sir. We take a very serious view of the matter. I was in communication with the Superintendent early this morning, sir, and he's requesting Scotland Yard to send an officer down to investigate."

"You mean that somebody deliberately set fire to the place!" said Mr. Pershore rather incredulously.

"I'm afraid it looks very like it, sir. The captain of the fire brigade is of the same opinion. I have interviewed Mrs. Adcorn, and she is unable to throw any light upon the origin of the fire."

"You can set your mind at rest about Mrs. Adcorn," said Mr. Pershore. "She didn't set fire to the place, I'll take my oath on that. And I can't imagine anybody else doing such a thing. I shouldn't be in the least surprised if it turned out that one of those confounded hop-pickers had got in and dropped matches about."

Wragge had no direct reply to this. He hesitated for a moment and then came out with his suspicions. "Lavis, who lives at Park Gate, was in your employ at one time, was he not, sir?"

"Lavis?" Mr. Pershore repeated in some surprise. "Why, yes, he was, some years ago. He was a lazy devil, I remember, and we had to discharge him. It was my own fault, for I took him on without proper references. He came to see me one day and told me he was out of a job and asked me if I could do anything for him. That was before the bungalow was built, when my wife and I used to take rooms in Matling for a week or so every summer. I asked him what he was used to, and he said travelling. As it happened, we wanted an additional traveller for this district and I said I'd give him a trial. But we wanted an energetic man, and Lavis turned out to be anything but that. We warned him once or twice, but it was no good, and in the end we had to get rid of him. I don't remember having set eyes on him since. I didn't even know that he was still in these parts."

"Yes, sir, he's still here," Wragge replied. "And he was heard to say that it served you right, when he was told that the bungalow was on fire."

Mr. Pershore smiled. "So you suspect Lavis of having done the trick, do you?" he said. "Have you any direct evidence against him?"

"Well, no sir, we haven't. And we know that Lavis can't have started the fire himself. But there was a burglary at Mr. Speight's of Paddock Croft on Saturday night."

Mr. Pershore interrupted him. "A burglary!" he exclaimed. "You seem suddenly to be overwhelmed by a wave of crime, Sergeant. But I don't quite see what a burglary at Paddock Croft has to do with a fire at my bungalow."

"We know the identity of the burglar, sir," replied Wragge with dignity. "And my investigations have proved that he and Lavis were acquainted."

Mr. Pershore shrugged his shoulders slightly. "I'm getting a bit out of my depth," he said. "As I understand it, the position is this. You believe that the bungalow was purposely set on fire. A man from Scotland Yard is coming down to look into the matter. If he wants to see me I shan't be far off. When Mr. Velley rang me up last night he offered to put me up for a day or two, and I accepted his offer. I shall look round here and make an inventory of the damage, and after that you'll find me at Hobb's Farm, and now if you like to take a lift back to Culverden with the car, you're welcome to do so."

Wragge accepted this offer gratefully enough. He returned home in the car to await the arrival of his visitor. Nor was this arrival long delayed. A couple of hours later there came a knock on his door and he rose to answer it himself. A tall pleasant-faced young man confronted him.

"Good-morning, Sergeant," he said. "We've talked to one another before, though we've never met. I'm from the Yard and my name's Waghorn. Can you spare me a few minutes to tell me your troubles?"

"Come in, sir," replied Wragge heartily. "And if you'd care for something to eat, the missus and I were just going to sit down to dinner."

"That's what I call a timely offer," Jimmy exclaimed. "If you've no objection I'll join you, and we can talk things over while we eat. But look here, let's get things straight from the start, I'm here to help, not to be a nuisance to you. And I'd much rather you'd drop the 'sir', and treat me just like a fellow policeman."

Wragge grinned. He liked this young man, so obviously devoid of airs in spite of his rank and superior education. "I'll do my best," he replied. "It won't take long to tell you all about it. There's a crook at large in this district somewhere. First that burglary you know about, and now this case of arson."

During dinner, a remarkably satisfying meal, Wragge unfolded to Jimmy the conclusions to which he had already arrived. Jimmy listened without comment, merely putting in a word here and there. The Sergeant's logic, though not altogether unassailable, appeared to him to be sound on the whole.

"Now I don't want to drag you about the country, Wragge," said Jimmy when the meal was over. "I'd like to have a look round this afternoon and take my bearings. I suppose there's somewhere in Culverden where I can hire a bicycle?"

"You needn't do that," Wragge replied. "I've got one here that I borrowed last night from Raymond of the Matling Chequers. He said I could keep it for a bit, and there's no reason why you shouldn't use it."

So Jimmy set forth on Mr. Raymond's bicycle. He had brought with him a map of the district, which he had studied in the train during his journey to Culverden. He owed his selection for the job to Hanslet. The Superintendent had received the telephone message from the local police, and had sent for Jimmy.

"Look here, my lad, you know something about this business already," he had said. "You had better go down and see what this new disturbance is about. If you think you can manage it on your own, sail in and win. If you find that you're up against it, just let me know and I'll come down and bear a hand. Off you go."

As Jimmy rode towards Hobb's Corner, he considered the information which Wragge had given him. That Elver and this man Lavis were in league seemed to him likely enough. Lavis probably knew of the place of Elver's concealment. But that Elver should at his instigation have consented to commit a second crime which would bring him no possible benefit, seemed rather unlikely. Obviously, the first thing was to investigate the origin of the fire. It might possibly turn out to have been accidental, in which case the situation would be simplified. It would then remain to organise a systematic man-hunt for Elver, whose presence in the neighbourhood seemed probable.

When Jimmy reached the bungalow, he found Mr. Pershore and Mrs. Adcorn already on the premises. He introduced himself, and Mr. Pershore glanced at him ironically.

"Well, Inspector, and do you share the belief that this is the work of a criminal?" he asked.

Jimmy laughed. "I don't form theories until I have had some opportunity of investigation," he replied. "I'd rather approach the matter from another direction.

I'd like to convince myself that the fire cannot have been started accidentally. Then I'll begin to look for the criminal."

Mr. Pershore nodded. "That's a very sensible remark, Inspector," he said approvingly. "Mrs. Adcorn and I have been over the whole place pretty thoroughly, and we can't understand how a fire can have been started by accident. There seems to be no doubt whatever that it originated in the lounge. Now, I know for a fact, and Mrs. Adcorn supports me, that there was nothing in that room likely to cause a fire. There is no fireplace nor are there any electric wires anywhere in the house. Come in and see for yourself."

Jimmy entered the lounge and looked round it. He could see that the fire had been fiercest against the wall which separated the lounge from the dining-room. The wooden panelling which had covered the wall on both sides had completely disappeared. The flooring against this wall was burnt away, though in other parts of the room it was comparatively slightly damaged by the fire. Further, the hole in the roof through which the flames had burst was exactly over this particular spot.

Mr. Pershore reported the list of the objects which had stood against this wall. "In this corner there was a divan," he said. "It was merely a low wooden frame, on which rested a box spring mattress. On the divan were half a dozen cushions. Next to it was a grandfather clock, one of my most cherished possessions. And next to that again was a small chair with a needlework seat. And at the farther end of the wall was a bureau, a tall one with a bookcase above it. How a fire can have started in any of these things passes my comprehension."

"Once the fire was started they would burn readily enough," Jimmy suggested.

"It looks like it," Mr. Pershore said ruefully. "There's precious little left of any of them, as you can see. Of course they were dry and made chiefly of wood. I can quite understand their burning, but not how they caught fire."

"There is such a thing as spontaneous combustion," said Jimmy. "All manner of things catch fire by themselves under certain conditions. A heap of coal dust or a bale of oily rags, for instance. Could you tell me what was in the bureau?"

"It was practically empty," Mr. Pershore replied. "I know that my wife used to keep supplies of stationery in the bottom drawer, but I don't think there was anything in any of the others. There may have been a few odd papers, but nothing else. The case above was full of books of various kinds but they weren't of any value."

"There were no matches or anything like that?" Jimmy asked.

"No, the only matches in the house were in the pantry. They are still there, for the matter of that. The fire didn't reach them. As for your coal dust and oily rags, there was nothing of the kind in the house, was there, Mrs. Adcorn?"

"No, sir, that there wasn't," Mrs. Adcorn replied. "There may have been a bushel of coke in the shed where the furnace is, but there was no oily rags anywhere. Why, I always bring over a rag of my own to do the lamps with, and throw it away when I've finished with it."

"Well, that seems to dispose of the spontaneous combustion," said Jimmy. "But there's another way that fires get started sometimes. The rays of the sun through a burning glass have often been responsible. Now I happen to have noticed that the windows of this room face south-west. Was the sun shining yesterday afternoon, Mrs. Adcorn?"

"Yes, sir, it was a beautiful day," said Mrs. Adcorn. "The sun was pouring in here when I shut up at six o'clock."

"Yesterday was September 3rd," said Jimmy. "The sun didn't set till six-forty Greenwich time, that's seven-forty summer time. The fire might have started smouldering then, and only burst into flames soon after eight."

Mrs. Adcorn shook her head. "The sun didn't come into this room after six o'clock, sir," she said. "That's when I shut the windows, and when I do that I always draw the curtains. And there was nothing smouldering then or I should have been bound to notice it."

"For the matter of that there wasn't a lens of any kind in the house," Mr. Pershore remarked.

"An actual lens isn't necessary," Jimmy replied. "Anything that acts as one will start a fire. A soda-water bottle left lying about has started a fire before now; and a carafe of water will concentrate the rays sufficiently. Are you quite sure there was nothing like that in the room?"

"I'm perfectly sure, sir," replied Mrs. Adcorn. "There were no glass ornaments or anything like that even, for I keep them put away in the pantry when the family aren't here."

Jimmy went across to the windows and looked out. They faced away from the road. In front of them was a narrow lawn, then the hedge separating this from the hop gardens. It seemed impossible that a spark should have been blown into the room from outside.

He turned back to Mrs. Adcorn. "You're perfectly certain that nothing could have been smouldering in here at six o'clock?" he asked.

"Perfectly certain, sir," she replied firmly. "If there had been I should have smelt it. I've got a very quick nose. I can tell if anything's caught in my kitchen when I'm outside the house. But I did fancy that there was a smell of paraffin about the place."

"Did you try and find out where the smell came from?" Jimmy asked.

"I had a good look round, sir, for I couldn't understand it. It didn't seem to be in any of the other rooms, only here. But I couldn't find any paraffin anywhere. I didn't know then that the drum was empty, for I never thought of looking. I put it down to the engine which had been running all the afternoon."

"Ah, we smelt that before," said Mr. Pershore. "You see, inspector, there's a water-pump driven by a paraffin engine behind the oast houses. It supplies the farm and this bungalow. And very often when the wind's the right way we get a distinct smell of paraffin in the house. I expect that was it, Mrs. Adcorn."

"That doesn't explain how the drum came to be empty," said Jimmy thoughtfully. "It doesn't leak, I suppose?"

"I have never known it to have done so," replied Mr. Pershore. "Still, I've had it a good long time, and these things do develop holes. Let's go and have a look."

They went into the scullery, and Mr. Pershore picked up the empty drum. He held it under the scullery tap and filled it with water. Then he put it beside the sink and the three of them watched it for a minute or two. No sign of a leak appeared. The drum was perfectly tight.

"That's one question answered," said Mr. Pershore. "I'm not inclined to attach much importance to the disappearance of the paraffin. Lots of the hop-pickers bring oil stoves and cans down with them, and they wouldn't be above helping themselves to paraffin if they knew where to get it. It would be easy enough to slip through the scullery window and out again."

"I've said so a dozen times before now, sir," said Mrs. Adcorn reproachfully.

"I know you have, Mrs. Adcorn," Mr. Pershore replied. "But I was ready to take the risk. Anything's better than coming down for a week-end to a house that hasn't been aired. And this is the first time that you've found anything missing, isn't it?"

"Well, yes, it is, sir," she said. "But it's been a terrible anxiety to know that all the windows were open and anybody might get in. Suppose they'd made off with some of the furniture?"

"And carried it across the countryside in broad daylight," said Mr. Pershore with a smile. "Well, Inspector, have you any other suggestions as to how the fire might have originated accidentally?"

"I should like to be absolutely satisfied on that point," replied Jimmy cautiously. "What we seem to have established is this. The fire cannot have started accidentally after Mrs. Adcorn shut the house up at six o'clock. That leaves us with two possible theories. One is that the fire was already smouldering at that time, though it could not be perceived. The other is that somebody broke in after six o'clock and set fire to the place. Now since it was less than an hour after sunset when the fire was observed, it can't have been very dark at the time. This house stands in full view on all sides. Were there many people about between six and half-past eight yesterday afternoon, Mrs. Adcorn?"

"Dozens of them," replied Mrs. Adcorn. "The hop-pickers knocked off at half-past five, and they were swarming all round the place. They're all respectable people, I will say that. They've been down here year after year and we've never had no trouble with them. I wouldn't say that they wouldn't pick up anything that lay handy, but they wouldn't break into a house that was shut up. And besides the pickers, there were all the chaps from the farm. My son Fred was to and from the oast all the time. And my other son Tom was in the hop gardens only just the other side of the hedge. Nobody could have broken in without somebody or other having seen him."

"Then something must have started smouldering earlier in the day, and you didn't notice it, Mrs. Adcorn. Some things -- like tinder, for instance -- will smoulder away with practically no smoke or smell."

"There wasn't any tinder in the house," replied Mrs. Adcorn stubbornly. "And if there'd been anything smouldering in here I should have found it when I was looking for the smell of paraffin, shouldn't I?"

This seemed unanswerable. In any case there was obviously nothing more to be got out of Mr. Pershore or Mrs. Adcorn.

"I'm still not altogether satisfied," said Jimmy. "I'd rather nothing here was touched until I've had time to get an expert down, Sergeant Wragge will send a constable over to keep watch, I dare say. I'll get back to Culverden and see him about it."

Mr. Pershore raised no objection to this course. Jimmy returned to the Sergeant to arrange for the presence of the constable at the bungalow. Then, rather to Wragge's disgust, he announced his intention of returning to London.

"There are two reasons for my going," he said. "One is that I want to consult an expert as to the origin of that fire. The other is concerned with Elver. It's only guesswork on our part that he's hiding about here somewhere. He may have got back to London, taking care to avoid his usual haunts. I'd like to get our people to comb out all the likely places."

Immediately upon his return to London that evening Jimmy went to the Yard, where he sought out Hanslet. The Superintendent raised his eyebrows at his entrance. "Hallo, what are you doing here?" he asked. "You haven't finished your case already, surely?"

"I've hardly begun it yet," Jimmy replied. "I came back mainly to seek your advice. There's a matter of a burnt-out bungalow and I can't make up my mind whether the fire was accidental or deliberate."

"I dare say you can't," Hanslet replied. "Arson is notoriously the most difficult of all crimes to detect. You may have your suspicions, but the proof is usually destroyed in the fire itself. You've been over the place pretty carefully, I suppose? Give me the particulars, and if I can form an opinion on them you're welcome to it."

Jimmy gave the Superintendent an account of his investigations at Hobb's Corner. "Always supposing that Mrs. Adcorn is speaking the truth, I seem to be up against it," he continued. "On the one hand it seems quite impossible that the fire should have been accidental. On the other hand, it seems equally impossible that any one should have started it. But there's no doubt about there having been a fire, and a pretty fierce one at that."

"Your problem sounds a bit of a brute," replied Hanslet thoughtfully. "I tell you what. I'll ring up the Professor and ask him if we can go round and see him this evening. He simply wallows in a problem like that, and he may be able to suggest a line to you to work on."

Permission for the evening's visit to Dr. Priestley was easily obtained. They were bidden to the house in Westbourne Terrace as soon after nine that evening as possible. Jimmy employed the evening in making the necessary arrangements for a thorough comb-out of Halibut Street and its environs; then he and Hanslet had supper together, after which they presented themselves at Dr. Priestley's house in Westbourne Terrace at the appointed time.

They were shown into the study, where they found Dr. Priestley and Harold Merefield.

"Very good of you to give up your time to us like this, Professor," said Hanslet. "Jimmy's got a bit of a problem and neither he nor I can see the way to a solution. Have you got time to listen to Jimmy's story of what he suspects may be a case of arson?"

"Certainly," replied Dr. Priestley. "But I would ask the Inspector to confine himself to facts."

Thus encouraged, Jimmy launched out into his story. He repeated the account which he had already given to the Superintendent and concluded by enunciating his dilemma. "It seems to me, sir, that the fire must have been accidental or maliciously started," he said. "And either theory seems impossible. I'm driven to believe that Mrs. Adcorn was lying to shield either herself or somebody else."

"I see no reason to suspect Mrs. Adcorn of untruthfulness," replied Dr. Priestley quietly. "What makes you say that it is impossible that the fire should have been started maliciously?"

"Why, just this, sir. Mrs. Adcorn declares that nothing in the house was smouldering at six o'clock that evening. At that time she closed the house, fastening all the windows and closing the doors. Local conditions were such that nobody could have broken into the house unobserved between that time and the discovery of the fire."

Dr. Priestley smiled. "I'm ready to share your conviction that nobody could have entered the house after Mrs. Adcorn left it," he said. "I am also prepared to accept her statement that nothing in the house was smouldering at six o'clock. And yet I see no objection to the theory that the fire was started maliciously."

"By somebody from outside the house, sir?" Jimmy ventured. "I don't see how that could have been done under the circumstances."

"The fire undoubtedly originated inside the house," Dr. Priestley replied. "You told us, I think, that you were satisfied that the fire started against one wall of the lounge. Will you tell us again what furniture stood against that wall?"

"A divan, a grandfather clock, a small chair and a bureau."

"Exactly," said Dr. Priestley in a tone of satisfaction. "This problem of yours is not without interest, Inspector. You said, I think, that you had arranged for nothing at the bungalow to be disturbed. If I may say so, that was a very wise precaution on your part. Now, since we have considered the possibilities of a crime having been committed, you may already have made some conjecture as to the identity of the criminal."

"As to that, I can only judge by what the local Sergeant told me, sir. He's inclined to suspect an inhabitant of the district, whose name is Lavis. Lavis is known to have had a grudge against Mr. Pershore, and when he heard of the fire he exclaimed that it served him right. But the difficulty is that Lavis himself can't have done it."

"Indeed!" exclaimed Dr. Priestley. "And why is that?"

"Because he was in the village when the fire broke out."

Again Dr. Priestley smiled. "I will refer to a handbook which should be in the hands of every detective, Inspector," he said. "Harold, would you be good enough to find me Grose's Criminal Investigation"

Harold selected from the book-shelves a volume which he handed to his employer. Dr. Priestley opened it and turned over the pages. "This is the passage I had in mind," he said. "'The incendiary will do all in his power to prove at the time of the conflagration that he was far enough away to make it impossible for the fire to be his work. To this end, he endeavours to start the fire after the lapse of a certain time, and unfortunately the means at his disposal are many; some are simple, some are very ingenious.

"'The most usual method is to light a candle, the bottom of which rests upon some hay or other inflammable substance. By the time the candle has burnt down to the hay, the criminal has time to get well away, and can prove that at the time of the outbreak he was, in the presence and to the knowledge of numerous witnesses, drinking in a distant house of refreshment, buying cattle at a market, or attending a ceremony.'

"I am not suggesting that so simple a method as a candle was used in the present case. Grose mentions several other methods by which the desired results may be obtained, but none of these, I fancy, is applicable to the present case. I would suggest, Inspector, that you should make a second and more detailed examination of the premises as soon as possible."

"I propose to go down there the first thing to-morrow morning, sir," replied Jimmy.

"And how will you proceed on your arrival?" Dr. Priestley asked.

"Well, sir, I shall look for some device which could have started a fire after a certain lapse of time. An infernal machine of some kind, I suppose. But surely if anything of the sort had been used, Mrs. Adcorn would have noticed its ticking."

"She probably did," replied Dr. Priestley casually. "As I remarked before, this case of yours is by no means devoid of interest. Inspector, Would it hamper your investigations in any way if I were to pay a visit to the premises to-morrow?"

"Hamper them, sir!" Jimmy exclaimed. "I haven't a doubt that you'd be able to spot the dodge at once, whatever it was."

"My powers of observation are by no means infallible. But I have had very little experience of incendiarism, and I should be glad to have the opportunity of studying such a subject on the spot. I think that the passage I have just read has convinced you that the theory of arson is by no means impossible. That being so, you should consider in advance all likely motives for such an act."

"In our experience, Professor, arson is usually committed with the object of drawing the insurance money," Hanslet remarked. "The owner himself, or some agent on his behalf, sets fire to the premises. This bungalow and its contents were insured, I suppose, Jimmy?"

"Mr. Pershore himself told Sergeant Wragge that that was the case," Jimmy replied. "On the other hand, Mr. Pershore emphasised that the articles were irreplacable."

"Nevertheless, some inquiry should be made into Mr. Pershore's antecedents," said Dr. Priestley. "It should always be remembered that the owner of the premises has advantages enjoyed by nobody else. He can enter or leave them unsuspected, and he is familiar with the internal arrangements. This applies not only to the owner, but to his family and servants as well."

"I am informed that no member of the family has visited the bungalow since August 10th, sir," Jimmy replied.

"You are informed!" exclaimed Dr. Priestley testily. "Have you taken any steps to confirm that information?"

"Well, no sir, not yet. But my impression of Mr. Pershore is that he is not at all a likely person to do such a thing. According to Sergeant Wragge he is a manufacturer in a very prosperous way of business."

"Even prosperous manufacturers have been known to stoop to crime," said Dr. Priestley. "Arson, however, is not invariably committed for the sake of the insurance money. Revenge, for instance, or the desire to take advantage of the fire to steal something from the premises in the confusion."

"This man Lavis imagined that he had a motive for revenge, sir," said Jimmy. "He is already the object of some suspicion. Again according to Sergeant Wragge, he recognised the photograph of Elver as soon as it was shown to him. His sister declared that Elver called at the house the previous Saturday afternoon and asked to see him."

"Eh, what's this?" Hanslet exclaimed. "You didn't tell me that part of the story, Jimmy."

"Because I don't see at present how it fits in," Jimmy replied. "I'm not altogether satisfied with Wragge's theory that Lavis put Elver up to the burglary at Paddock Croft. And I'm still less satisfied with his suggestion that Elver set fire to the bungalow at Lavis's instigation."

"Well, I don't know," said Hanslet doubtfully. "What do you think, Professor?"

"You must remember that I am in ignorance of Sergeant Wragge's reasons for his suggestion," Dr. Priestley replied. "Perhaps the Inspector will repeat exactly what passed between them at their interview."

Jimmy replied to this invitation by repeating all that Wragge had told him that morning. Dr. Priestley listened attentively, putting in questions here and there.

"This is most interesting," he said when Jimmy had finished. "You have a burglary in which the facts appear indisputable. You also have a fire, which I strongly suspect to have been the work of an incendiary. I would like to offer two points for your consideration. One is, the identity of the burglar appears to be definitely established. The other is that the act of the incendiary may have taken place immediately before or after the burglary. However, as you are well aware, I'm not over-fond of indulging in conjecture. It appears to me that further investigation is urgently required."

"I have your promise to come down and help, sir?" asked Jimmy.

"That promise shall be fulfilled. I will hire a car and Harold will drive me down to Hobb's Corner to-morrow morning. Would it be convenient to you if we arrived there at eleven o'clock?"

"It would suit me perfectly, sir," Jimmy replied enthusiastically.

"Then we waste no further words on the matter to-night," said Dr. Priestley. And taking this hint Hanslet and Jimmy departed.

CHAPTER IX

ITH his usual punctuality, Dr. Priestley reached Hobb's Corner at five minutes to eleven on Tuesday morning. He was accompanied by Harold Merefield and found Jimmy awaiting him. Mr. Pershore and Mrs. Adcorn were in attendance. Jimmy introduced Dr. Priestley to them, knowing that they would take him to be the expert whom he had mentioned on the previous day.

Dr. Priestley's first request was to be taken to the point where the fire had originated. He and Jimmy entered the bungalow together and the latter led the way into the lounge. Dr. Priestley spent some little time in examining the debris. At last he pointed to one particular spot on the wall dividing the lounge from the dining-room.

"The fire appears to have been more fierce here than anywhere else," he said. "It is also the centre of the damage. We shall probably be correct in assuming that it is the point of origin. Will you be good enough to ask Mr. Pershore and Mrs. Adcorn to join us?"

Jimmy called to them, and Dr. Priestley indicated the point on the wall which he had selected. "Can you tell us, Mr. Pershore, what piece of furniture stood there?" he asked.

Mr. Pershore measured the distance from the corner with his eyes. "The divan was just over six foot long," he said. "It stood with its head right up against the corner. A few inches from the foot of it was the grandfather clock. That means that the clock was standing against the wall at the point you mean."

Dr. Priestley turned to Mrs. Adcorn. "Was the clock in that position at six o'clock on Tuesday evening?" he asked.

"Yes, sir," replied Mrs. Adcorn. "I never move the clock. Mr. Pershore gave me particular orders not to touch it."

"A grandfather clock should never be moved," said Mr. Pershore. "Once one has got it to go in a certain position, the slightest movement will very often stop it. And it takes some adjustment to get it going again."

"That is exactly my theory, Mr. Pershore," said Dr. Priestley courteously. "I have also found that it is very bad for a grandfather clock to be allowed to stop for any length of time."

"Quite right," replied Mr. Pershore. "That's just what I've always told Mrs. Adcorn. She has instructions to wind all the clocks in the house, including this one, on Saturday mornings."

"And did you carry out these instructions, Mrs. Adcorn?" Dr. Priestley asked.

"Yes, sir, I was very careful to wind the clocks first thing when I came on Saturday mornings."

"Did you wind this clock as usual last Saturday morning?"

"Yes, sir, I distinctly remember doing it."

"Did you touch the clock again between that time and the fire?"

"No, sir, except perhaps just to flick a duster over it. Mr. Pershore had told me not to interfere with it in any way."

"That's right," said Mr. Pershore. "About once every six months or so I used to take the hood off and clean the movement. If the clock wanted regulating, which it very rarely did, I used to do it then. But nobody else was allowed to touch it."

"You regulated it in the ordinary way, by screwing the bob of the pendulum up or down?"

"Yes, but I don't think I've touched the pendulum for over a year now."

"Can you describe to me how the movement was driven?"

"Yes, by two weights, one to rotate the hands and the other to actuate the striking mechanism. These weights were supported on strands of gut. When the clock was fully wound, the weights were at the top of the case just below the movement. It took rather more than eight days for the weights to reach the bottom of the case."

"There was the usual door, I suppose, occupying practically the whole of the front of the case?"

"Yes, and I always kept that door locked to prevent the door popping open accidentally. The key was kept on a ledge at the top of the hood, together with the key for winding the clock."

"Have you ever opened the door, Mrs. Adcorn?" Dr. Priestley asked.

"Never sir," she replied emphatically. "I didn't even know that the key was where Mr. Pershore says it was."

"You are perfectly certain that you did not open the door between six o'clock on Saturday evening and the time of the fire?"

"Perfectly certain, sir. There was no occasion for it, I didn't know where the key was, and, if I had, I know that Mr. Pershore wouldn't have liked me to open it."

"I'm not so sure that it wasn't opened," muttered Dr. Priestley. Then turning to Jimmy: "It might be worth our while to examine the debris where the clock stood, Inspector."

Against the foot of the wall the debris was many inches thick. It had dried to some extent since the previous day, and was no longer of the consistency of mud. The floor had been entirely burnt away, leaving a cavity full of rubbish. Jimmy knelt down and began to lift this out with his hands.

Most of the rubbish consisted of fine ash, now damp and pasty. But as Jimmy proceeded he brought other substances to light. First of all, a few fragments of charred wood which might or might not have been the remains of the clock-case. It was not until he had gone deeper that he fished out some pieces of metal which were still recognisable as parts of the movement.

Mr. Pershore surveyed these ruefully. "They're past hope," he said. "The greater part of the movement was of brass -- fairly soft brass at that -- and most of it seems to have been melted away by the heat of the fire. There are one or two steel pinions, and I dare say they can be made serviceable again. But there's no possibility of restoring the original movement."

Under Dr. Priestley's eyes Jimmy continued his excavations. He had very nearly reached the level of the foundations of the wall when he picked up some curved blackened fragments which were certainly not metal or wood. Dr. Priestley seized upon these with sudden interest. He took them to the window and rubbed one of them with his handkerchief.

"Earthenware!" he exclaimed. "Apparently portions of some shallow vessel such as a saucer. Can you account for their presence, Mr. Pershore?"

"No, I can't," replied Mr. Pershore without any great show of interest. "Perhaps Mrs. Adcorn can enlighten us. Did you leave a saucer standing on the clock or anywhere near it, Mrs. Adcorn?"

"No, that I didn't, sir," said Mrs. Adcorn. "I always kept all the crockery and that in the pantry."

"And yet we found this saucer under the remains of the clock movement," said Dr. Priestley thoughtfully. "That suggests that it must have been inside the clock-case when the fire took place. You are certain, Mr. Pershore, that you never put a saucer inside the case for any purpose?"

"Perfectly certain," replied Mr. Pershore. "I cannot imagine any reason for doing such a thing."

Meanwhile Jimmy had cleared out the last of the debris on the spot where the clock had stood. His last finds were a long piece of stout iron wire, and a shapeless mass of lead weighing several pounds. Mr. Pershore identified the wire as the stem of the pendulum, and the lead had probably run together as the result of the melting of the weights and the pendulum bobs. Dr. Priestley seemed perfectly satisfied with the result of his investigations. He turned to Mr. Pershore.

"There is no need to detain you and Mrs. Adcorn any longer," he said politely.

They left the bungalow. Dr. Priestley collected the fragments of the earthenware which Jimmy had found and regarded them almost lovingly. "You need have no further doubts that this fire was the work of an incendiary, Inspector," he said.

But Jimmy was still puzzled. "I'm afraid I shall have to ask you to make it a bit clearer sir," he said.

"These fragments of earthenware, which were once a saucer, form the clue," Dr. Priestley replied. "You spoke yesterday evening of an infernal machine. But you were reluctant to believe in its existence, for the reason that Mrs. Adcorn must have heard it ticking. She did, without her suspicions being in any way aroused. For the grandfather clock had been most ingeniously converted into such a machine.

"You heard Mr. Pershore explain the mechanism of the clock. When Mrs. Adcorn wound it on Saturday morning, she raised the weights to the top of the case. The remainder of the case would then be empty, except for the pendulum, which swung, I expect, about half an inch from the back.

"The criminal's procedure, unless I am greatly mistaken, was this. He entered the house some time between Saturday morning and six o'clock on Tuesday evening. Apparently, since the windows were habitually left open during the daytime, he would find little difficulty in doing this. He had supplied himself with a quantity of rags, paper, wood-wool or some similar material. He opened the door of the clock-case with the key so readily to hand, packed the bottom of the case with the rags and sprinkled these with paraffin from the drum. You will remember that Mrs. Adcorn told you that she detected the smell of paraffin in this room on Tuesday morning. Upon these rags he placed a support, such as a block of wood, and on this he balanced a saucer in such a way that one of the weights on its descent would fall upon the edge of the saucer and so upset it.

"This was the only mechanism necessary. You are doubtless aware that there are several substances which upon being brought into contact burst into flames. Those most commonly employed are sulphuric acid on the one hand and a mixture of sugar and chlorate of potash on the other. We will suppose that the criminal selected these for his purpose. He sprinkled the oily rags liberally with a mixture of chlorate of potash and sugar. The saucer he filled with sulphuric acid. Now, you can see for yourself what must actually have happened. The weight in its descent would tip over the saucer, thus pouring the sulphuric acid on to the chlorate of potash and sugar. Flames would immediately ensue, which in turn would ignite the oily rags. They, burning fiercely, would set fire to the case of the clock and in time to the panelling of the wall behind it. Within a very short period the furniture and the wall itself would be in a blaze. I cannot help feeling gratified that my suspicions have been confirmed."

"Well, sir, that's infernally ingenious," exclaimed Jimmy, admiringly. "The next thing is to find out who did it."

"That may be a matter of some difficulty," replied Dr. Priestley gravely. "One of the first necessities in criminal investigation is to establish the time at which the crime was committed. That is usually possible within certain narrow limits. But it is not so in this case. We have Mrs. Adcorn's statement that she wound the clock on Saturday morning. The exact time at which she did so is important. We may assume for our present purposes that the weights were at their highest point at noon that day.

"The fire is said to have been first observed at twenty minutes past eight on Tuesday evening. We do not know how long before this it actually started, nor is the point material. We can be certain, however, that it had not started at six o'clock when Mrs. Adcorn shut up the house.

"What I wish to impress upon you, Inspector, is this. The apparatus for starting the fire may have been put into position at any time during that period of seventy-eight hours. This very wide limit must necessarily handicap your investigations. A further complication is the ease with which the house could be entered during the hours of daylight. The windows were opened in the morning and were not closed again until the evening. Any one, by watching for a suitable opportunity, could easily slip in and out unobserved.

"This suggests to me another point. Normally one would conclude that the crime had been committed with somebody legally familiar with the house. By legally familiar I mean the occupant, his family, his servants or his visitors. One would argue that no stranger would be familiar with the existence of the grandfather clock and the drum of paraffin. But in this case, any stranger might have effected an illegal entry and so acquired the necessary knowledge. That again must considerably widen the field of your investigations.

"You will be tempted, I imagine, to connect the fire with the burglary at Paddock Croft. But, strictly speaking, there is absolutely no proof of any such connection. There appears to be little room for doubt that Elver was the burglar. But was he also the incendiary? There is nothing whatever to suggest it.

"The fact that the burning of Mr. Pershore's bungalow was deliberate must not be lost sight of. Many acts of incendiarism are committed more or less on the spur of the moment. For instance, a labourer has a grudge against a farmer. He finds himself alone by one of the latter's haystacks and sets fire to it with a box of matches he happens to be carrying in his pocket. But in this case certain preparations had to be made. When the incendiary entered the bungalow, he was already in possession of rags or some similar material, and also the substances the combination of which produced the fire. The saucer and the paraffin probably originated in the bungalow itself. I said just now that he employed a block of wood on which to support the saucer. He may, however, have employed one or two books taken from the case above the bureau. These would serve his purpose equally well.

"Unfortunately none of these articles is in any way difficult to procure. Rags, waste paper, or wood-wool are available to almost anybody. Sulphuric acid is used for so many purposes, wireless batteries for instance, that its purchase would excite no comment. Sugar is to be found in every household. Chlorate of potash is sold by every chemist in the form of throat lozenges. Yet some person must have collected these different substances for the purpose of causing the fire. What was the motive?" Dr. Priestley paused as though expecting an answer to his question.

"Well, sir," replied Jimmy hesitatingly. "The only motive we've got to work on so far is revenge. Lavis had been employed by Mr. Pershore's firm and had been discharged. This may have rankled with him until he made up his mind to do Mr. Pershore an ill turn. Knowing the pride which Mr. Pershore took in his antique furniture, the idea of setting fire to the bungalow may have occurred to him. He was heard to express satisfaction when he learnt of the fire. He was seen to take the path leading to Hobb's Corner on Saturday evening. He evinced uneasiness when taxed with this by Sergeant Wragge. It seems to me, sir, that Lavis must be the first person to be suspected."

"Certainly," Dr. Priestley replied. "But do not commit the error of concentrating suspicion on one person alone, to the exclusion of all other possibilities. In the meanwhile you will, I suppose, undertake the investigation of the burglary at Paddock Croft?"

"Sergeant Wragge is anxious that I should do so, sir," Jimmy replied. "I confess I'm rather surprised that Elver hasn't been found yet. The Sergeant is convinced that Lavis knows where he is concealed."

"That may or may not be the case. It is certainly significant that Elver called at Lavis's house on Saturday afternoon. It is, of course, no evidence that the two acted in collusion in the matter of the burglary. It seems to me that there is one thing worthy of investigation. How did Elver become acquainted with Lavis's whereabouts?"

"They must have been in communication since Elver's release, sir," replied Jimmy promptly.

"Not necessarily. You assume that because Elver called at Lavis's house, it was for the purpose of doing so that Elver came here on Saturday. But he may have come here with a very different purpose, and after his arrival have learnt by chance that Lavis was in the neighbourhood."

"Then he must first have spoken to somebody else in the district, sir," exclaimed Jimmy.

"He may have done so, and in that fact may lie a useful clue. I would recommend you, Inspector, to make further inquiries into Elver's past history. Now, since I can be of no further assistance to you, and my curiosity as to the origin of the fire is satisfied, I shall return to London. I need hardly assure you that my advice is at your disposal whenever you care to seek it."

Jimmy escorted Dr. Priestley to the car where Harold was waiting for him, and watched them drive away. Then he mounted Mr. Raymond's bicycle, which he still retained, and rode back to Culverden.

Wragge was very much impressed by the ingenuity with which the fire had been contrived. "Clever old boy that expert of yours seems to be," he said. "Well, that pretty well settles it. Lavis is our man, there's not a shadow of doubt about that. But how are we going to bring it home to him, that's what I want to know?"

"We'll have to do our best," Jimmy replied. "Perhaps when we lay our hands upon Elver he'll be able to tell us something useful. I'm inclined to think that's the first thing to be done."

Wragge laughed. "I thought that all along," he said. "But I've failed so far and it's up to you now. Have you got the London folk to work on the job?"

"I had a chat with the Superintendent of M Division last night. He promised to organise a man-hunt straight away. My idea is that Elver may have slipped back to his usual haunts somehow, and that with some of the proceeds of the burglary he's bribed somebody to hide him. M Division will comb out the neighbourhood practically house by house. The Superintendent promised to let me know at once if he heard anything of him, and in any case to ring me up here at five o'clock this evening."

"Well, there's no message come through yet. The best thing you can do now is to sit down and have a bit of dinner with us. And when you've done that you might like to have a look round the hop fields. They're worth seeing, for any one coming down here for the first time."

Jimmy readily fell in with this suggestion. And since the neighbourhood of Hobb's Corner had a particular interest for him, he chose the hop gardens belonging to Hobb's Farm as the scene of his explorations.

When he arrived there he found work in full swing. His first call was at the farm-house, where he introduced himself to Mr. Velley and asked his permission to look round the hop gardens.

"You're welcome to go where you like, Inspector," replied Mr. Velley heartily. "I'm just going to take a turn round myself. Perhaps you'd like to come with me, and I can tell you what it's all about."

Jimmy accepted this invitation gratefully, and the two set out together. "Hops aren't like any other crops," said Mr. Velley, as they walked towards the garden in which the pickers were working that afternoon. "Take corn for instance. You can grow as many acres as you like, reap it with a tractor, and thresh the corn from the ears afterwards by machinery. Nowadays you want very little more labour at harvest time than you do at any other time of the year. And what extra labour you want you can always get locally. There's always somebody who's ready to come in and earn a bit by lending a hand.

"But with hops it's different. For one thing they are a permanent crop. The actual plants, or hills as we call them, remain in the same place from year to year. They always want a certain amount of labour, keeping the ground in proper condition, manuring and so forth. Then when the young shoots begin to grow in spring, there's a good deal of work in tying them to their supports. Nowadays hop-poles aren't used so much. The shoots have separate bits of twine up which they are trained. The shoots aren't tied to the twine, merely twisted round it, like you've seen a runner bean growing up a stick. Hop-twiddling we call it. But there's no reason to send far afield for extra labour like that. The wives and families of the chaps on the farm do the most of it. Then there's the washing and spraying and so forth, but that doesn't call for any extra help.

"It's when the hops are ready to pick that the rush comes. You see, you can't start picking them until they are ready, and you mustn't leave them too long after that. You've got to get your picking done in a certain time after the hops are in the proper condition. And you can't just cut the vines down and thresh the hops off them. Each separate hop has got to be picked off by hand, there's no machine yet invented that will do the job for you. So, during hop-picking time you want an enormous amount of extra labour, and most of it has to come from the towns, mainly London."

"How do you get hold of these extra hands?" Jimmy asked.

"Oh, it's quite easy enough now. It's very different from what it was in the old days. There were a lot more hops grown then than there are now, and you had to take on anybody who offered themselves, and glad to do so. But now since the quota system has been introduced you can pick and choose. You see, the acreage of hops is strictly limited. I'm only allowed to grow so many hundredweight of hops a year, for which I'm guaranteed a standard price. If for any reason my crop doesn't come up to my quota, I'm allowed to sell my surplus quota to anybody who happens to have more hops than he's entitled to. For instance, suppose my neighbour and I both have a quota for a thousand hundredweight. My crop turns out at nine hundredweight, and his at eleven hundredweight. He's a hundredweight surplus to his quota. I'm the same amount short. I'm allowed to sell him that amount of my quota, so that he can market all the hops that he's produced. But the permanent quota remains the same. I mustn't plant any more hops than have been allowed me. It's a queer business in its way, but it works out pretty well on the whole."

"I've got that," said Jimmy. "It comes to this, I take it. You've got to employ practically the same number of pickers every year."

"That's it, and now you'll be able to understand when I tell you how I get them. I don't have to go to an employment exchange or anything like that. Anybody who wants to come hop-picking writes to one or other of the farmers in the neighbourhood that they've heard about. Their friends tell them their names, I suppose. I get hundreds of letters myself in the course of the year. And from those letters I pick out a certain number, giving preference to people who've been down here before and who've behaved themselves. Anybody who's been a nuisance to me or my neighbours gets struck off the list at once. Actually, the same people come down year after year. It isn't so much the money they're after, though if they give their minds to it they can earn a good bit. They like a holiday in the country at the pleasant time of the year."

"You don't have much trouble with them?" Jimmy suggested.

"Wonderfully little, and no serious trouble at that. Some people treat them like dirt, because they come from the poorer parts of London. I won't say that their ways are everything you might wish. They're noisy, they break the hedges, they over-run the countryside like a plague of locusts. The amount of litter they leave behind them would break your heart to see. But they're thoroughly decent, respectable people at heart, and, speaking for myself, I've little fault to find with them. The greater part of the money they earn they spend in the district, which means a lot in a place like this. It isn't only the shops and the pubs that benefit, either. There isn't a cottage round about that doesn't sell them flowers, or fruit or vegetables or eggs, or maybe a chicken now and then. We may be glad to see the back of them, but we've got to admit that we couldn't do without them. We shouldn't get our hops picked if it wasn't that we had those folks to call on."

"You've got to provide accommodation for them, of course?"

"Yes, that we have, and there are Inspectors to see that we do it properly too. They've got to have decent weatherproof huts, plenty of dry litter to lay their beds on, a water supply and somewhere to cook their grub. Then they have to have their firing. Some of us have provided great cauldrons to boil water, and we supply a man to look after them and keep the camp as tidy as possible. Like everything else it is all a matter of organisation. I decide upon the number of pickers I want, just before I'm ready upon the day that I'm going to start picking. Then I send cards to those I've selected, telling them to come down the day before. We also notify the railway company, and they arrange special trains. But a lot of them come down by road, and a queer sight it is to see them arrive. Perhaps a couple of families will club together and arrange with a man who owns a motor lorry to bring them down. Then they pack themselves and their children and their mattresses and their pots and pans into the lorry, until it looks like a proper Noah's Ark. You'd laugh to see them sort themselves out when they get to the huts. Of course there are lots of them who won't run to the expense of a lorry. Some of them walk it all the way from London. Pushing perambulators with them, too, stacked up with their goods and chattels. I often wonder how some of them get here at all, but they all seem to manage it somehow."

"Who are these folks when they are at home?" Jimmy asked.

"It's hard to say. Women and children mostly. The wives and families of small traders and hawkers mainly, I imagine. All I know is that there's no decline in the birth rate where they come from. You never in your life saw so many children as they bring with them. I believe they bring their neighbour's brats with them just for the holiday. And the children are a bit of a nuisance sometimes. They very soon get tired of picking hops and wander off about the countryside. Mischievous little devils they are too, some of them. However, it does them good, I suppose. They look very different when they go away from when they came down."

By this time they had reached the edge of the garden where the pickers were at work. "Now you can see for yourself how we set about it," said Mr. Velley. "There are the hops ready to be picked, with the vines still growing up the sticks which support them. The strings are tied at the top to a framework of wire, supported on wooden posts. The wires and posts are permanent and remain there from year to year. But if you left the hops like that you'd want a ladder to pick the upper ones. So they have to be brought within the picker's reach. Every morning a couple of my regular chaps go round and cut the strings so that the vines fall to the ground. We only cut as much as can be picked during the day. And we don't waste anything either. We find a use for the vines after the hops have been picked off them. We dry them and use them next year as litter for the pickers to put their mattresses on. Some of them don't worry to bring their mattresses down. They just lie on the litter itself. There you are, now you can see them at work on the vines which were cut down this morning."

Jimmy concentrated his attention upon the group nearest to him. It consisted of an elderly woman, two girls whose likeness to her suggested that they were her daughters, and three or four children whose ages varied from eleven to fifteen. Each member of this group was assiduously picking hops. Jimmy marvelled at the dexterity which they had acquired during long practice. A quick twist of the wrist detached a luxurious spray of hops from the vine. Then adroit fingers plucked separate hops from the spray and cast them into the receptacle designed to receive them. This was a piece of sacking supported like a hammock from a wooden framework. Both sides of the framework extended at either end so that the whole concern could be picked up and moved as the hoppers advanced.

"Bins we call them," said Mr. Velley as he put his hand into one and ran through his fingers the hops it contained. "Each group works in a straight line up the garden picking from the rows on either side. And each has its own bin which it carries with it. That's how we keep a check on what each group picks. See, here comes the measurer. Well, Tom, how are we getting on this afternoon?"

"Nicely, sir," replied Tom Adcorn. "We'll be knocking off about half-past five as usual, I expect. The hops in this garden are the best samples we've picked so far."

Tom Adcorn had a bushel basket with him. This he proceeded to fill from the bins which the group were working. The members of the group watched him with anxious eyes. "Now mister, don't you press them down so hard as that," said the old lady reprovingly. "Some of you chaps try to get two bushels into a basket that's only meant for one. How do you think me and my poor orphan daughters is going to get a living that way? It's robbing the poor, that's what you're doing, more shame to you."

Tom was clearly accustomed to that sort of thing. "All right, mother," he replied cheerfully. "Fair's fair and a bushel's a bushel whichever way you look at it. It's more hops you want to pick if you want to make more money."

"I'd have you mind your manners, young man," she said with dignity. "I'd have you know that I was picking hops before your father made the mistake that turned out to be you. And if I was to start telling you all I think of you, these gentlemen here would learn something I reckon."

All this without a moment's hesitation in her dexterous picking. Her hands were yellow with the sticky juice of the ripe fruit, and her wrinkled face moistened with the September sun which poured down upon it.

The two girls tittered, caught Jimmy's eye and laughed impudently. He noticed that they were good-looking enough, in a bold artificial way. But Tom, fully inured to the pickers' broad humour, took no notice whatever. He continued filling his basket from the bin, then carried it to an enormous sack into which he emptied it.

"It holds ten bushels," said Mr. Velley towards the sack. "A poke we call it. That's how we keep a tally on the pickers. They're paid by piece-work, of course. So much for every poke they fill. When all the hops are picked, we reckon up what each family has earned, then pay them off."

"What do they live on meanwhile?" asked Jimmy, as they strolled across towards another group of pickers.

"Oh, they borrow on their expectations. Subbing they call it. Some of them sub up to the limit and have nothing left when it comes to paying-off day. I've known cases before now where a family found itself absolutely without money and had to walk home. Some of them manage to keep a tidy bit in hand, but not many. As I said before, it isn't altogether the money that appeals to the most of them. So long as they get a country holiday which pays for itself, they're content."

They stopped to watch a second group. Four young women, this time, of ages varying from twenty to thirty-five. They were talking and laughing among themselves and paid very little attention to Mr. Velley and his companion. One of them, apparently the eldest, looked up and nodded familiarly.

"Afternoon, Mr. Velley," she said.

"Good-afternoon, Miss Rivers," replied the farmer politely. "Enjoying yourself down here this year?"

It seemed to Jimmy that the girl blushed at the apparently innocent question. "Oh, not too bad," she said as she turned away to continue her picking.

Once more they moved on. "Come and have a look round the huts," said Mr. Velley. "They're quite close and you'll find them well worth a visit. That girl I spoke to just now is one of my oldest hands. She's been down here to my farm for the last fifteen years at least. You asked me just now what these people are at home. Well, she works in a tannery somewhere in Bermondsey. Very decent girl she is, from what I know of her. And I'm not the only one who thinks so. Tom could tell you quite a lot about her, I dare say."

"Tom?" repeated Jimmy inquiringly.

"Tom Adcorn, the weigher you saw just now. I suspected for the last year or two that Tom had been smitten. It's a joke among the pickers that he always gets more bushels out of her bin than anybody else's. Tom's a steady lad and so's his brother. I've often wondered that neither of them have got married before this. Too comfortable at home with mother, I expect."

"Does it often happen that a local man marries one of the pickers?" Jimmy asked.

"Not very often. As a rule the locals and the pickers are like oil and water. They don't mix. But it does sometimes happen that one of the chaps falls for a fascinating hop-picker. I rather hope that Tom won't marry Miss Rivers, though."

"Not a suitable match, you think?"

"It isn't that so much. But in my experience those sort of weddings never turn out a success. The girl comes down to the country for three weeks of hop-picking a year and thinks she's in heaven. It's light work, plenty of fresh air, and all the freedom she wants. She imagines that if she marries a countryman she'll be able to enjoy that sort of thing all the year round. She hasn't the least idea what it means to be a farm labourer's wife. But she very quickly gets disillusioned. She is lonely, since the man is out at work all day. She misses the pavements, the shops and the neighbours next door. Then she finds that most of her time is spent in cooking and housework to which she isn't accustomed. And she always seems aggrieved when the children arrive, which they do at the most inconvenient moments. No, in my opinion, a farm labourer had much better marry a country girl who knows what she is in for when she accepts him. And there are plenty of girls round here who would be glad to many either of the Adcorns. And there's another thing about that Rivers girl. She's got no parents."

Jimmy laughed. "I shouldn't have thought that was necessarily a bar to matrimonial happiness," he said.

"On the contrary, it's very often an advantage. But when I said that the Rivers girl had no parents, I meant something rather different. She's a foundling, and nobody knows who were her parents. You remember the story of Moses and the bulrushes? Well, hers is somewhat similar. Only it wasn't Pharaoh's daughter but an elderly stevedore who found her. As he was coming to work one morning he noticed a shopping basket standing on the doorstep of a warehouse in Pickle Herring Street. He picked it up and found a live baby in it, not more than a few hours old. Not having any use for perishable articles of that nature, he took it to the nearest policeman, and the policeman in turn passed it on to the guardians, who christened it Kate Rivers. Rivers, I suppose, because the child had been found by the river side. In due course a job was found for her in the tannery, and she was boarded out with a family by the name of Sheares. The Sheares girl nearly always comes hop-picking with her. She was in that group we saw just now."

"I don't see that her origin is any bar to her marrying whom she likes," said Jimmy.

"I dare say you don't. Nor do I. But country folk, or the majority of them, aren't quite so broad-minded. They think that no foundling has any right to become a respectable married woman. She wouldn't be nice to know, in fact. She'd be made to feel that, I'm afraid, if she ever came to live here as Tom Adcorn's wife. It's all very silly, no doubt, but you can't change people's outlook. Well, here are the huts. Like to have a look round them?"

Jimmy looked at his watch and found that the time was already half-past four; "Thanks very much, Mr. Velley," he replied. "But I've got to be back at Culverden by five and it's time I was getting on. Perhaps you will be good enough to let me have a look round some other day?"

"Delighted to see you whenever you care to come," Mr. Velley replied. "Any news of the chap who broke into Paddock Croft last Saturday, by the way?"

"I'm expecting news of him any time now," Jimmy replied.

He thanked Mr. Velley and walked back to the farmhouse, where he had left his bicycle, and rode away.

CHAPTER X

THE call from the Superintendent of M Division came through punctually. But his report was entirely negative. Everybody with whom Elver had been associated had been questioned, without result. His movements could be traced with accuracy up till about noon on the previous Saturday. He had actually been seen at London Bridge Station waiting for an excursion train bound for the hop-fields. But since then all trace of him had been lost.

"I think you can take it that your man hasn't come back to these parts," said the Superintendent. "Of course we'll keep our eyes and ears open, and if anything is heard of him I'll let you know at once. This piece of information may be useful to you. He doesn't seem to have made many friends since his release. By which I mean that he hasn't become friendly with any family living in the neighbourhood. He seems only to have spoken to the Pilbeams, where he lodged, and to the chaps he worked with. I'm pretty certain that nobody in the district knew him well enough to take the risk of sheltering him."

Jimmy concluded the conversation, which he repeated to Wragge who was standing by. "If he hasn't gone back to London I don't know where else he could have gone," he said. "A man isn't likely to go wandering off to a strange place with his pockets full of stolen jewellery. It seems to me far more likely that he's hiding about here somewhere."

"Then I'll wager my best pair of boots that Lavis knows where he is," said Wragge decisively.

"I think it's about time that I made Lavis's acquaintance," said Jimmy.

"You'll find him an obstinate customer to deal with. Still, you may be luckier than I was. Now just you sit down and have a cup of tea and a bite of the missus' plum cake. And after that, if you're set on it, you can ride over to Park Gate. You should find Lavis at home by that time. Where are you going to sleep to-night, by the way?"

"Oh, I thought of getting a room at one of the local pubs," Jimmy replied.

"In hop-picking time?" said Wragge scornfully. "You'd hardly be made welcome, I'm afraid. The pubs have got as much as they can do just now without taking in visitors, even though they happen to be Inspectors from Scotland Yard. You must stay here with us. I was asking the missus about it this afternoon, and she'll be glad to have you. I don't say that we can make you as comfortable as you're accustomed to, but we'll do our best."

"I'm sure I shall be more comfortable than I've ever been in my life," replied Jimmy heartily. "It's really awfully kind of you and Mrs. Wragge. Are you quite sure I won't be a nuisance?"

"You're not the sort to be a nuisance," said Wragge with a chuckle. "Now you come along and have that tea. It's been waiting for you since you came in."

After tea Jimmy set out once more on Mr. Raymond's bicycle, this time for Park Gate. Mrs. Creach opened the door to him. He fancied that as he introduced himself a flicker of anxiety came into her eyes. But she informed him that her brother was at home and admitted him rather grudgingly. Lavis was evidently on the point of going out and scowled ungraciously at the intruder.

As he had ridden over Jimmy had decided upon the line that he would take with the man. Wragge had tried intimidation and failed. A subtler method might be successful. He would not treat Lavis as a suspect, but as a trustworthy individual who might be able to give useful information. And he had not forgotten the hint which Dr. Priestley had dropped that morning.

"Good-evening, Mr. Lavis," he said. "I'm sorry to break in upon you like this, but I believe that you may be able to help me. I'm looking for information about a certain Christopher Elver, who was once known as Sea Joe. Since he is a discharged convict the police are rather interested in him. Between ourselves, he's disappeared and nobody seems to know what has happened to him. You knew him at one time, didn't you?"

"Well, we did meet once or twice in a way of business," Lavis replied cautiously. "He was a steward on a ship, you see. He used to deal with the firm I was representing at the time."

"So I understand. Now what I want to know is this. Was he always perfectly honest and above-board in his business dealings with you?"

Lavis seemed surprised at this question. "Why yes," he replied. "He never tried any tricks that I know of. He always seemed to me a straight-forward young chap, and I could hardly believe my eyes when I read in the papers that he'd been arrested for dope smuggling."

"You never can tell what some people are up to on the quiet," said Jimmy sagely. "I expect you remember the case well enough, don't you?"

"Well, I can't say that I do. I read all about it in the papers at the time, but that's many years ago, and it's mostly slipped my memory now."

"He used to deliver the stuff to a woman who kept a shop in Lambeth. She was imprisoned too, and died before her sentence had run out. Her name was Mrs. Hawkins, and she posed as Sea Joe's aunt. You never met her by any chance, did you, Mr. Lavis?"

Jimmy saw at once that this chance shot had told. Lavis winced and his reply was hesitant and unconvincing. "Met her!" he exclaimed. "How should I have met her? I wasn't in the habit of calling on my customers' relations."

"Oh, I thought you might, that's all," said Jimmy. "I always understood that ships' chandlers tried to look after their customers to some extent. They entertain them now and again, for instance, just for the sake of goodwill. I expect that was your custom, wasn't it?"

"Well, maybe I'd stand my customers a drink once in a way," Lavis replied.

"I thought that there was just a chance that Sea Joe might have brought his aunt along to have a drink with you. You and he did drop into a pub sometimes together, I dare say?"

"Maybe we did. In fact, I wouldn't say that we didn't. But it was only in the way of business, you understand. I'd go aboard his ship and take his order, then I'd ask him to come ashore and have a drink with me. But he never told me anything about himself, much less his aunt, that I'm sure of."

That Elver should seek Lavis out, after so casual an acquaintanceship so rudely interrupted, was incredible. Already Jimmy suspected that Lavis knew more about Mrs. Hawkins than he cared to reveal. But he felt the need of proceeding cautiously.

"Did Sea Joe ever bring any friends with him on these occasions?" he asked.

"Perhaps now and again he'd bring one of his chums from the ship with him. And once, I remember, we met a girl on the quayside and she came with us."

A girl! This was interesting, though obviously merely a side issue. Jimmy remembered Hanslet's account of the case. Mrs. Hawkins had mentioned a girl whose existence Elver had strenuously denied. It would be amazing if, after all these years, her identity and her connection with Elver should be revealed. And from such an unexpected source.

"You met this girl casually on the quayside?" Jimmy asked.

"Well, no, not that exactly," Lavis replied. "She seemed to me to be waiting there for Sea Joe. Anyhow he knew her, and it seemed to me that he wasn't best pleased to see her. So far as I recollect, he didn't introduce her but just said to me that she was a friend of his. Then he told her that we were just going to have a drink and that she'd better come along too."

"Did you happen to hear her name?" asked Jimmy casually.

"No, that I didn't. Never set eyes on her since, and I shouldn't know her again if I did. I didn't take any particular notice of her and I was glad when she cleared off, after he'd promised to meet her again later."

"You were glad, Mr. Lavis!" Jimmy exclaimed. "Rather unchivalrous of you, wasn't it?"

Lavis fidgeted as though he felt he'd made a slip. "Well, you see, he and I hadn't finished our business," he replied. "He hadn't given me the whole of his order when we were on board ship, and there were a few more things he had to mention. We were going to talk it over quietly in the pub, and we couldn't very well do that with that girl there."

"I see," said Jimmy. "Women are apt to be in the way sometimes, aren't they? You never saw this girl again, you say?"

Lavis shook his head vigorously. "No, and I never saw Sea Joe again neither," he replied. "His ship sailed again a day or two later, and the next thing I heard of him was that he had been arrested."

"It must have been a bit of a shock to you, Mr. Lavis," said Jimmy sympathetically.

Again the shifty look came into Lavis's eyes. "What do you mean?" he replied. "It didn't affect me one way or the other whether Sea Joe was put in quod or not. The firm lost a customer, that was all. The next steward might have carried on as before, I don't know."

"You didn't hear anything from him at the time of his release two years ago?"

"Why, I had forgotten all about him by then. And he's probably forgotten all about me, too. Why should he want to get in touch with me again, or if he did how was he going to set about it? I left the ships' chandlers soon after he was arrested and came here to live with my sister. I don't suppose they even know my address now, so it wouldn't have been any good Sea Joe going to them and asking them."

"And yet he turns up here on Saturday afternoon," said Jimmy quietly.

Lavis shot a savage glance at his sister, who had been standing by the doorway, a silent witness of their conversation.

"There's only a woman's word for that," he replied. "And women are that fanciful you can never rely on what they say. I dare say a chap did come here on Saturday afternoon to see me. I've got plenty of friends around the countryside whom my sister doesn't know by sight. And I dare say he wasn't unlike the photograph the sergeant showed us. But you'll never make me believe that it was Sea Joe that came."

"Would one of your friends from the countryside come to call upon you wearing a paper hat?" Jimmy asked.

"I don't see that anything's to prevent them. They might have picked it up and put it on by way of a joke. Anyway, I didn't see the chap then, or at any other time."

Jimmy shook his head. "I think it was Sea Joe, just the same," he said. "When I next meet him I shall have to ask him what his business with you was."

Lavis recoiled slightly in his chair before this veiled threat. "Why you'd never believe what an expired convict told you!" he exclaimed. "He'd make up some sort of yarn, likely enough. Some story that he'd been friendly with me at one time and wanted me to do something for him now. That is if it had been Sea Joe who came here, but it wasn't."

"And yet I happen to know that Sea Joe was in Matling on Saturday evening." Jimmy was aware of Lavis's searching gaze upon him, and that the man was trying to determine whether this was sheer bluff or not. "That's perfectly true," he continued. "He has quite a lot to explain when I come up with him, including his visit to you. It would be a great pity, Mr. Lavis, if your name got mixed up in the affair. Of course, if you could help me to get in touch with him it would be an entirely different thing."

Lavis shook his head violently. "I don't know anything about the chap, I tell you," he exclaimed. "I've never set eyes on him since that day we met the girl on the quayside. And what's more I've never heard a word from him. It's no use you and the Sergeant tormenting me in this way. I can't tell you more than what's the truth, can I?"

In spite of Jimmy's conviction that Lavis was something of a rogue, the sincerity of his declaration impressed him. Certainly the man was not telling the whole truth and nothing but the truth. The relations between him and Sea Joe had at one time been deeper than he cared to admit. But still there was the possibility that the two had not met since Sea Joe's arrest. And if so, Lavis was probably unaware of his present whereabouts.

Jimmy left the house feeling that he had made remarkably little headway. He really had learnt nothing more than Wragge already knew. Except about that girl. It seemed now that her existence must be accepted as a fact. Lavis had mentioned her casually, without any suggestion on Jimmy's part. Why should he have mentioned the incident of meeting her on the quayside if it had never occurred? He could have nothing whatever to gain by doing so.

Yet, as Jimmy was well aware, the point was of academic interest only. Hanslet would be interested to hear that she had turned up again, that was all. There was no question that she was in any way implicated in that almost forgotten drug trafficking business. That Elver had got in touch with her again since his release seemed unlikely. The Superintendent of M Division had expressly stated that he had no acquaintances except the people he lodged with and his fellow workmen. If he had cultivated the friendship of a girl, M Division would have known about it at once. It is a maxim of police methods that a girl friend very often proves to be a most useful informant.

On the other hand, Lavis's conscience was by no means clear. Jimmy had watched him closely enough during their conversation to be sure of that. But this uneasiness originated probably in the days before Elver's arrest. Jimmy had noticed that Lavis's uneasiness only betrayed itself when those days were under discussion.

Jimmy was still wondering what step he should take next when he reached the Chequers. The sign suspended before the house reminded him of one obvious duty. He could not go on using Mr. Raymond's bicycle indefinitely. He might just as well give it back to him now and walk the couple of miles into Culverden. As he walked an idea might occur to him.

It was now nearly seven o'clock. The sky had become overcast and a light drizzle followed the fine afternoon. It had kept many of the hop-pickers in their huts and the scene outside the Chequers was not so lively as usual. Certainly the stalls were arranged beneath the elm tree, but their proprietors looked dispirited. Their flow of customers was scanty. A few women with shawls muffled round their heads made random purchases and then hurried away. Even round the windows of the bar parlour the applicants were scarce. It was not at all the sort of evening to sit out and enjoy the open air.

As Jimmy dismounted from his borrowed bicycle, two men approached the door of the other room, opened it and passed inside. Jimmy recognised one of them as the measurer he had seen that afternoon. Tom Adcorn, Mr. Velley had called him. Jimmy, seeking Mr. Raymond, decided to follow their example. He in turn approached the door of the other room, but a figure appeared suddenly and confronted him. "Not in there," he said brusquely. "You just go along to that window and they'll serve you."

The experience of being refused admittance to a pub was a new one to Jimmy. It rather amused him than otherwise. "Sorry," he replied, "I didn't know the rules. Do you think I can have a word with Mr. Raymond?"

The other glanced at him suspiciously. Alf Mailing had been specially chosen as doorkeeper by Mr. Raymond on account of his extensive local knowledge. But now he regarded this stranger with no little perplexity. He wasn't one of the home-dwellers, for there was nobody who lived within twenty miles of Matling that Alf didn't know. And he certainly didn't look like a hop-picker or one of their hangers-on. He turned towards the arbour and pointed.

"There's the guv'nor over there," he said. "Him that's putting the tarpaulin' up on the framework. If you want a word with him I dare say he'll listen to you."

Mr. Raymond was obviously busy. Mounted on a stepladder he was drawing an enormous tarpaulin across the wooden rafters erected above the tables and benches. The tarpaulin was heavy and resisted his efforts. As he approached Jimmy could hear him mumbling beneath his breath.

It seemed an opportunity not to be missed. "Here, let me give you a hand," Jimmy exclaimed. And before Mr. Raymond could reply to this unexpected offer his unknown assistant climbed upon the table and caught hold of one corner of the tarpaulin. Mr. Raymond, like a wise man ready to accept the blessings of heaven without a too minute inquiry, asked no questions.

"A little more over this way," he said. "Steady now, we don't want to tear the dratted thing between us. That's right. Now pull out straight. And tie your corner down securely so that if the wind comes up it won't blow away."

Between them they got the tarpaulin into position. Mr. Raymond descended from his steps and regarded Jimmy gratefully.

"Now, that's what I call real neighbourly," he said. "I'd have got Alf yonder to bear me a hand, but he's got a poisoned arm, see, and that's why he can't go to work this week. And that tarpaulin's terrible heavy for one to set up. It's always like this in hop-picking. You won't catch me staying here another year, not if the brewers paid me for it. It comes on a sudden shower like this and the pickers get that spiteful if they can't sit somewhere in the dry. So the old tarpaulin has got to go up and never mind the wear and tear. You're a stranger to these parts, if I may make so bold to ask?"

"Quite right," Jimmy replied. "But although I'm a stranger I've been riding your bicycle about all day. I've just come to return it, with many thanks."

Mr. Raymond laughed heartily. "There, I did think there was something familiar about the old bike," he said. "You'll be a friend of Sergeant Wragge's then, over at Culverden? It was him that borrowed it yesterday morning, and I told him he could keep it as long as was convenient."

"Yes, I'm a friend of his. In fact, I'm staying with him for a day or two. I'll leave the bicycle with you and get on my way back."

"You'll do nothing of the kind," said Mr. Raymond firmly. "You'll have a drink with me before going back all that way. Why, it's two miles and not a yard less. You come along inside with me."

He led the way round the house, which they entered by the back door. "I'm fair sick of this hop-picking," he exclaimed. "Not a corner of the house that a man can call his own. The bar parlour's full of barrels and the home-dwellers are playing darts in the other room. I'd ask you into the kitchen, but mother's washing the glasses in there, and there's not room to sit down. Let's come into the cellar, if you don't mind."

"The cellar sounds a very good place," Jimmy replied. "You seem pretty busy, Mr. Raymond."

"Busy!" exclaimed Mr. Raymond contemptuously. "If I don't get no busier than this, I shan't be able to pay the brewers' bill. That's hop-picking all over. You turn the house upside down and then the rain comes and keeps the customers away. But never mind. It'll all be the same a thousand years hence, I suppose. Now what are you going to have? A drop of Scotch to keep the damp out?"

"I'd rather have a drop of beer, if it's all the same to you," Jimmy replied. "Beer's better for a man than whisky, if he can take it."

"You're right there," agreed Mr. Raymond as he drew a generous pint from one of the barrels. "Beer is best, as the advertisement says, especially if you're going to do a bit of walking afterwards."

He handed the pint to Jimmy and drew another for himself. "Talking of beer reminds me of a couple of toffs who were in here a month or two back. They'd got one of them sports cars with them. Noisy thing that you could hear a couple of parishes away. They was talking about how many miles she could do to the gallon. I listened to them for a while, and then I said to them, 'Gentlemen', I said, 'I don't know anything about your car, but I know what my consumption is.' They looked at me and one of them said, 'Well, let's hear about it.' 'A pint to a mile,' I said, 'that's what I do. You won't catch me walking no farther than Culverden and that's two miles, isn't it? Well, I have a couple of pints before I start out, and a couple more at one of the pubs there before I come home again. If that doesn't work out at a pint a mile, there's something gone wrong with my arithmetic.' You're staying with the Sergeant, you say. Maybe you might happen to be in the police yourself?"

Jimmy had no reason to conceal his identity. In any case it would very soon become public property. "Yes, I'm a policeman,' he replied. "In fact I'm an Inspector from Scotland Yard. Waghorn, my name is, and I've been sent down to see about this business at Paddock Croft."

"I'm sure I'm very pleased to meet you, Inspector," said Mr. Raymond. "That was a bad business up at Paddock Croft. You haven't found the chap yet, then? The Sergeant was telling me that it was known who did it."

"We haven't found him yet," Jimmy replied. "We have reason to believe that he's still hanging around these parts somewhere."

"Likely enough," said Mr. Raymond. "But there's so many strangers hanging round here just now that one more or less wouldn't be noticed. But I don't like the idea. I'll see to it that I lock up securely every evening. Between ourselves, there's more money in the house than I care about. In a place like this you can't bank your takings every day. And I dare say that chap knows it well enough."

"You'll be wise to take all precautions, Mr. Raymond. He might be tempted to try and break in."

"He'll not break in here without some trouble. The doors are stout and the locks are good. This place has been standing some hundreds of years, and they knew how to build then. Not like that flimsy bungalow concern of Mr. Pershore's. I've been thinking that the chap who broke into Paddock Croft is the most likely to have set fire to that."

"It's not impossible, though it's difficult to see what he hoped to gain by it. I was at the bungalow myself this morning having a look round with Mr. Pershore. He seems to me a very decent sort of fellow."

"Oh, he's well enough liked around here. Not like Mr. Speight up at Paddock Croft, whom nobody seems able to get on with. Speaking for myself, I've always found Mr. Pershore as pleasant as you could wish. I serve him with whatever he wants in the way of drink whenever he's at the bungalow. And often enough he'll drop in here of a Saturday morning and have a chat. And there's no standoffishness about him either. He'll just walk into the bar parlour, sit down among the men, and as likely as not stand drinks round. He'll be terribly upset by that fire, I make no doubt."

"He certainly seems to be," Jimmy replied. "You know him pretty well, I expect?"

"Well, only from seeing him now and again. But there's Alf Mailing now. He knows him as well as anybody in these parts. He keeps the bungalow garden in order for him and has done ever since the place was built. You sit where you are for a minute and I'll call him in."

Mr. Raymond went out and returned a minute or two later with Alf Mailing. "Sit down Alf, and I dare say I can find a pint or two for you," he said. "There won't be so many folk round this evening that you need stop out there all the time. This gentleman's asking about Mr. Pershore, and I said maybe you could tell him more than I can."

Alf shook his head despondently. "Ah, he's terrible put out over that fire," he replied. "I heard that he was staying up at Hobb's Farm, so I went round there this afternoon to see him. I wanted to know if he'd like me to put the mess straight and tidy the place up a bit as soon as my arm's better. He said that I could clean the place up outside, but that I wasn't to touch anything inside until he let me know. Said the police weren't satisfied about the fire as yet. Mrs. Adcorn she's fair broke up about it. She keeps saying that Mr. Pershore is sure to blame her for what happened. It's no good telling her that Mr. Pershore is too kind a gentleman to blame anybody for what they couldn't help."

"He's pretty well off, isn't he?" Jimmy asked.

Alf laughed. "Well off!" he exclaimed. "Why, he's got more money than most folks would know what to do with. He knows all right what to do with it, does Mr. Pershore. If he hears of anybody who's in any trouble or want he's the first to put his hand in his pocket. Many's the time he's called me to him and asked if there's anybody about the place who needed any help. And as soon as I give him a hint then he goes to see what can be done. You remember the case of that kid of young Bill Gunter's?"

Mr. Raymond nodded. "I remember well enough," he replied. "Sent him up to London to a nursing home for a couple of months. Saw to it that he wanted for nothing while he was there, didn't he?"

"That's right. And that's only one of the cases I could name. It isn't the damage to the bungalow that upsets him so much. That's insured, and even if it wasn't he could build a dozen more like it without feeling it. But it's them old pieces of furniture that he put in it. If he took a fancy to a thing like that he'd buy it, no matter what it cost. And as he was telling me, if a thing like that's destroyed you may never find another one like it so long as you live. I reckon there's not a soul about that isn't sorry for what's happened. They'd all go a long way to prevent anything happening to upset Mr. Pershore."

"And yet even a man of his type can't please everybody," Jimmy suggested.

"There's no pleasing some folk and that's a fact," Alf replied. "But it's only trash like that Lavis that would bear a grudge against him. Said the fire served Mr. Pershore right, I'm told. I wish I'd heard him. I'd have given him a bit of my mind, and a bit of my fist as well. After the way Mr. Pershore has treated him and all."

"He was employed by Mr. Pershore at one time, wasn't he?"

"He was that. It was like this, you see. Mr. Pershore used to stay in the village here before he built the bungalow. It was then that I first knew him, for I used to work for the ladies of the house where he stayed in. And he came out to me one day as I was sticking the runners in the garden. 'Alf,' he said -- he always calls me Alf -- 'Do you know anything about a fellow called Lavis who lives at Park Gate?'"

"Well, I didn't know much about Lavis then, except that he'd been travelling for a firm of sewing machine makers and lost his job. And so I told Mr. Pershore. 'Well,' he says, 'he's been to see me and asked if I could do anything for him. He says that he's a commercial traveller but that he has lost his job owing to the firm he worked for going out of business.'

"Well, I knew that wasn't true for a start. The firm hadn't gone out of business and they'd got a new traveller in Lavis's place. But I didn't say anything, because I thought it was none of my business. And a week or so later Mr. Pershore spoke to me again. He told me that he had decided to take on Lavis as a representative of his firm. The next thing I knew there was Lavis going round selling manure for Pershore and Huggins."

"That's so, I remember it well enough," said Mr. Raymond.

"Well, I could tell that Lavis wasn't a man to suit a firm like Pershore and Huggins. They wanted an energetic sort of man who'd go round and talk to the farmers properly. And Lavis wasn't that sort. He'd rather sit round in the pub drinking, and let the farmers come to him if they wanted his stuff. And as you know, guv'nor, farmers aren't made that way."

"They're not and that's a fact," Mr. Raymond agreed.

"Mr. Pershore found this out soon enough," Alf continued. "He's the sort that finds out what he wants to know without poking and prying into anybody's business. I know for a fact that he went to see Lavis and put it up to him that he had to mend his ways. But it wasn't a bit of good. Lavis went on just the same until one fine day he got a letter from the manager of Pershore and Huggins giving him a month's notice. And by the same post he got another letter which just shows where Mr. Pershore's kindness comes in. It was from Mr. Pershore himself, with a five pound note inside it. And the letter said how sorry he was that the experiment had not been a success, but he hoped that the money would come in useful until he found another job. And he's the chap that says it serves Mr. Pershore right that his bungalow was burnt. Pah!" Alf spat disgustedly and then hastily rubbed the spot with his boot. "He's a wrong un, is Lavis," he added darkly. "And unless I'm very much mistaken he's up to no good now."

"Up to no good!" exclaimed Mr. Raymond. "What do you mean by that, Alf?"

"I wouldn't like to say anything that I wasn't sure of," Alf replied cautiously. "But he's a lot too thick with the hoppers for my liking. Not that I've got anything against the hoppers, mind. They're a bit rough and the language the women use is disgusting, but I dare say they're all right when you get to know them. I'm glad I'm not a Londoner, that's all."

"Oh, they're all right," said Mr. Raymond tolerantly. "Their ways are different to ours and we don't understand them, that's all. Lavis worked in London before he came down here, they tell me, and I dare say he gets on with them better than we do."

"That may be," said Alf without conviction. "But what does he want hanging about the hopper huts at night, that's what I want to know? He's been doing that more than once, especially round about the week-ends. Talking to the folk that come down to see the hoppers, and they're a rum lot, you won't deny. What's he got to say to them? They don't buy his knives or whatever it is that he carries round with him, I reckon."

"He's usually too fuddled at the week-end to talk much to anybody," said Mr. Raymond contemptuously.

"He? Don't make any mistake about that. That's just one of his little dodges, as I know for a fact. Why, I've seen him come out of the Bell at Culverden to all eyes as drunk as the farmer's sow. It was one Saturday night last hop-picking. He got on his bike, wobbled along for a yard or two and then fell off it. Then he got on it again and did the same thing. There was a crowd of hoppers there, all laughing at him fit to burst their sides. I happened to be there, and as I was coming home this way I thought I'd follow him in case he came to some harm. And this is as true as gospel. As soon as he was clear of the village he got on to that bike and rode off along the road as straight as an arrow. There wasn't much the matter with Lavis that night, you can take my word for it."

"Why, whatever did he want to go and do a thing like that for?" Mr. Raymond exclaimed. "Making himself a laughing stock before all them strangers. You'd think a man would have more sense."

"It isn't sense he lacks. He's got some reason for making people think he was properly tucked that night. Like you said just now, guv'nor. A man in that state wouldn't be fit for any mischief. Likely he'd fall into a ditch on the way home and go to sleep there."

"Well, that takes the biscuit," said Mr. Raymond. "He's no good about the place, I've always known that. It's that sister of his I'm sorry for. She's a decent hard-working woman, and it must be a sore trial for her to have to keep that good-for-nothing brother."

"Yes, she's all right. Can't think why she puts up with that chap Lavis. The house they live in at Park Gate belongs to her. There's nothing to prevent her from telling him to clear out whenever she wants to. Doesn't want to leave the neighbourhood, I suppose, though nobody goes to the house when they think her brother's there."

"Well, it's time I was getting the gas over the door lighted," said Mr. Raymond. "If you'd like to stop and have another one. Inspector, you're welcome, I'm sure."

Jimmy declined the invitation, and the three of them left the house together. They found that the drizzle had ceased and that the evening sky was now perfectly clear. The pickers had taken advantage of this and were now thronging the space in front of the Chequers. The stalls were doing a roaring trade, and Mrs. Raymond and her daughter had their work cut out to supply their customers at the window of the bar parlour. "Things look a bit brighter now, guv'nor," said Alf.

"And I've had my trouble with them dratted tarpaulins for nothing," replied Mr. Raymond pessimistically.

He lighted the gas lamp over the front door and Alf resumed his duties as guardian angel. Jimmy said good-night to them both and set off at a smart pace along the road to Culverden. A few yards from the Chequers he overtook a group strolling slowly in the same direction. Tom Adcorn and another man so like him that he must surely be his brother Fred. A girl whom Jimmy recognised as Miss Rivers. The fourth member of the party was also a girl. Probably Molly Sheares of whom Mr. Velley had spoken. They were laughing and talking very happily together, and took no notice of Jimmy, who passed on.

Before they went to bed that evening, he and Wragge discussed the situation as it appeared to them.

"It's a bit of a rum go," said the Sergeant reflectively. "Take that affair at Paddock Croft to begin with. From all we hear, Lavis ought to have done it, but we know that he didn't. Mind you, I've always suspected that Lavis was a shady sort of customer. Though I can't say that I've ever had any definite complaints against him. Raymond up at the Chequers grumbles at him for getting drunk in his house and using bad language. Now we've got this chap Alf Mailing saying that he only pretends to get drunk for some reason of his own. And there's the fire at Mr. Pershore's bungalow. You tell me that that may have been arranged any time since last Saturday morning. Well then, did Lavis do that or didn't he?"

"I don't know," Jimmy replied. "Lavis is a bit of a puzzle, there's no denying it. But, do you know, I'm very much inclined to believe him when he says that he has no idea where Elver is now."

"Somebody must know where Elver is," said Wragge stubbornly.

"I know. The trouble is that neither you nor I are that somebody. Look here, it's five days since the burglary took place. We know who did it and we have a list of the things that were taken. Yet we haven't found a trace of the man or of the jewellery. It isn't as though we were looking for an unknown criminal. By this time pretty well every policeman in the county must have studied the description of Elver and his photograph. And I don't see how he can possibly have disposed of the jewellery. Which means that he is still wandering about somewhere with the stuff in his pocket."

Wragge lighted a fresh pipe. "You say that you don't believe that Lavis is hiding him," he replied. "Well, perhaps you're right. I'm inclined to think that if he was he'd own up to save his own skin. But it doesn't follow that he isn't taking care of the jewellery for him."

"That's an idea," said Jimmy. "What about applying for a search warrant and having a good look round that house at Park Gate? It's worth trying, I fancy."

"I was going to suggest it. I'll see about the warrant first thing in the morning, unless, of course, you'd rather do it yourself."

"No, I'd rather you did," Jimmy said. "I want to arrange for the ashes in the bungalow to be taken away for analysis. There's just a chance that that may give us a clue. But I'm afraid, after all, it won't help us to lay our hands on Elver, which is our main object."

"It's this hop-picking that's our difficulty," said Wragge. "With the countryside over-run with strangers like this, you can't expect us to put our finger on a single man. It's like looking for a needle in a haystack."

CHAPTER XI

J IMMY, in spite of the solid comforts provided by the hospitable Sergeant and his wife, spent a sleepless night. It was the first time that he had been entrusted with a really independent investigation. In all other cases since he had joined the force he acted as Hanslet's lieutenant. The Superintendent had always been at his elbow, so to speak, giving him the benefit of his advice and experience. He felt that the mysterious affair in which he now found himself involved was, in effect, a test of his ability.

His training had taught him that the first thing to do was to select one particular thread of the tangle and follow it up. Which thread was he to select? He had two crimes to investigate -- the burglary at Paddock Croft and the arson of Mr. Pershore's bungalow. Were these two crimes connected, or were they entirely independent of one another?

As he lay awake, Jimmy tried to make up his mind on that point. He reviewed the evidence in favour of the crimes being connected. They had occurred in the same district and at about the same time. The identity of the burglar was known. It seemed at least possible that Lavis was the incendiary. These men had once been acquainted, as Lavis himself admitted. Elver had almost certainly called at Lavis's house on the previous Saturday afternoon.

On the other hand, it was difficult to suggest any common motive for the crime. The motive of the burglary was understandable. The jewellery was stolen for the sake of its value. It had been stolen by a man who was a stranger to the district. But that such a stranger should go to considerable trouble to burn down Mr. Pershore's bungalow was hard to believe. Further, Lavis declared that he had not met Elver since the latter's arrest nine years earlier. And though Lavis was manifestly a liar, and, if local report was to be credited, a doubtful character in other respects, Jimmy was inclined to believe him on this one point. He believed, in fact, that Lavis had his own reasons for wishing to avoid Elver rather than seek a renewal of their acquaintanceship.

Out of this tangle emerged only one thread which appeared at all hopeful. This was the practical certainty that Elver had been the burglar. Jimmy knew enough about the science of fingerprints to dismiss the possibility that those on the silver box might have been faked. He also knew that the chances of the fingerprint department having been mistaken in their identification were negligible. It might be argued that the presence of Elver's fingerprints on the box did not prove conclusively that he had abstracted its contents.

But it did prove that he had handled the box and for that purpose he must have entered Paddock Croft. Elver's presence in Matling on that night was therefore established. This Jimmy felt was the obvious thread to be followed up.

He tried to put himself in the criminal's place. To begin with, what had brought Elver down to Matling? He was apparently penniless and had been given notice. Though his situation was not acutely desperate he might well have been disheartened. Since his discharge from prison his conduct had been beyond reproach, and he had held more than one job. According to the foreman under whom he had last worked, he had given satisfaction. But he had never succeeded in becoming more than a mere labourer, and he might have come to the conclusion that honesty was not the best policy, after all. His earlier criminal career had been terminated by an unhappy accident, but while it had lasted it had proved very remunerative. Might it not be a better policy to abandon the paths of rectitude for a second time?

If this had been Elver's process of thought, his mind would naturally have turned to his former associates in crime. His alleged aunt, Mrs. Hawkins, was dead. Her clientèle was probably dispersed long ago. But there still existed one companion of the old days who might prove useful could he but find him again.

Now what had been the true relationship between Elver and Lavis? That it had been more than a straightforward matter of business, Jimmy felt certain. Lavis had betrayed obvious uneasiness whenever the point was touched upon. Although he had denied all knowledge of Mrs. Hawkins, he had started at the mention of her name. It seemed quite possible that their business transactions had been the cloak for something more sinister. It did not follow that Lavis had necessarily been involved in the drug traffic. But it might well be that he and Elver had been associated in some other form of dishonest practice. It was certain that he had manifested a dislike of the subject of Elver's earlier years. He must already have regretted the sudden impulse which had led him to betray his knowledge of the origin of the photograph.

This seemed to Jimmy rather an interesting psychological point. If Lavis had seen Elver within the last few days he would have been on his guard. He would have anticipated inquiries being made about him, and would have been prepared to deny any knowledge of his existence. On the other hand, if he had not seen him for nine years, if he was unaware of his presence in the district, a sudden production of the photograph might well have startled him into momentary indiscretion. It would have reminded him of matters which he was doing his best to forget. Hence his almost involuntary exclamation.

To return to Elver again. The exact nature of his former transactions with Lavis scarcely mattered. He had somehow discovered the latter's present whereabouts, and had determined to seek him out. Whether for the purposes of blackmail or not, it was impossible to say. Perhaps he had thought out a scheme by which they might both profit, which depended upon Lavis for the necessary capital. It was improbable, Jimmy thought, that the idea of the burglary had been in Elver's mind before he left London.

Elver had called at Lavis's house and found him away from home. How had he occupied his time between that visit and the burglary? Why had he never returned to Park Gate in pursuance of his original plan? These were questions which Jimmy found it very difficult to answer.

He put the matter to himself in another way. Why had Elver abandoned the idea of meeting Lavis and committed a burglary instead? Had some one suggested the burglary to him, or had he thought of it himself? The first alternative seemed unlikely. Elver was a total stranger to the neighbourhood and was not likely to have so confiding a friend in the course of a few hours. On the other hand if he had thought it out for himself, he must have noticed the possibilities of Paddock Croft during the hours of daylight.

And he might well have done so. Anybody using the path from the village to Hobb's Corner might observe the position of the house. From one point in that path, the ladder and the temptingly open window were in full view. A very short study would be sufficient to show that if the window remained open at night it could be entered without much fear of observation. Elver might well have postponed his visit to Lavis and determined to try his hand at burglary instead.

So far so good. It was Elver's subsequent behaviour that seemed inexplicable. He could not have been aware that he had left his fingerprints on the silver box or he would have found means to obliterate them. He had successfully acquired quite a valuable collection of jewellery. There was no reason, so far as he knew, why he should ever be associated with the burglary. The only way in which he could possibly incur suspicion would be to hang about Matling with no apparent motive. One would have thought that his natural instinct would have led him to return to London as soon as possible, not only in the interests of his own safety but in order to find the means of disposing of his booty.

That he had not in fact returned to London Jimmy was perfectly satisfied. Elver was so well known as to be almost a familiar friend of the officers of M Division. They had carried out a very careful search for him and failed to find him. And where else could he have gone with that distressingly incriminating evidence in his pocket? Since he had not returned to London he must still be lingering in the neighbourhood of Matling.

Which, when you came to think of it, was a most extraordinary proceeding on his part. He could not procure the necessities of existence without being in communication with somebody or other. He must by now have learnt that the identity of the Paddock Croft burglar was known. Wragge had mentioned it to Mr. Raymond of the Chequers, and, as Jimmy knew, once a thing is whispered in a village bar it immediately becomes public property. Had Elver bribed any of the hop-pickers to shelter him? He could only have done so by offering them a share in the proceeds of the burglary. That any of them would accept such a bribe seemed highly improbable. And yet the supposition offered the only reasonable solution to the mystery.

Jimmy's mind went back a few steps. He had noted already that Elver, had he taken the path from the village to Hobb's Corner, might have noticed the possibilities of Paddock Croft. But why should he have used the path? It did not lead to Park Gate, which had presumably been his original destination. Of course he might have lost his way and taken it under a misapprehension. On the other hand, he might have wished to reach Hobb's Corner for some purpose. Mr. Pershore's bungalow stood there, and some malefactor had certainly set fire to it.

But this idea merely tightened the knots in the tangle. Why on earth should Elver have designs on the bungalow? Who had told him of its existence? Who had provided him with the necessary materials for producing the outbreak? Jimmy felt that he had better leave the bungalow out of the question, at all events for the present. What other reason could have led Elver to Hobb's Corner? Beside the bungalow there was only Hobb's Farm and the surrounding hop gardens. Had Elver, for any reason, already decided to take shelter among the pickers?

Jimmy had seen those very pickers for himself not many hours earlier. Although he knew the danger of judging by appearances, it seemed to him very unlikely that any of them would deliberately shelter a criminal. They were nearly all women, he had noticed, in fact he did not remember seeing a single man among them. The old lady who had exchanged such lively badinage with Tom Adcorn, for instance. Would she be likely to afford shelter to the fugitive? The idea was almost ludicrous. If he had approached her, she would possibly not have reported the matter to the police, but she would have driven him away with the liveliest recrimination.

And then a wild and fantastic idea entered Jimmy's brain. That elusive girl whose existence was vouched for by both Mrs. Hawkins and Lavis, but so strenuously denied by Elver? Was it within the bounds of possibility that she was to be found among the hop-pickers?

If so, an entirely new field of conjecture was thrown open. Elver, upon his arrest, had denied her existence with a definite object in view. He had no wish that her identity should become known to the police. This did not necessarily mean that she was in any way involved in his crime. He might have counted upon making some use of her in some way after his release. And finding himself in financial distress, he had, on the previous Saturday, determined to avail himself of her services.

This theory put an entirely new complexion on his relations with Lavis. It also disposed of the difficulty of the discovery of Lavis's whereabouts. He had no knowledge of his presence in the neighbourhood until his arrival at Matling. It had been this unknown girl who had informed him of the fact. Beyond this point speculation was useless. It only remained to find the girl and question her. And it seemed at least possible that the girl might be found among the pickers at Hobb's Farm.

So comforting did Jimmy find this fresh inspiration that he went off to sleep almost immediately.

He said nothing to Wragge next morning about his intentions. He was already provided with a copy of Elver's description and photographs and with these he set out immediately after breakfast. His first call was at the local garage, where he had no difficulty in hiring a bicycle; mounted upon this he rode to Hobbs's Farm and obtained Mr. Velley's permission to explore the hop gardens for the second time.

Having arrived there he approached each group of pickers in turn and showed them the photographs. Naturally he had to endure much good-natured chaff: the pickers commented upon the appearance of the photograph, usually in disparaging terms. They wanted to know if Jimmy was looking for his long-lost brother, who had disappeared from home, taking the children's money box with him? They invented pretexts for Jimmy's search which positively made him blush. They found entirely fanciful resemblances between the subject of the photographs and well-known film stars. But beneath all this Jimmy detected a note of sincerity. They weren't trying to hide the man. They simply didn't recognise him.

As it happened, the group to which Miss Rivers belonged worked at the farther end of the garden and Jimmy did not reach it until he had exhausted all the rest. Without much hope of success he held out the photographs for their inspection. "Have any of you people ever seen anybody like this?" he asked.

They desisted from their picking and gathered round him inquisitively.

"Well, he's no beauty, I must say," said one.

Another giggled. "Not half so handsome as the gentleman himself."

And then Miss Rivers' hand went suddenly to her throat. "Oh," she gasped.

Jimmy turned upon her swiftly. "You recognise the photograph?" he asked.

"No, no," she replied urgently. "It's a mistake, of course. I thought for a moment it looked like somebody I once knew. But it isn't, of course. It's all a mistake."

Her demeanour belied her words. She had gone deadly pale and her hands, despite her efforts to control them, were trembling violently. Jimmy drew her aside.

"We've met before, Miss Rivers," he said cheerily. "I was round here yesterday afternoon with Mr. Velley, if you remember. I wonder if you would mind if I had a little talk with you." He started away from the little group, and she followed him meekly and with obvious reluctance. Their departure was a signal for a burst of derisive laughter from her companions.

"Mind what you're about, mister! Don't let Tom Adcorn see you, or he'll have something to say." "I'm surprised at you leading an innocent girl astray like that." The comments continued until they were out of earshot. Jimmy led the way to a deserted corner of the garden, where a grassy bank bordered the high framework from which the hops had been taken down.

"Sit down, Miss Rivers," he said quietly. "There's no reason at all for you to be frightened. I only want to know what you can tell me about Christopher Elver."

Certainly the name had no pleasant associations for her. She shuddered violently. "What right have you to ask me that?" she replied in a scarcely audible voice.

I'm an officer from Scotland Yard," said Jimmy. "Elver has disappeared from his lodgings in Halibut Street, and we want to know where he is. I'm quite sure you can help us and if so we should be grateful. You knew him before his arrest nine years ago, didn't you?"

She raised her eyes and looked at him searchingly. "Who told you that?" she asked.

"Oh, we manage to pick up a lot of things, you know," replied Jimmy with a disarming smile. "Most of it is of no particular importance, but sometimes a bit here and there comes in useful. You knew Elver when he was a steward on the Etrurian, didn't you?"

"Yes, I knew him," she said in a dull voice, and then with sudden ferocity, "I wish to God that he had never crossed my path!"

Until now she had been standing, facing Jimmy half-defiantly. All at once she sat down on the grass bank beside him. He was conscious of her close scrutiny but was careful to appear not to notice it.

"I expect you smoke, don't you. Miss Rivers?" he said, producing his cigarette case. "Try one of these. They aren't too bad, considering all things."

She took a cigarette, which Jimmy lighted for her. Then she laughed shortly. "Well, here we are, sitting close together like a pair of lovers," she said. "You seem a decent sort, though you are a cop. What is it you want to know?"

"I want you to tell me everything you can about Christopher Elver," Jimmy replied.

Her face darkened. "I don't care to talk about him and that's a fact," she said. "It was so long ago that I'd almost forgotten. And I honestly thought he had, until last Saturday."

Jimmy nodded sympathetically. "Things one wants to forget have a habit of turning up at awkward moments," he said. "I wonder if you'd care to tell me how you first met him?"

"How I first met Chris? Why, just by accident, as you might say. It was about a year after I'd gone to lodge with Mrs. Sheares and been found a job in the tannery. I dare say you know already that I was a foundling. I never make any secret of that, for what's the good?"

"Mr. Velley did happen to mention it to me," Jimmy replied.

"Well, I was brought up in the workhouse. I dare say I was better off than many a girl outside. Enough to eat and drink, and clothes to wear, and that sort of thing. And I was pretty well-behaved and gave no trouble. At all events they told me so when they let me out. They found me a job which I have been working at ever since, and they got Mrs. Sheares to take me in. Nobody could be kinder to me than she's been. That's her daughter Molly who's working with me. We're like two sisters together, except that we don't squabble so much. Molly's a good sort, just the same as her mother and father.

"As I was telling you, I was a foundling. They picked me up down by the riverside. I don't know who left me there, and, if you want the truth, I don't very much care. They had to give me a name of some kind so they called me Rivers. Kate Rivers. It was as good a name as any other, I suppose. Anyway, the river's in my blood, as folk say."

"You mean you're fond of the river?" Jimmy asked encouragingly.

"Fond of it! I'm that fond of it I can hardly keep away from it. I've been like that ever since I was a kid. That's why I liked going to the Sheares. They live in the top floor of one of those tenement houses, and from the window of the room where Molly and I sleep you can see the masts of the shipping in the Surrey Docks."

She stretched her arms out with a gesture of disdain.

"Look at this!" she exclaimed. "The girls are always saying how lovely the country is. Well, they can have my share and keep it. It's always the same, nothing ever seems to change. I've been down here hop-picking every year for goodness knows how long, and nothing's ever altered since I can remember. Except that bungalow that was burnt out the other evening. That's been put up since I can remember. But the hops and the grass and the hill yonder over towards Matling, they never change. And what's more, I don't believe they ever will."

"You'd find the countryside looking very different if you came down at another time of year," Jimmy remarked.

"I dare say I should. But I haven't got the curiosity to come and see. It might be a different colour but it would still be the same shape, with the same things in the same places. Now the river's not like that. It never looks the same two days running. It's the ships that do that, I suppose. They keep on changing. And you can't tell where they've come from, or where they're going to. I don't know, I'm a silly fool, I suppose. But I never could keep away from the river. I shall end by jumping into it some day, I shouldn't wonder."

"Not for a very long time, I hope," said Jimmy. "Was it down by the riverside that you first happened to meet Elver?"

"You've guessed it. It was the worst trick that the river ever played me. It was one summer evening, and after I'd knocked off in the tannery I went down to the river to get a breath of air. I walked as far as Tower Bridge and there I stood up against the parapet looking right over the Pool.

"It was tide-time, I remember, and all the ships were moving about. I could see them going in and out of London Docks and the tugs and lighters bumping about all around them. And then a ship came up the river and began to hoot. I knew well enough that that meant that she wanted to pass through the bridge.

"I always liked to watch the ships come through the bridge. It's just like somebody coming home. The door opens for them and then shuts again behind them. I always used to fancy that ships must be tired when they came in, and could rest more comfortably above the bridge with the door closed behind them. But there, you don't want to listen to me talking all this nonsense."

"It isn't nonsense," said Jimmy. "It's a jolly fine idea, I think. So you watched this ship come through the bridge?"

"I watched her like I'd watched dozens like her before. She came through the bridge and then a tug got hold of her and pushed her against the wharf just below where I was standing. I don't know how it was, but I must have been feeling romantic or something that evening. I kept looking at the ship long after she'd tied up. I could read her name plainly enough, Etrurian, and I wondered where she'd been and what she had got in her hold. And then I saw a young fellow dressed in a posh suit and hat. He came on deck and looked about him. Then he must have caught sight of me looking at him, for he waved and smiled. Seeing him all dressed up like that I thought he must be the captain.

"Well, I don't know what took hold of me. I'd never done such a thing before, and I'd give twenty years of my life not to have done it then. He came towards the gangway and I could see that he was going ashore. And I thought what a wonderful thing it would be if he would only talk to me and tell me about the ship and her voyage.

"I knew the waterside pretty well by then. I knew that there was only one way off the wharf up a narrow passage into Tooley Street. So I slipped off the bridge and round the corner to the end of the passage.

"He came out just as I got there and he didn't seem a bit surprised to see me. He just took off his hat and said good-evening. And all of a sudden I came over all sort of shy. I didn't know what to say and the words seemed to come out of themselves. 'Good-evening,' I said to him. 'You're the captain, aren't you?'

"He laughed like anything at that, and I saw that I had made a fool of myself. 'The old man would be flattered if he heard you,' he said. 'No, I'm not the captain, I'm only the steward. But that's no reason why you shouldn't walk as far as London Bridge with me, is it?'

"Oh, I remember every word of all that. And then I asked him about his ship and he told me. He said that he traded regularly between London and Hamburg. She came into London every fortnight and stayed two or three days discharging and loading again. He told me about Hamburg and what a fine place it was. And I listened, like the little fool I was. Thought how nice it was to be talking with a real sailor. I walked as far as London Bridge with him, and there he told me that he was on his way to see his aunt at Lambeth."

Jimmy must have made some sudden movement at this remark, for she nodded her head gravely. "Yes, I know," she said. "But I didn't know then. It wasn't until I saw it in the papers that I knew what that little shop was really for. And Chris said that evening that he didn't see any reason why I shouldn't go with him. His aunt would give us both a cup of tea and we could stay there for half an hour or so. I told him that I couldn't think of such a thing, but he managed to persuade me in the end. He had a way with him, when he wanted to, that could make anybody do anything."

"So that's how you came to meet Mrs. Hawkins, is it?" said Jimmy reflectively. "You may not know it, but she talked a lot about you after her arrest. Elver, however, denied all knowledge of you. The police were inclined to believe him and never made any great effort to find you."

"So Chris wasn't lying then, on Saturday. He swore that he never let on that he knew anything about me. But of course I didn't know that at the time. I was expecting every minute that a cop would come round and ask me a lot of questions. And if he'd done that I'd have chucked myself in the river right away. Straight I would."

"We've hardly come to that point yet, have we?" said Jimmy. "You went with Elver to Mrs. Hawkins' shop. I'd very much like to know what happened when you got there."

"Nothing that seemed to be much out of the ordinary. Chris introduced me to his aunt, as he called her. I thought at the time that she wasn't over-pleased to see me, but she made herself pleasant enough. And then Chris thought he'd go upstairs and change his coat. Off he went and a minute or two later Mrs. Hawkins said she'd better go up and see him. She'd hung his clothes up in a cupboard where he mightn't be able to find them. A minute or two later they both came down together and I saw that Chris had a different coat and waistcoat on. We all had a cup of tea, and then Chris brought me back on the bus as far as London Bridge. And there he left me to go back to his ship. But he asked me to meet him a fortnight later when she next came in. He said she always came to the same berth and anybody would tell me what time high water was."

"And you met him again then?" Jimmy asked.

"Yes, I met him again," she replied slowly. "I was a good deal younger then than I am now, and perhaps I didn't know things that other girls did. You see, I hadn't knocked about as a kid like they had. They taught us quite a lot of things in the workhouse, I may, tell you. Some of them were useful enough, I dare say. But the most useful things of all they kept to themselves. Well, I don't blame them. A girl's got to look out for herself, wherever she's been brought up.

"Oh, yes, I met him again. I liked Chris well enough, I'm not going to pretend I didn't. But I wasn't in love with him, then or at any other time. I don't know what it was. He was somehow different to the chaps I used to meet down Bermondsey way. He had a nice way of speaking and treated me just as he would have treated a lady. And after that I used to meet him every time the ship came in. We'd always go to his aunt's shop for a cup of tea and I noticed he always went upstairs and changed his coat and waistcoat. He told me that he kept two sets so that his aunt could brush and clean one of them while he was away. Sometimes he'd take leave from his ship for a bit longer than usual so that when we'd had tea he'd take me to the pictures.

"That went on for the best part of the year, and I was happy enough. I didn't trouble my head about Chris while he was away, I hardly thought of him. That'll show you that he didn't mean over-much to me. We were just friends, that's all. But I enjoyed the days when his ship came in, just to listen to his talk and maybe go to the pictures with him or something like that. I never mentioned a word about him to Molly or anybody else. I thought they'd laugh at me taking up with a chap like him. They always did laugh at me wanting to go along the river all by myself. Besides, Chris didn't belong to my everyday life, if you see what I mean. He was different, and I didn't want to mix him up with the girls and the chaps I knew."

Jimmy nodded. "I can understand that," he said. "It's often better to keep one's friends apart. Sometimes they don't mix and then one feels uncomfortable. You continued to meet Elver until his arrest, I suppose?"

For a minute or two she made no reply. She sat very still, staring fixedly in front of her. In the distance, against the background of the yet-standing hops, were the pickers. The confused sound of their laughter and talk came almost unsubdued to the bank upon which Jimmy and Kate were sitting. But it was plain that she neither saw nor heard them. A very different scene was before her, and, by the light in her eyes, Jimmy could tell that it was not a pleasant one.

She answered his question at last. "It happened before then," she said in a curiously hard voice. 'You'll laugh when I tell you and say it serves me right. So it did. But that doesn't make it any better to bear. I've only got myself to thank for the position I'm in, I know that well enough."

"I won't laugh, I promise you that," Jimmy replied fervently. "Perhaps if you tell me I may be able to think of some way of helping you."

"That's very kind of you, I'm sure, but I'm past help, as you'll see for yourself. I'll tell you about that evening, though you're the only soul I've mentioned it to before. I met Chris as usual, and we'd gone to his aunt's to have tea. His ship had only just caught the tide. It would be after nine o'clock when we'd finished tea. And then something came over me, a new sort of feeling altogether. I felt all happy and excited as though I had the world for my own. Then Chris said that it was too late to go to the pictures, and that he'd take me as far as London Bridge on his way back to the ship.

"I don't remember that journey. Nor do I remember what happened when we got to London Bridge. But somehow we were walking along Tooley Street together on the way to the wharf and Chris was telling me that if I wanted to see the ship, as I'd often said, now was the chance. Nearly everybody would be ashore and those that weren't would be asleep. There was only the watchman, and he was probably faster asleep than any of them. He said that 'fast asleep as a ship's watchman' was a proverb along the waterside. And I was still feeling all excited, as though nothing mattered. So I let him take me on board. Nobody saw us, I'm certain of that. And we went to his cabin and I stopped there until after midnight."

She paused and then turned upon Jimmy almost fiercely. "Oh, you can guess for yourself what happened," she exclaimed. "I'm sure I don't know what made me do it. I didn't want to really, I know that well enough. But I didn't seem to know what I was doing that evening. And Chris went on persuading me. It would be great fun. I should enjoy it. It wouldn't matter to anybody. Not a soul would ever know anything about it. I dare say you've said the very same things to a girl in your time. Anyway it did happen, and at last Chris put me ashore again, and I went home and slept that night like a dead woman.

"But next morning I got up with such a tearing headache that I could scarcely drag myself to work. I didn't remember until I'd got out of bed and began dressing myself. And then it all came back to me with a rush. And I was frightened. More frightened than I'd ever been before in my life."

"Pretty rotten trick to play on you," said Jimmy sympathetically. "Has it never occurred to you that the tea you drank at Mrs. Hawkins' shop was probably doped?"

Her hand went to her throat as she uttered a queer choking sound. "You're a real brick," she said gratefully. "Any one else would have laughed and said it was my own fault. No, I hadn't thought of that, though when I read about the cocaine in the papers I might have guessed. That accounts for the way I felt that night, I suppose."

"And for the way you felt the next morning," said Jimmy brightly. "What did you say to Elver when you next met?"

"I'm coming to that. You won't understand the state I was in that morning. At first I didn't seem to be able to understand what had happened. You might think that a girl like me, brought up as I was and working among a lot of other girls and fellows, would understand all about these things. But I didn't. I'd heard them talk about it, of course, but it had never happened to me before. It wasn't that I felt that I'd done anything wrong. For all that I was only a foundling, my body was my own to do as I liked with. I didn't feel a bit like running round to the missionaries and telling them what a bad girl I'd been. It wasn't that I was scared of. It was just that I'd made sure that I should have a baby. That meant that I should lose my job and that the Sheares would turn me out. There would be nothing for it then but the workhouse again. And I'm much too fond of my life outside to want to go back there.

"I was in a terrible state for the next couple of days. I wouldn't say a word to a soul, not even to Molly Sheares, although I used to tell her pretty well everything. And I couldn't face Chris again just then. I knew well enough what he'd say. He'd just laugh and tell me it was all right. It had only been a joke. And I wanted somebody to help me, not to make fun of me like that. I went down to the river once, after his ship had left. And I didn't mean to come back again that time. But it looked so black and cold that I couldn't just bring myself to do it. And I had a sort of fancy that the lights all round me were beckoning to me, telling me to clench my teeth and stick it. So I went back to think it out all over again.

"It wasn't until after that that I saw a way out. And even then I couldn't bring myself to think of it for a bit. It wasn't what I wanted, and it didn't depend on myself alone. But after a while I persuaded myself that it wouldn't be so bad after all. You see, Chris was away eleven days out of the fourteen, and until the baby came at least I could go on as I was."

A sudden light burst upon Jimmy. "You mean that you thought of marrying Elver?" he exclaimed.

"More than thought of it," she replied tranquilly. "I married him a month later and left him that very day."

CHAPTER XII

JIMMY sprang to his feet and began to pace up and down in front of her. So this girl was Elver's wife! Surely that fact must simplify the situation? Naturally whether or not she was aware that he had committed the burglary, she must feel bound to shelter him. But how and where? Jimmy felt that he would have to proceed very cautiously. Difficult ground lay ahead of him. She might be ready enough to tell her story up to a point, but beyond that it would be very difficult to make her go. Jimmy became suddenly resentful of his youth and comparative inexperience.

It was Kate herself who interrupted his meditations. "Sit down," she said. "I haven't finished yet. It surprised you to hear that I was Mrs. Christopher Elver, didn't it?"

Jimmy resumed his place by her side. "It did surprise me," he replied, and then in a sudden burst of confidence he added, "And it isn't going to make things any easier for me, you know."

She looked at him in astonishment. "I don't see how it can make any difference to you," she said. "I'm the one that suffers for it. You're the only person besides Chris that knows we're married. I didn't feel so good about it that I went round shouting the news to everybody, I can tell you."

Only then did it occur to Jimmy to wonder whether her statement was true. There was something so natural about the way she had told her story that he had never thought of doubting it. But now an obvious difficulty occurred to him. Surely at the time of Elver's arrest, the fact of his marriage must have transpired? A marriage must be made in the presence of witnesses, and a record made of the event. With all the publicity which had been given to Elver's trial, surely one of those witnesses would have communicated his or her knowledge to the police.

"You say that you are married to Elver," said Jimmy with a touch of sternness in his tone. "When and where did the ceremony take place?"

She laughed rather bitterly. "Chris was no more anxious to make a song and dance about than I was," she replied. "By the next time his ship came in I'd made up my mind what I was going to do. I was pretty nearly desperate, and it seemed to me that my only chance was for me to marry Chris whether he wanted it or not. And when I met him I told him straight. I said that after what had happened we'd got to get married at once. Chris wouldn't listen to me at first. He laughed as I knew he would, said it was all rot. He'd other things to do with his money than spend it on a wife. It meant his having a house on shore and he couldn't afford it and didn't mean to. And he told me that I could put the idea out of my head for good and all.

"Then I told him that I didn't want to get married any more than he did. What's more I said I wouldn't live with him. But we'd have to be married just the same. I didn't want to touch his precious money, I could earn enough for myself and the baby when it came. Until then nobody need know anything about it. I'd go on living with the Sheares and then when I couldn't hide it any longer I'd tell them that I'd been married quietly and show them the certificate. It would be the same with the people at the tannery. I'd got a pound or two saved and I knew I could go into a maternity home somewhere. Then when it was all over, Mrs. Sheares would look after the baby and I could go back to my work. Oh, I'd got it all mapped out, I promise you that. Still, Chris wouldn't listen. He said that once we were married he'd be responsible. I might get tired of work and then I could come down on him for maintenance. And then I turned on him good and proper. I told him that if he wouldn't marry me I'd see the captain of the ship and the owners and everybody else. I'd tell them what had happened and I'd make out that he'd forced me to it. And if that didn't cost him his job I'd know the reason why.

"Well, that staggered him a bit. I didn't know then that his job was so important to him. He might have got another ship, but if his new one hadn't been trading with Hamburg he couldn't have gone on with the dope smuggling. So I was a bit surprised that he came round so quickly. He said that he'd see about it, and that we could be married the very next time the ship came in. But he said that it was no use telling anybody else about it. It wouldn't do him any good or me either. I was to leave it to him and meet him the next fortnight. Then he'd tell me what to do."

"You met him the next time the ship came in?" Jimmy asked.

"You bet your life I did. I'd tied him down to it and I meant to see it through. But as it happened it was an early tide that day and I didn't get down until perhaps an hour or two after the ship had been tied up. And Chris wasn't there on the quayside. I wasn't going aboard. He made it clear enough that he didn't want me to do that. So I waited on the wharf there wondering what he'd say to me when he came. And I think I knew then that if he'd acknowledge the child I'd forgive him.

"Well, he came off at last. It was the child I was thinking about, not him or me. You won't believe me when I say it, but he was even then no more to me than any of the chaps I met every day of my life. He came ashore at last and there was a chap with him. I heard him mention his name. It was a name I'd heard before. Mr. Lavis he called him."

Jimmy nodded. "You've met Mr. Lavis again since then, haven't you?" he asked.

She glanced at him knowingly. "You've met him for yourself, perhaps?" she replied.

"Yes, I've met him," Jimmy replied easily. "I'm not altogether sure that I like the look of him. What did you make of him?"

"I didn't like the look of him either. One of those cunning fly-by-night sort of blokes, I thought. Mind you, that wasn't the first time I'd heard of him. Chris had often spoken of him to me. He hinted all sorts of things that I didn't rightly understand. Lavis, Lavis, he dinned the name into my ears until I was sick of it. 'He's a useful man,' he used to say. 'He and I are on a thing or two together. We know where there's a spot of money to be made.' But he'd never tell me how. Well, to tell you the truth I never asked him, I wasn't interested."

"Tell me about that meeting with Lavis," said Jimmy quietly.

"Oh, that! I didn't know who he was at first, but I very soon guessed, though Chris didn't introduce us. Chris had spoken of him before as the man he bought the ship's stores from and that kind of thing. And he hinted that there was more in it than that. I thought that it was something to do with betting, or that sort of thing. Any way I never met Lavis until that evening. I saw that he had something to say to Chris, but I wasn't going to be put off. My business was more important than his, any way. And Chris said that he and Lavis were going to have a drink and that I'd better come along too."

Jimmy nodded. This confirmed Lavis's statement, almost word for word. "You went along, I suppose?" he asked.

"Yes, I went along, wondering when Lavis would take himself off and I should get Chris to myself. We went to a pub, I forget the name of it now, and there we sat. At last Chris managed to whisper to me that I'd better leave them and meet him again at the corner of Tooley Street in a couple of hours' time. So I went off and left them to it."

"You didn't see Lavis again that evening?"

"I never set eyes on him again until next hop-picking. You see, ever since I've been living with the Sheares I've come down to the Hobbs' Farm every year. Mrs. Sheares used to pick regularly for the farmer who was here before Mr. Velley. And then when Molly was old enough she used to come instead. And when I went to live with them, Molly wrote to Mr. Velley and asked if she might bring me with her next time. Mr. Velley said she might, and that's how I started down here."

"You didn't expect to meet Lavis, of course?"

"No, that I didn't. It gave me a pretty nasty turn when I saw him prowling about among the huts. You see, I wasn't anxious that anybody should know that I'd ever had anything to do with Chris. And as Molly and I were coming back from work one evening we ran straight into Lavis. I knew him straight away. I never forget a face that I've once seen. But as soon as he looked at me, I knew that he hadn't recognised me. I suppose he hadn't taken any particular notice of me that evening at the pub. I've often met him since then, but he's never taken any notice of me. I'm sure he doesn't know that I'm the girl he met with Chris that evening.

"Well, I didn't altogether trust Chris. I thought he might slip off somewhere and leave me waiting for him. But when I came back to the corner of Tooley Street, there he was all right. He told me that he'd got everything fixed up. We were to be married at a registry office in Stepney next morning at ten o'clock. But he said that we'd have to be married under his right name or it wouldn't be legal."

"He was wrong there," said Jimmy. "A marriage if properly performed is legal whether a false name has been given or not. What is his right name, by the way?"

"Oh, he spun me a long yarn about that. He said that his real name was Jack Croft and that he'd run away to sea as a boy. He'd given a false name in case his parents might fetch him back again. He told me where the register office was and what to do when I got there. So I met him next morning and we were married... . They gave me a copy of the marriage lines. I've got it now."

She spoke without a trace of emotion. It was plain to Jimmy that this singularly unromantic wedding had been to her a pure matter of business. As to the man's correct name that was a mere detail. He may have been telling the truth or he might have invented the name of Jack Croft on the spur of the moment. Perhaps he was not anxious that his associates in crime should become aware of his marriage. They might have regarded his wife as a potential danger. But the change of name explained why his marriage had remained a secret at the time of his arrest.

"That's how I came to marry Chris," she continued, after a pause. "But although I married him he was never my husband. I'd asked for the morning off on the excuse that I wanted to go to a friend's wedding. And after we'd been married I went back to my work and Chris went back to his ship. I didn't see him again before he sailed. I didn't seem to want to, somehow.

"And then only a day or two later I heard that Mrs. Hawkins had been arrested. Mr. Sheares always reads the paper after supper and if there's anything exciting in it, he tells us all about it. I thought they'd find out that I'd been to the shop and that they'd come and ask me questions. I used to jump whenever I met a stranger in case he was a detective come after me. But when nothing happened I began to feel a bit better. After all, it had nothing to do with me. And just before Chris was due home again I saw that I wasn't out of the wood by a very long way."

"You guessed, I suppose, that he had something to do with the drug business?"

"I didn't think of it at first. It came to me all of a rush the day before I expected him. I saw that the first thing he always did when his ship came in was to go and see

Mrs. Hawkins. And I made sure that he'd go there again and that the police would be waiting for him.

"I nearly went crazy wondering what to do. If the police got him they'd find out that I was his wife and would naturally think that I was in it too. Even if they believed me when I told them that I wasn't I shouldn't have made things any better for myself. I should be marked down as the wife of a crook for the rest of my life, and all the plans I'd made would come to nothing.

"At last I made up my mind what I'd do. I'd meet the ship when she came in and warn Chris not to go to Mrs. Hawkins. Of course, I didn't know whether she'd given him away or not. There had been nothing about him in the papers, I was sure of that. So it seemed to me that if I warned him, there was just a chance that he might keep out of it.

"I went down to the wharf long before I knew that the Etrurian could get alongside. But there was a man there waiting even before I got there. He was trying to keep out of sight, I could see that at once. And I knew somehow that he was waiting for Chris. I thought at first that it might be Lavis, but I very soon saw that it wasn't. He was a much bigger man and I knew that he must be a detective."

Jimmy smiled. Hanslet would hardly be flattered if he knew his identity had been so easily guessed. "This man didn't see you?" he asked.

"I don't think so. He didn't take any notice of me if he did. I cleared away from the wharf and went round on to the Tower Bridge, the very place I'd been standing when I first saw Chris. From there I could see the Etrurian as she came in. I was expecting the man to go on board and fetch Chris, but he didn't. I began to wonder if perhaps I'd been a fool and the man had no business with Chris after all.

"It often happened that Chris couldn't leave the ship at once. He had to get the officers' tea and tidy up and things like that. So it was that evening. He didn't come off for a long time. And I began to wonder whether I couldn't somehow get on board and tell him. But I saw that the man was still waiting on the wharf and I didn't like to. And then at last Chris came off and the man went up and spoke to him. And when I saw them go off the wharf together with the man holding Chris by the arm, I knew it was all up.

"I nearly went out of my mind with worry that next day or two. I thought the police were bound to make inquiries and find out about me. My heart used to stand still when Mr. Sheares read the paper to us in the evening. It had been pretty bad after Mrs. Hawkins' arrest, but it was ten times worse now. I've never understood to this day how it was they didn't find me."

Jimmy smiled. "It's simple enough, really," he said. "Mrs. Hawkins spoke about you, but she didn't know your name. Elver denied that he even knew a girl, much less that he'd married her."

"So Chris wasn't lying when he told me that on Saturday," she replied thoughtfully. "Well, I don't suppose that he wanted to have any more to do with me than I did with him. And then, after he'd been sentenced, I began to think that I wouldn't be brought into it after all. I started to wonder what I was going to do now if the baby came. Either I had to keep quiet about my marriage and take the consequences, or I'd have to say that I was the wife of Jack Croft, and show my marriage lines. And when they asked me who this Jack Croft was, I should have to tell them that he was in prison under the name of Chris Elver."

"A most unpleasant dilemma," said Jimmy. "You chose the first alternative and said nothing, I suppose?"

"I never had any cause to say anything. There was no sign of a baby after all, and I saw what a little fool I'd been. Just because I'd let myself be scared for no reason, I'd tied myself up to a crook for life. And I began to wonder what would happen when Chris came out of gaol. He'd be out of a job and I made sure he'd look me up and expect me to keep him. And somehow I hadn't the pluck to run away. I was perfectly comfortable as I was and I didn't know how I'd be able to make another start all over again."

"What did actually happen when he was released?" Jimmy asked.

"Nothing. I don't even know when he was let out. I knew he'd got seven years of course, but I thought that I'd better make the best of them. But after the seven years were up I didn't know a moment's peace. I thought whenever there was a tap on the door that Chris was coming after me. But he never came forward or wrote anything. And it wasn't until last Saturday that I set eyes on him again."

"How did you meet him?" Jimmy asked.

"It was like this. We'd knocked off at one o'clock and had our dinner. Then Molly went into Matling to buy a few things and I stayed in the hut to tidy round. I'd just about finished and was wondering whether I'd go off to Matling myself and find Molly when somebody came and stood in the doorway of the hut. My heart sort of stopped even before I looked up. I seemed to know that it was Chris got me at last. And when I did look up at him I knew him at once, though it was nine years since I'd last seen him.

"I'd often wondered what I would say to him when it did happen. But I found that I couldn't say anything at all. I just stood there staring at him like a fool. And he laughed in that careless sort of way I remembered so well. 'Hallo, Kitty,' he said. 'So you're alone, are you? Well, I'm in luck, for I want a word with you.'

"He came in and sat down just as if the place belonged to him. He was wearing one of those paper caps the chaps wear when they come down here to see their friends. But otherwise he looked just the same as he had all those years before. A bit older, perhaps, and not nearly so well-dressed. But there was no difference in the way he talked.

"I managed to get my voice back at last and asked him what he wanted with me. He said that depended. He'd heard nothing of me for a long time and didn't know how I was fixed. He had made inquiries if I was still living with the Sheares and had been told that I was, but was away hop-picking. That was all he knew. He was pleased when I told him that there'd been no baby. Then he said that he'd lost his job, and wanted a quid or two to tide him over."

"Did you give him any money?" Jimmy asked quickly. If Elver had managed to secure funds, his evasion of justice was more easily explained.

"No, I didn't, though I would have if I'd thought it would have got rid of him. As it happened I hadn't any to spare. I'd brought none with me down here and Molly and I had only subbed enough to keep us going. I told him this, though I don't think he believed me. He just laughed and said that he'd have to get some money somewhere. He said that though I might have forgotten that we were married, he hadn't. And if I was so short of money, I had only to go to Mr. Velley and tell him that my husband had come down unexpectedly. Chris said that he didn't doubt that he'd let me have a quid or so."

"Naturally you didn't want to break the news of your marriage quite in that fashion," Jimmy remarked.

She blushed crimson. "I didn't and that's a fact," she replied. "I didn't want anybody to know I was married, let alone the folk down here. I'd begun to hope I'd never see Chris again and that somehow ... Well, that doesn't matter now.

"And then I thought of something. I don't know what put it into my head like that, but I was desperate to get Chris out of the way before Molly or anybody else saw him. 'I can't do anything for you,' I said. 'You'd better go and see your pal Lavis and get him to help you.'

"He seemed more taken aback than I'd ever known him. 'Lavis!' he exclaimed. 'Whatever makes you think of him after all this time? You haven't taken up with him surely?'

"'I haven't so much as spoken to him,' I said. 'But he's living in these parts with his sister up at Park Gate. Don't tell me you didn't know that.'

"'I didn't know it, straight,' he said. 'But I'm very glad to hear it. Seems like my luck's in this afternoon, after all. You're sure it's Lavis, the chap I used to deal with when I was on the Etrurian?'

"I told him that I was sure enough of that. And then he asked me where Park Gate was and I told him it was quite close. He said he'd go off and see Lavis straight away. But he told me that I needn't think that I'd got rid of him so easily as all that. If it turned out that Lavis couldn't help him I should have to, that was flat. He went off, and I've never set eyes on him since. But I know that as soon as he wants anything he'll be round worrying me again."

"Where is he now?" Jimmy asked.

She shrugged her shoulders. "I don't know, and what's more I don't care," she replied. "Perhaps Lavis gave him some money and he's gone back to London. He's kept away from me, and that's all I want of him."

"What time was it that he left you on Saturday afternoon?"

"I couldn't say for certain. Somewhere between three and four, I should think."

"And you're perfectly certain that you haven't seen or heard of him since?"

"I'm certain of that. I should have reason to remember it if I had, shouldn't I? I'm hoping that he won't come worrying me again until I get back home, but I can't be too sure of that."

"I don't think that he's likely to worry you for a considerable time," said Jimmy quietly. "You've heard that there was a burglary close here on Saturday night, I expect?"

"I heard them talking about it, but I didn't pay any attention to it with Chris turning up like that."

"Well, I'm sorry to have to tell you that your husband was the burglar," said Jimmy.

She looked at him wide-eyed. It was some moments before the full significance of the words dawned upon her. "You mean that when you find him he'll go to prison again?" she said at last in a strained voice.

"I'm afraid he will," replied Jimmy simply.

"Then I'll be rid of him again for a time," she said slowly, and then with sudden violence, "A burglary!" she exclaimed. Why didn't he kill somebody and have done with it? Then he'd have been hanged and I'd have been rid of him for ever."

"Not a very edifying sentiment," said Jimmy reprovingly. "How about the unfortunate victim? Wouldn't you have been a little bit sorry for him?"

She became suddenly contrite. "I didn't mean that. Inspector, really I didn't," she said. "Only I'd give everything I've got to be sure that I'd never see Chris again. Now it'll be just the same as it was last time. Waiting and waiting until he's let out, knowing that then I'll see his shadow in the door again. Only this time it'll be worse, because I shall have to say that he came to see me here. Then it'll come out that we're married."

"Not necessarily," said Jimmy slowly. "However, we can see about that when we get him. By the way, did any one see you talking to him on Saturday?"

"I don't think so. You see, there weren't many folk about when he came along. I dare say somebody might have seen him coming to my hut, but there was nobody near enough to recognise him."

"Have you told any one about his visit to you?"

She shook her head violently. "I never said a word to a soul," she replied. "Not even to Molly. I just hadn't the heart. I was afraid it would all come out soon enough without anything said by me."

"You wouldn't hide him if he came and asked you to?"

"Of course not!" she exclaimed. "How could I do that even if I wanted to? There's no place here that I can call my own except the hut, and that Molly shares with me. She wouldn't have him hiding in there, that 1 can promise you."

"I'd like to have a look round that hut all the same," said Jimmy. "I wonder if you'd take me along there now?"

"You can come and see it and welcome," she replied. She rose and with a sudden gesture laid her hands upon his shoulders. "You're a good sort, I do believe," she said. "I've told you what I've never spoken a word of to a soul before. You won't go about telling everybody that I'm married to Chris, will you?"

Jimmy smiled. "I shan't tell anybody outside the force, you may be sure of that," he replied, "and it's not the custom of the police to go about blabbing other people's secrets. Of course, if Elver brings your name up I can't help that."

She raised herself on tip-toe and kissed him swiftly on the cheek. "Good enough," she said. "Now come along if you want to and I'll show you round the hut."

Their way took them round the unoccupied end of the hop garden, across the road and so into a meadow belonging to Hobb's Farm. This meadow was roughly square, and three sides of it were occupied by what appeared at first sight to be long corrugated iron sheds. Since the pickers were at work the meadow was practically untenanted. Outside of the sheds three old women, seated on wooden stools, were engaged in earnest conversation. One of them Jimmy noticed was peeling potatoes, apparently for a large family. An enamel slop pail which stood in front of her was nearly half full. One of the others was darning a red flannel petticoat with patches of material apparently filched from some other garment. The colours clashed horribly, but that. Jimmy supposed, hardly mattered, since the petticoat would not be seen.

He entered the hut which she indicated and looked around. There was no sign of Elver, and no indication of male occupancy. "What did you do after you saw Elver?" he asked Kate, who had come in with him.

"Molly and I went for a bit of a walk, then we fell in with two of the boys we know down here. As soon as the Chequers opened they took us there and stood us a drink. I dare say we sat out there in the arbour for an hour or two. Then we bought a few things from the men at the stalls and came home and cooked a bit of supper. And after that we went to bed. I can't say that I slept much that night. I was expecting Chris to turn up every minute. But he never came, and, as I say, I haven't set eyes on him since that day. And I'll be a happy woman if I never set eyes on him again."

Jimmy emerged from the hut. "Well, I'm very grateful to you for the help you've given me," he said. "I want you to promise me something. If you see or hear anything of Elver you'll let me know at once, won't you? I shall be hanging about here off and on for the next few days, I expect. And if you don't see me you've only got to send me word. I'm staying with Sergeant Wragge at Culverden."

Kate nodded. "I'll let you know, quick enough," she replied. "You've been decent to me and I'll be glad to be the same to you. Now if you've nothing more to say, I'd better be getting back to the picking. They'll be wondering what's become of me all this time."

They parted at the entrance to the meadow. Jimmy strolled slowly towards Hobb's Farm to pick up his bicycle. The story which he had just heard had profoundly impressed him. He never for a moment doubted the truth of it. It fitted in so well with the facts which he had learnt from other sources. The motive for Elver's journey to Matling was now fully established. But it seemed to Jimmy that the problem of his present whereabouts remained as obscure as ever.

Elver's actions up to a point might reasonably be surmised. Finding himself out of funds and with the prospect of losing his job, he had determined to get in touch with Kate again. He had apparently found out that she was still living with the Sheares but that she was then away hop-picking. Kate had been in the habit of picking at Hobb's Farm before she met Elver. No doubt she had mentioned this to him, and he had remembered it. He must have known at least roughly the situation of the farm. He had probably taken the train to Culverden as being the nearest station. Thence he had walked to Matling and so by the path to Hobb's Corner. During his journey he had noticed the open windows of Paddock Croft and the ladder hung up against the garden wall. Possibly the idea of entering the place had occurred to him then as a last resort to be used in case of emergency.

He had found Kate, but had failed to extract any money from her. He had, however, acquired a piece of information which might prove even more valuable. His old associate Lavis was living in the neighbourhood. Lavis had practically betrayed the fact that there was more in their association than appeared on the surface. This fully confirmed the theory that Elver had hoped to be able to extort money from him. But Lavis had been away from home, and, as far as could be ascertained, the two had never met. Elver might then have returned to Kate's hut, only to find her absent and the place locked up. He might then have decided that the burglary was, after all his best speculation. If he had, his natural instinct would have been to keep out of the way until after dark.

So far it was comparatively plain sailing. But his actions after the burglary became inexplicable. Surely, if he really had some sort of influence over Lavis he would have gone at once to him and demanded shelter and assistance. But this apparently he had not done. He had somehow managed to vanish into thin air, taking the proceeds of the burglary with him.

Jimmy, having retrieved his bicycle, paid another visit to Mr. Pershore's bungalow. He found a constable on guard and exchanged a few words with him.

Then, since it was now dinner time, he rode back to Culverden. But he said nothing to Wragge of his conversation with Kate. After all, she had told him nothing which bore directly upon the burglary.

Fortunately, Wragge was not inquisitive. He was too full of his own adventures for that. He had obtained a search warrant and examined Lavis's house from cellar to attic.

"I don't think there was a corner of the place I didn't ransack," he said. "Lavis wasn't there, but Mrs. Creach was, and she watched me like a cat watches a mouse. But I didn't find what I was looking for, and I'm ready to swear it wasn't there."

"You thought you might come across some of the stolen jewellery, I dare say," Jimmy suggested.

"That's about it. But not a thing of that sort could I find. It wasn't until I got up into the roof that I found anything at all out of the way. And I'll lay you'll never guess what that was."

Jimmy shook his head. "I'm no good at guessing," he said. "A dark lantern and a set of housebreaker's tools, perhaps."

Wragge chuckled. "That wouldn't have surprised me," he replied. "No, it wasn't that. When I climbed up into the attic through a sort of hole in the ceiling, I looked about and saw that one of the boards in the floor was loose. Well, I just lifted it up and there were rows and rows of medicine bottles. They hadn't any labels on them, but they were all corked and full of something or other. I uncorked one of them and smelt the stuff inside. And whatever do you think it was?"

Jimmy smiled. "Collier's Certain Cure for Constipation, perhaps," he replied.

"Not it," Wragge exclaimed. "It was spirit, and jolly strong stuff, by the smell of it. Well, I counted those bottles quick. There were forty-six of them, but there aren't now. I slipped one of the bottles into my pocket, then I came down out of the attic. Mrs. Creach hadn't followed me up there, but she was standing in the kitchen looking pretty white about the gills when I came down. But I didn't let on to her. 'Sorry to have given you all this trouble, Mrs. Creach,' I said. 'You'll understand that we don't enjoy having to do this sort of thing. But duty's duty, you know. I haven't found anything out of order, you can tell your brother so when he comes home.' She looked that relieved I could hardly keep from laughing."

"Well done!" Jimmy exclaimed. "There's something queer about those medicine bottles, I'll wager. Have you any idea where the spirit came from?"

"I dropped in at the Chequers on my way home," Wragge replied. "There I asked Mr. Raymond, casual like, if Lavis ever bought spirit from him. He said to the best of his recollection he'd never sold him a drop. So the stuff didn't come from the Chequers, that's pretty certain."

"Perhaps we'll be able to find out where it comes from and where it goes to," said Jimmy. "Now I've got to arrange about the analysis of those ashes from Mr.

Pershore's bungalow. I wonder if you'd get one of your chaps to shovel it into sacks? Then it can be sent up to the Yard, addressed to me. I'll slip up this afternoon, warn them it's coming, and tell them what to look for. It's possible that I may stay in town for the night. But if I do, I'll come down again first thing in the morning."

CHAPTER XIII

JIMMY'S expectation that he would spend the night in London was fulfilled. After consultation with Hanslet, it was decided that they should again seek the advice of Dr. Priestley. They called upon him by appointment at nine o'clock that evening.

"It's queer how things crop up years after one's almost forgotten about them," said Hanslet, when they were installed in Dr. Priestley's study. "You remember me telling you the other night about Sea Joe and the way I arrested him? There was talk then of there being some girl or other in the background. I didn't pay much attention to it at the time. But, would you believe it, Jimmy stumbled across her this very morning. And she told him that she'd been married to Elver about a fortnight before his arrest."

"And there's no doubt that her story's true," Jimmy added. "I've been round to the registrar's office in Stepney myself. And I found the entry almost at once. Jack Croft and Kate Rivers. The date is correct and everything."

"Very interesting," said Dr. Priestley. "Would it have made any difference had you ascertained the fact of this marriage at the time?"

"I don't think so," Hanslet replied. "From what Jimmy tells me this girl had nothing whatever to do with the dope business. It's rather a queer story, in its way. Perhaps you'd like to hear Jimmy tell it in his own words, Professor?"

"If the Inspector cares to tell me, I shall be happy to listen," said Dr. Priestley.

Jimmy repeated accurately his conversation with Kate. "The girl was telling the truth, I'm pretty sure of that, sir," he concluded. "She told me that she was married to Elver without the slightest prompting on my part. And the details of her story seem to fit in with everything we already know. Unfortunately, she couldn't throw any light upon the burglary or, what is even more important, upon Elver's present whereabouts."

"It's extraordinary how that chap manages to keep out of the way," said Hanslet. "I agree that this girl Kate has nothing to do with it. I'm only interested in her because I confess that I always believed that she was an invention of Mrs. Hawkins."

"What steps did you take to trace this man Elver?" Dr. Priestley asked.

"We've done everything we can think of," Hanslet replied. "You know as much about our methods as I do myself, Professor. The police all over the country are on the look out for him and for the stolen jewellery. And up to date nobody has found so much as a hint of either."

Dr. Priestley shook his head a trifle impatiently. "There is one obvious explanation which has apparently not occurred to you," he remarked.

"You mean that he somehow managed to slip out of the country, Professor?" Hanslet replied. "But that for a man in his circumstances is the next thing to impossible."

"That is not my meaning at all," said Dr. Priestley. "Has it never occurred to you that Elver may be dead?"

"Well, no, I'm bound to confess that it hasn't," Hanslet replied. "And after all, Professor, people don't die without attracting some sort of attention. If anybody runs across the body of an unknown man an inquest is sure to follow."

"His body may not yet have been found -- indeed, it is possible that it may have been deliberately concealed."

Hanslet laughed. "I wish you'd tell us exactly what's in your mind, Professor," he said.

"It is in my mind that Elver may have been murdered," replied Dr. Priestley quietly. "I am of course, aware that there is no evidence whatever in support of this suggestion. Usually in a case of murder one is confronted with the fact though the motives are not apparent. Here the fact is unconfirmed, but the motives, one might almost say, stand out with startling clearness.

"Consider the situation when Elver appeared in the neighbourhood of Matling last Saturday. To his wife, his appearance was little short of a disaster. Her happiness, as she explained to the Inspector, depended upon her connection with Elver remaining unknown. He was the shadow hanging over her life, and, when the shadow became the substance, she might well give way to despair.

"She seems never to have felt the slightest love for her husband. In a way he fascinated her, perhaps because she was only able to see him once a fortnight. Nor apparently was Elver infatuated with her. It is true that he seduced her, and I agree with the Inspector that the administration of cocaine probably played a large part in that seduction. But his subsequent conduct seems to show that his passion for her was merely temporary.

"I have no doubt that her statement to the Inspector is perfectly true, in one respect, at least. She married Elver, not because she cared for him in the least, but in order to escape the consequences of her error. These consequences never ensued, and meanwhile Elver was removed from her life for a term of at least seven years. She had never desired marriage, and to find herself not only a wife, but the wife of a convict, must have seriously perturbed her.

"Still, there was nothing for her to do. She could only wait for events to develop. One can easily understand the horror with which she anticipated Elver's release. But when Elver was once more a free man he made no attempt to communicate with her. He could easily have done so, since she had not changed her address or her mode of life. It is probable that he had no desire to assume the responsibilities of marriage. Or it may be that he had some other reason for keeping away from all those who had known him in former days. His motive, is not I think, of great importance. The result of his silence was that his wife must have begun to believe that she would never see him again.

"And then, when she expected it least, he appeared in the doorway of her hut. This must have seemed to her the beginning of a life which she had so long dreaded. If he were to proclaim the fact that they were married she would have no option but to ally herself with him and with his fortunes. This, for many reasons, would have been utterly distasteful to her. Her husband alive was a perpetual menace to her. But if once he were dead she could again call herself a free woman."

Dr. Priestley paused, and Hanslet nodded his head in rather doubtful agreement. "There may be something in that, Professor," he said. "But how, when and where did she murder the man? And above all, how did she dispose of the body?"

"I do not say that this woman murdered her husband," Dr. Priestley replied. "I merely point out that she had a very definite motive for doing so. And she was not the only person who possessed such a motive. The position of the man Lavis must be considered.

"As I remarked just now, Elver after his release, did not get into communication with any of his former friends. But I am inclined to think that there was one person with whom he would have been glad to get in touch. It is perfectly clear, from what the Inspector has told us, that the relationship between Elver and Lavis was not confined to the transaction of honest business. They were engaged together in certain secret transactions, the nature of which has not yet been revealed. Elver may have made unsuccessful attempts to find Lavis. The latter had given up his post as a ships' chandler's agent and retired to the country. It is highly probable that Elver was unable to discover his whereabouts.

"His behaviour when his wife told him that Lavis was living at Park Gate is to me highly significant. He immediately abandoned all attempts to extract money from her, and apparently proceeded at once to Lavis's house. This suggests that he considered Lavis to be a more promising source of supply than his wife. It would interest me, Superintendent, to learn whether Elver was in possession of any funds at the time of his arrest?"

"We were never able to discover any," Hanslet replied. "I thought at the time that he must have made a bit out of the dope-smuggling business, but he swore that he had always spent the money he had received as fast as he got it. Anyway, when I arrested him, he had no more than a pound or two in his pocket. We found another ten pounds or so locked up in his cabin in the Etrurian, but that was all."

"That seems a very small sum to represent the proceeds of drug smuggling," said Dr. Priestley. "We now have reason to suspect that Elver was engaged in other enterprises as well. He probably derived a profit from his transactions with Lavis, whatever they were. And I cannot help wondering whether Lavis acted as his banker."

"By Jove, that's an idea, Professor!" Hanslet exclaimed. "It would account for his anxiety to get hold of Lavis at once. And it might account for something else, too. Although Lavis denied it so strenuously, we must remember the possibility that the two men actually met. If at that interview Lavis supplied Elver with money, the difficulty of his disappearance would be explained."

"That may be," said Dr. Priestley. "But what I wish to point out is this; Lavis had perhaps believed himself safe from discovery by Elver. Now that this discovery had been made, Lavis's position was decidedly uncomfortable. Elver could not, of course, sue him for the return of money illegally earned. But he could threaten to reveal their former intimacy to the police. We do not know what crime could have been laid to Lavis's charge, but we may assume that he would have found himself in trouble as the result of a revelation on Elver's part. Here, then, is a second person to whom Elver's existence was a menace. His death would relieve Lavis of considerable anxiety."

"Well, then I'll ask the same question as I did before, Professor. How, when and where did Lavis murder Elver? And having done so, how did he dispose of the body?"

"It is not my habit to indulge in conjecture," Dr. Priestley replied. "Perhaps the Inspector could formulate a theory which would supply the answer to your question."

Jimmy hesitated before replying to this invitation. "The idea hadn't occurred to me before, sir," he said at last. "But I see now that it is by no means impossible. How, when and where did Lavis murder Elver? How, I can't say, but there's one method which occurs to me. Lavis is at present acting for a firm in Sheffield which manufactures butchers' knives. He carries parcels of these knives about the country with him on his bicycle. Last Saturday evening when he left the Chequers at ten o'clock these samples were in his possession. He is said to have fallen off his bicycle, and in doing so to have scattered the knives by the roadside, Sergeant Wragge certainly picked up a knife next morning at the spot where the accident occurred. He has shown it to me. It is new, as one would expect a sample to be, but the blade is stained and encrusted with what may possibly be blood."

Hanslet chuckled. "You're getting on, Jimmy," he said. "You have produced the weapon and traced it to the criminal. Lavis killed Elver by cutting his throat with one of those sample knives of his. It's as simple as A B C so far. Carry on."

Jimmy glanced at Dr. Priestley. "I don't say that that theory is proved, sir," he said hastily. "I'm simply repeating the facts as I've heard them. They provide a possible answer to the question 'how'. Then we come to 'when'. On leaving the Chequers Lavis did not go straight home. Instead of taking the direct road to Park Gate he made a detour by Hobb's Corner. In doing so, he would pass close to Paddock Croft, the scene of the burglary. The explanation he gave to Sergeant Wragge for making this detour was that he was too drunk to know what he was doing. But there is reason to believe that he was in the habit of assuming drunkenness for his own purposes. If this is the case, he probably had some deliberate motive for taking the path to Hobb's Corner. This motive may have been his desire to meet Elver. We cannot say accurately when such a meeting would have taken place. But we can place it between ten o'clock, when he left the Chequers, and midnight when the Speights returned home.

"Then comes the question where the murder may have been committed. I'm afraid I can't make any suggestions about that. It may have taken place immediately the two men met, which they probably did on the path in the neighbourhood of Paddock Croft. Or they may have walked some distance together until the murderer found a suitable spot for his purpose. We do not know when Lavis returned home that night, since his bare statement cannot be accepted. But appearances would suggest that if a murder was committed it was within a comparatively short radius of Matling."

"That's all right, Jimmy," said Hanslet. "Your imagination does you credit. But now you've got the most difficult question of all to answer. How was the body disposed of?"

Jimmy shook his head. I've nothing whatever to guide me on that point," he replied. "Any attempt on my part to theorise about it would be merely guesswork."

"Then you are fully justified in not attempting to form a theory," said Dr. Priestley approvingly. "But are you sure that you have no facts to guide you? We will imagine, purely as an intellectual exercise, that the theory you have suggested is correct. We will suppose that Lavis murdered Elver some time between ten and twelve on Saturday night in a comparatively short radius of Matling. Since no body has been found, Lavis must have disposed of it in some way. He could not carry it very far, say to the sea for instance. He was obliged to dispose of it within a very limited area. Had you been faced with such a problem, Inspector, how would you have solved it?"

"I'm sure I don't know, sir," replied Jimmy thoughtfully. "I shouldn't have buried it, for I should have been afraid that some one would have noticed the place where the ground had been disturbed. I shouldn't have thrown it into Mr. Velley's pond, or it would have been bound to come to the surface sooner or later. I might have cut it up with one of the butchers' knives, and then I don't quite know what I should have done with the pieces. In fact, I'm afraid I should still have the body on my hands, wondering what to do with it."

"Surely it would have occurred to you that the safest way of disposing of a human body is to destroy it completely by fire?"

"It might have occurred to me sir, but where should I have found a fire of sufficient intensity at that time of night? I couldn't very well have collected fuel and lighted one. The blaze would have attracted attention." Jimmy paused suddenly and then stared at Dr. Priestley with wide eyes. "Mr. Pershore's bungalow!" he exclaimed. "But how?"

"Hallo," Hanslet exclaimed, "this is getting interesting. That fire a couple of days later always seemed to me a bit queer. Was the bungalow set on fire in order to consume Elver's body? It's a most intriguing theory, anyway."

"I don't quite see how that can have been the case," said Jimmy. "We're supposing that Elver was murdered on Saturday night. The bungalow did not catch fire until the following Tuesday afternoon. Where was the body during that period? We're supposing that the man was killed some time during Saturday night. According to Mrs. Adcorn she was in the habit of visiting the bungalow at least twice a day. That means that she entered it at least six times between Saturday and the time of the fire. And since she was nervous about the windows being left open she always examined the place thoroughly. She had her last look round, before the fire, at six o'clock on Tuesday afternoon. It seems to me quite impossible that she could have overlooked a dead body had there been one in the house."

Hanslet shrugged his shoulders. "Well, you've been down there and I haven't," he replied. "But let me tell you this, Jimmy my lad. The Professor has often dropped me a hint which I've rejected because it seemed to suggest the impossible. And it has always turned out that he has thought of something which I hadn't. I expect it's the same again this time, isn't it, professor?"

"My suggestion is merely that the fire at Mr. Pershore's bungalow might be considered in the light of a murder having been committed," Dr. Priestley replied. "I must impress upon you, however, that there are no facts to prove that Elver is dead. Both you and the Inspector are puzzled by the fact that he has not shown himself. I have suggested as a possible explanation that he is no longer alive. I have endeavoured to show that his death would be very welcome to certain persons.

"I think the possibility that he was killed between the time of the burglary and that of the fire must be taken into consideration. It seems to me to be established beyond much doubt that the fire was caused maliciously. The object of this crime may have been the destruction of Elver's body. The Inspector has raised a very serious objection to this theory. He maintains that the body cannot have remained concealed in the bungalow from Saturday night until Tuesday evening. How can that objection be overcome?"

Hanslet, to whom this question was addressed, considered it for a few moments in silence. "I think I can see one way," he replied. "You say, Jimmy, that this woman Mrs. Adcorn was in charge of the bungalow. She opened it up every morning and closed it again in the evening. Did she go alone on these occasions or did anybody go with her?"

"She said nothing about anybody going with her." Jimmy replied. "I didn't ask her the question directly, I must admit. But from what I've seen of the place, I think it almost certain that she did go alone. Hop-picking's a very busy time in that part of the world and everybody seems to have a job of one kind or another connected with it. Mrs. Adcorn's two sons, for instance, are hard at work from early till late. At this time of the year I don't think that any one would have leisure to help Mrs. Adcorn, even supposing that she wanted help."

"Well, that makes it probable that Mrs. Adcorn was always alone when she visited the bungalow. So, don't you see, there's no means of verifying her statement. She told you that everything was in order at six o'clock on Tuesday evening. But you've only got her bare word for that. It's not impossible that she knew something about the murder and was not prepared to disclose the presence of the body in the bungalow. How does that idea appeal to you, Professor?"

"Not very forcibly," Dr. Priestley replied. "I will admit that Mrs. Adcorn may have been aware of the presence of the body. But I am inclined to think it extremely unlikely. Her connivance would have involved her in too much risk. The windows of the bungalow were always kept open during the daytime, and it would have been easy enough for any passer-by to enter the place. If the body had thus been discovered, Mrs. Adcorn would have been the first to be called upon for an explanation."

"Besides, Mrs. Adcorn doesn't strike me as the sort of person who would connive at the concealment of dead bodies," Jimmy remarked.

"It's not always safe to judge by appearances," said Hanslet. "However, if you don't like the theory of Mrs. Adcorn's complicity, I'll try to get round your objection in another way. Is there any reason why Elver's body should have been hidden in the bungalow during the whole period between his death and the time of the fire?"

"That is a very good point," said Dr. Priestley approvingly.

I'm glad you think so, Professor. The question of the concealment of the body, whole or dismembered, is worth going into. There are two cases to be considered. The first is when the police know that a murder has been committed and are looking for the body. Then admittedly it's a devilishly awkward thing to hide. It's heavy, and it takes up a lot of space. Given that the police know that the body must lie within a reasonably limited area, they are pretty well bound to find it.

"But the second case is altogether different. It occurs when the body itself is the only evidence of a crime having been committed. The criminal has arranged matters in such a way that, so long as the body remains undiscovered, no suspicion of murder will arise. His task is made easier by the fact that no one is looking for a body. He can dispose of it at his leisure, using such means as his ingenuity suggests.

"Now, apart from its bulk and its weight, the human body presents another difficulty to any one wishing to conceal it. Sooner or later it will decompose, and in so doing is very likely to make its presence known. And it has been shown often enough that only an expert can arrest decomposition for any length of time. But a period of at least two or three days must elapse after death before the body gives itself away, so to speak. At least, in this climate and under normal conditions.

"Now during that period, a body which no one is looking for is comparatively easy to conceal. It might be rolled up in a carpet and put away in a lumber room, for instance. The criminal meanwhile can be making preparations for its destruction. I expect you see what I'm getting at, Jimmy."

"You mean that Elver's body may have lain somewhere unobserved, in a ditch perhaps, until shortly before the fire," Jimmy replied. "That's possible, I dare say, but it doesn't overcome my objection. When and how was the body conveyed to the bungalow? If you accept Mrs. Adcorn's statement, it was not there at six o'clock on Tuesday evening. I have already made up my mind that it would have been impossible for any one to enter the bungalow unobserved between that time and the fire. And I absolutely refuse to believe that any one could have done so with a body slung over their shoulders."

"Dr. Priestley smiled. "This discussion is by no means devoid of interest," he said. "May I suggest that it is extremely difficult entirely to consume a human body? A very fierce fire is required, to which the body must be exposed for a considerable time. Unless these conditions are fulfilled, only the softer tissues will be consumed. The bones, or parts of them, will remain in recognisable form. I do not think that the fire at Mr. Pershore's bungalow can have been sufficiently intense, nor did it last long enough, for the complete consumption of a human body."

"There's another thing, sir," said Jimmy. "You saw me rake through the ashes. I certainly didn't find anything that looked like bits of bone."

"That may be," Dr. Priestley replied. "You might not have recognised them as such. Charred bone upon casual inspection is not unlike charred wood."

"The point will soon be settled, sir," said Jimmy. "I've arranged for the ashes to be collected and sent up to the Yard for expert examination. I confess that I hadn't any idea of human remains in my mind when I did so. My idea was that the means used to start the fire might be discovered."

"I shall be interested to hear the results of that examination. But you realise, I hope, that the absence of human remains in the ashes will not refute the theory of Elver's death. You should, I think, explore very carefully the neighbourhood of Hobb's Corner. In the course of this exploration the means of disposal of a body may suggest itself to you. Meanwhile, further discussion of what is, after all, merely a tentative suggestion appears to me somewhat futile."

The hint was sufficient for Hanslet and Jimmy. A few minutes later they said good-night to Dr. Priestley and left the house. Since it was too late to return to Culverden that evening Jimmy went home to his quarters. There, while smoking a final cigarette before turning in, he considered the suggestion which Dr. Priestley had made.

That there was something in it he was quite willing to admit. It seemed impossible that Elver alive should have escaped detection. A living man must somehow or other obtain the means of sustenance. But a dead man had no such requirements. Elver might well have been murdered and his body disposed of. Dr. Priestley had pointed out that at least two people had motives for such a crime.

Kate, to begin with. She had every reason to desire the removal of Elver from her path. But his conversation with her had impressed him very favourably. She had, without any pressure on his part, revealed her past to him with a sincerity which it was very difficult to doubt. Would she have done so if she had killed her husband? It seemed incredible. Besides, what opportunity could a woman situated as she was have had of disposing a body?

It seemed far more likely that Lavis had been the criminal. Elver's unexpected reappearance on the scene must have been most unwelcome to him. Jimmy was tempted to reconstruct the crime with Elver as the victim and Lavis as the criminal. Upon his return home on Saturday evening, Mrs. Creach had informed Lavis of the afternoon visitor. She had no doubt described his appearance. From her description Lavis had recognised Sea Joe. When had the two met? Before the burglary, Jimmy had no doubt. Else how could Lavis have known that Elver was to be found that night on the path leading to Hobb's Corner? It was significant that Lavis should have taken his samples with him when he went out that evening. He could scarcely have hoped to meet a likely customer for a butcher's knife on Saturday night. But a heavy, sharp knife was a very useful weapon. And it would come in very useful later for dismembering a body. Lavis's actions were already a matter for suspicion. It seemed highly probable that he held the key to Elver's disappearance.

Jimmy got up early on the following morning, Saturday, and took the first train to Culverden.

On the whole he thought it better not to take Sergeant Wragge too deeply into his confidence for the present. He merely asked to be shown the knife, which was still in Wragge's possession.

"These look to me not unlike bloodstains," he remarked casually, as he examined it. "What about sending the knife up to the Yard for the people there to have a look at?"

Wragge chuckled. "You seem fond of sending things up to the Yard," he replied. "They've got something to get on with as it is. I despatched a couple of hundredweight of ashes from the station here yesterday evening. I've no objection to your sending the knife up too, if you like. But even if the chaps at the Yard say they are bloodstains, I don't see that it gets us any further."

"Perhaps not," replied Jimmy cheerfully. "But if those marks turn out to be blood we shall have to ask Lavis how they got there. You've heard nothing fresh since I've been away, I suppose?"

"Nothing to do with the burglary or the fire, if that's what you mean. I don't mind telling you that I'm beginning to get a bit worried. It's a week to-night since the burglary, and I don't see that we're any nearer laying our hands on that chap Elver than ever we were."

"Oh, we must possess our souls in patience," said Jimmy lightly. "Meanwhile, there's our friend Lavis to be reckoned with. You haven't found out yet where he got all that spirit from, I suppose?"

"I'm waiting for you to do that. But I've found out something about it. Yesterday evening I took the bottle to our local excise man for him to have a look at. He sat up and took a bit of notice, I can tell you. He says that the stuff is about ten under proof, which means that Lavis can't have come by it honestly. He'll be very glad when we can tell him a bit more about it."

"We'll do our best," Jimmy replied. "But I don't think I'll worry myself about Lavis just yet. This evening will be time enough. Meanwhile, I'm going to pay another visit to Hobb's Corner. I find quite a lot of things to interest me in that direction."

CHAPTER XIV

THIS, the second Saturday of hop-picking, was a busy day at the Chequers. Early in the afternoon the Raymond clan gathered to the fray. By four o'clock they were all assembled, fourteen strong. Mr. Raymond, with Mary as his chief of staff, directed operations.

Under his directions the bar parlour was filled with barrels to its utmost capacity. Beside these were arranged crates of bottles and sacks of packets of cigarettes. Hundreds of glasses were arranged on shelves handy to the serving window. Since it was a fine day with no prospect of rain, there was no need to put up the tarpaulin above the arbour. By the time all preparations had been made a thirsty and impatient crowd was assembled outside the house.

Mr. Raymond gave his final instructions to old Alf Mailing, the doorkeeper. "Now, you keep your wits about you, Alf," he said. "You know as well as I do what some of these home-dwellers are. If they think that any of the hoppers have a bob or two to spend, they try to get them into the other room. On the chance that they'll be stood a drink, that's what they're after. But I won't have any of the pickers inside the house if I can help it. I don't trust these Londoners. For one thing they make a terrible litter, which I've got to clear up. And for another once they get into the other room, they pinch the glasses. So you watch out and see that none of them slip in behind your back. Don't let anybody into the other room that you don't know."

"That's all right, guv'nor," Alf replied. "There's nobody won't get into that room that I don't know. And if any of the chaps want to take them in, why they'll have to get past me first, that's all."

By this time it was a quarter to six. The stalls had been set up under the elm tree long ago, and were doing a roaring trade. Saturday was the recognised shopping night and the pickers had more money than usual to spend. Besides, their friends, who seemed to outnumber them by two to one, had not come down with empty pockets. Not only the open space in front of the Chequers, but the road beyond it, was thronged with the vociferous multitudes. The press was thickest round the still closed windows of the bar parlour.

Mr. Raymond with Mary went to survey the scene from an upper window. He shook his head despondently. "They're a rough-looking lot and no mistake!" he exclaimed. "What beats me is where they all come from. You wouldn't think there was places for them all to live, no not even in London. And just look at the way they're scattering their litter all over the front. Well, this'll be the last hop-picking that'll find me here, you mark my word. I've said so before this, but your mother's always talked me round. This time I mean it. I'll go and see the brewers the minute that hop-picking's over."

"Nonsense, dad," replied Mary briskly. "You'll forget about it as soon as it's over. Besides, look at the money you'll be taking this evening. A couple of hundred pounds and more, I'll bet."

"I dare say I'll take it, but what's the good of that?" said Mr. Raymond. "Precious little of it sticks to my fingers, as you know well enough. I've got to pay the brewers for the beer, haven't I? Then there's rent, rates, taxes and licence. If I clear enough to buy the Sunday dinner, I'll be lucky. It's not worth all the upset to a man's home, that it isn't."

"Well, if it wasn't for hop-picking you'd never see us all home together, dad," said Mary.

Mr. Raymond smiled. "Well, that's one good thing about it," he replied. "If it wasn't for you boys and girls your mother and I'd never be able to manage it. And I sometimes believe that you enjoy it."

"Oh, it's not bad fun once in a way," said Mary cheerfully. "And if you don't like it you shouldn't have taken a pub in the hop-picking country. Come along, it's just on six. We'd better slip down and open those windows."

The opening of the windows was greeted with a deafening cheer by those outside. And for the next half hour the four servers, two at each window, had their work cut out. After their first customers' requirements were satisfied, others took their place clamouring for liquid refreshment. So closely were they packed outside the house that any movement seemed impossible. Yet somehow those whose glasses had been filled forced their way through the mob to find a seat at the fringes of the crowd. The benches under the arbour could not accommodate a quarter of them. The rest sat down where they could, on the grass under the elm tree, on the banks beside the road, even if needs must on the gravel itself. But nobody complained of over-crowding. It was a fine warm evening and they were all out to enjoy themselves.

A rough lot they might be, as Mr. Raymond had described them, but their appearance belied his words. The girl hop-pickers had put on all their finery in honour of their friends' visit. Without exception they showed a penchant for bright colours and gaudy jewellery. The older women had assumed black dresses of surprising shininess, and had adorned themselves with beads of every description. The male visitors were equally resplendent. They were wearing their best suits, of astonishing pattern and cut. Watch-chains adorned their waistcoats, their ties were of dazzling shades. Nearly all of them wore paper caps as symbols of festivity. They had come by train, by charabanc, by bicycle, bringing bottles of beer long since empty in their pockets. Now they clamoured for more beer with which to fill them.

Jimmy arrived on the scene about eight o'clock. He was immediately recognised by Alf Mailing who let him into the other room without question. This was full of home-dwellers but Jimmy saw nobody whom he recognised. A rapid glance assured him that Lavis was not present. He was looking for a corner in which to install himself when Mr. Raymond saw him from the passage outside. He beckoned to him mysteriously.

"Come along into the cellar, Inspector," he whispered hoarsely. "There's a seat in there and you'll be more comfortable. And you'll be able to see how a Saturday night in hop-picking turns a decent country pub into a bear garden."

Jimmy suffered himself to be led into the cellar and ordered a pint of beer. In a sense he found himself alone, like a man raised on a pinnacle above a surging mob. There were no other customers in the cellar, but it was a scene of unceasing activity. The bar parlour and the other room had to be kept supplied. And there were the wives of the home-dwellers to be thought of. These were allowed by Alf Mailing to come round to the back of the house. Their presence was resented in the other room, since ladies in a pub are rather apt to cramp a man's style. So they came round to the back door, where they tendered bottles and jugs for filling. Those members of the Raymond family who were not on duty in the bar parlour passed continually in and out of the cellar, attending to the various demands made upon them from all sides.

Jimmy watched the proceedings with considerable amusement. There was something inspiring in all the energy surrounding him. He had spent the day in exploring the neighbourhood of Hobb's Corner as Dr. Priestley had suggested. But he had found nothing which had suggested to him the disposal of a body. The most obvious place had been Mr. Velley's pond, but upon inspection this had proved disappointing. The demands made upon it by the fire engine on the previous Tuesday evening had very nearly emptied it. It now contained a little more than a few inches of water, tenanted only by a flock of disconsolate ducks. The farms and out-buildings of Hobb's Farm were certainly extensive. With Mr. Velley's permission Jimmy had examined all of them. But no sign of a dead body could he find. Obviously there was no room in the hopper huts for more than their temporary population. Indeed, it was miraculous how so many people could contrive to find shelter in so small a space. And as for the hop gardens themselves, deserted on Saturday afternoon, there was no corner in their whole extent where a body could be concealed.

Jimmy was feeling despondent as a result of his day's work. Dr. Priestley's suggestion had sounded extraordinarily hopeful. It had seemed to offer a solution to the problem. But Elver dead appeared as elusive as Elver alive. And as Dr. Priestley had insisted, there was no proof that he was dead. One could only suppose that the wretched man had found a way of rendering himself invisible and so eluding the hounds of justice.

Lavis was the only hope, and that a very vague one. It had not even been established that Lavis and Elver had met since the latter's arrest seven years before. The only certainty was that Lavis was up to no good. Perhaps in endeavouring to trace his misdeeds, Jimmy might light upon some clue to the burglary or the fire. But it would be the merest chance if that clue led to the discovery of the missing Elver.

Jimmy had been in the cellar about half an hour when Mr. Raymond came in again. "Enjoying yourself, Inspector?" he asked. And then in a lower tone he added, "Is there anybody you're looking for specially?"

"I was rather expecting Lavis to drop in this evening," Jimmy replied.

"I thought you might be. That's what I came in here to say. He's just gone into the other room. Came in by himself like he always does, and he's ordered a pint of cider. You won't catch him treating any of the other chaps when he's flush of money."

"Thanks," said Jimmy. "It's very good of you to give me the tip, Mr. Raymond. How did he come?"

"Oh, on his bike, I expect, like he mostly does. I didn't see him come myself. I wasn't by the window. If you like to slip out and ask Alf, he'll tell you. It was him that let him into the other room."

Jimmy made his way by the back door to the front of the house. He found Alf on duty and accosted him. "You saw Lavis come in just now, I expect," he asked.

"Aye, I saw him right enough, sir," replied Alf. "I wonder the guv'nor lets him come inside the house. I wouldn't."

"He won't come to any harm where he is. Did you notice if he came on his bicycle?"

"Yes, he had his bike and that great bag he carries round with him tied to it. I can't make out why he doesn't leave it at home when he comes out of an evening."

"Doesn't like to be parted from it, I dare say," said Jimmy. "Where is the bicycle now?"

"He took it round to the back. It wouldn't do to leave it out here with all these hoppers about. I expect he's put it in the lodge. Nobody would get at it there to interfere with it."

Jimmy walked round the Chequers until he found the door of the outhouse known as the lodge. It was shut but not locked. Jimmy passed through the doorway and found himself in a fair-sized shed, almost full of empty barrels. Against these barrels stood a bicycle to which was firmly strapped a heavy leather bag.

Jimmy's intention was to examine the contents of the bag. The lodge was ideal for the purpose, since when he shut the door nobody could see what he was doing. He did so and switched on his torch; then he loosened the straps of the bag and endeavoured to open it. To his annoyance he found that it was securely locked. He took a bunch of keys from his pocket and tried each of them in the lock in turn, but none of them would fit and he was faced with the problem of what to do next.

He could, of course, have forced the lock. There was a large screwdriver lying amongst the barrels which would have served his purpose admirably. But if he forced the lock he would have been unable to make it fasten again, and he did not want to arouse Lavis's suspicions. Better leave the bag unopened and take other steps to discover the nature of its contents.

Jimmy returned to the cellar, where he ordered a second pint of beer. He found that from one particular corner of the cellar he could see into the other room. In this corner he placed an empty crate and seated himself upon it. He was now satisfied that Lavis could not leave the Chequers unperceived by him.

As the evening wore on the rush of customers abated a little. The pickers began to drift away to their huts, followed in some cases by their visitors. One by one the stall-holders began to pack up and disappear. But even so, the gas lamp over the front door revealed a busy enough scene. The benches beneath the arbour were still packed, and the male chorus had assembled under the elm tree. Their singing came to Jimmy in bursts of sound whenever the outer door of the other room was opened. And almost drowning it came a continuous roar of voices from those assembled outside the windows of the bar parlour. The home-dwellers in the other room kept themselves aloof from all this. At the centre table a couple were playing cribbage, regardless of the advice showered upon them by a dozen spectators. Others sat upon the benches ranged round the walls, drinking beer or cider, and discussing the quality of the hops and the date upon which picking was likely to end. Now and then, in spite of the accompanying din, Jimmy was able to catch snatches of their conversation. It was borne in upon him that hop-picking was the only thing that mattered in Matling. While that was in progress a world war or a revolution was scarcely worthy of attention. Far less such a minor matter as a burglary or a fire. Not a single reference did Jimmy hear to either of these events.

From where he sat he could not actually see Lavis. Once, in order to assure himself that the man had not left the house, he got up and peeped through the door of the other room. Lavis was sitting in a corner by himself, with a pint of cider before him. The rest of the company seemed to ignore his presence. He took no part in the conversation and hardly seemed to be listening to it. He sat very still staring at the table in front of him. Now and then he would raise his glass to his lips and set it down again quietly, almost stealthily.

So it must have been exactly a week earlier, Jimmy thought. Lavis must have been sitting in the same corner, silent, unregarded, and steadily imbibing cider. At closing time, ten o'clock, he had gone out with the rest. By that time he was apparently very drunk. Apparently, because Alf Mailing had maintained that he feigned drunkenness for his own mysterious purposes. Anyhow he had somehow got himself in a row outside. The usual pointless row between men who had indulged a little too freely. The two Adcorn brothers had been mixed up in it, which was rather curious since on all hands they were acclaimed as a thoroughly steady pair. Mr. Raymond had put an end to the disturbance, and the group had dispersed. Lavis had mounted his bicycle, only to tumble off it a short distance away. Had he done so merely in order to afford proof of his inebriety? And then he had taken the path which led to Hobb's Corner.

Lavis's movements could be checked during the period of the evening. But what about Elver? Where had he been at this time? Had he met Lavis before the latter's visit to the Chequers? Say some time between six and eight in the evening? It seemed almost certain that he must have done so, else why should Lavis have taken the path which led him past the scene of the burglary? Or was it possible that business of quite another kind had taken Lavis to Hobb's Corner?

Jimmy was still pondering the matter when he heard Mr. Raymond's stentorian voice from the bar parlour. "Now then, give your last orders, please. Only ten minutes to closing time!" A confused medley of shouted orders replied to him.

"Here y'are, three pints of bitter -- we've got the glasses. Two gins and peppermint. A pot of mild and see that it's full up this time."

The activity within the house became once more intense. The home-dwellers, warned by the summons, hammered their empty glasses upon the table. Hot and perspiring members of the Raymond family hastened to fill them. A few stragglers from among their womenfolk urgently passed their jugs in through the back door. Jimmy finished his beer and slipped out unobserved. He walked round the house and took up a position at the farther side of the road where he was hidden by the deep shadow thrown by the hedge.

But although he could not be seen, he commanded an excellent view of the Chequers. The gas-lamp was sufficiently bright for him to be able to see the doors of the house and the crowd assembled round the windows of the bar parlour. He watched the latter as it swayed tumultuously. By now there was no hope of getting another drink. But there was money to be recovered on the glasses. Frantic hands thrust these through the windows, demanding the return of threepences. The clamour was at its height when once more Mr. Raymond's voice rang out. "Time, gentlemen, please."

The crowd began to melt away. Groups of half a dozen drifted off up and down the road with linked arms. They sang discordantly as they went. Then the door of the other room opened, shedding a path of yellow light across the open space. The home-dwellers came out singly or in pairs, their gravity contrasting oddly with the uproariousness of the strangers. They disappeared with heavy footsteps into the darkness of the night.

Lavis was the last to emerge. To all appearances he was as drunk as an owl. He paused for a moment or two on the threshold of the door, swaying perilously on his feet. Then he began to stagger forward, steering a devious course until he reached the edge of the grass under the trees. He tripped over this and sat down heavily. Those of the strangers who had not yet dispersed greeted his proceedings with hilarious laughter.

"Coo! Look at him. There's a bloke what's been spendin' his money properly. Reckon he feels like as if he was sittin' on one of them there joy wheels. Hi, mate, stand up and tell us what it feels like."

Lavis took no notice of this ribaldry. He got up slowly and with immense dignity. Then he brushed his knees and the seat of his trousers with his hands. He seemed uncertain what to do next. But after a few moment's hesitation he lurched off in the direction of the lodge.

The last glasses had by now been handed in and the windows of the bar parlour closed with a bang. A few moments later Mr. Raymond appeared at the front of the house.

"Now then," he said, "you folk had best clear off. I don't want you hanging about around the house making a racket and keeping decent folks awake. And, besides, I'm going to turn out the light and then where will you be?"

A shrill female voice replied to him. "All right, guv'nor, we'll be good." There was a burst of laughter at this, followed by a snatch of unmelodious song. Then the last of the strangers moved off, whistling to the accompaniment of a mouth organ. Mr. Raymond watched them until they had gone some little distance down the road. Then he turned off the gas, leaving the front of the house in darkness.

Jimmy remained motionless, secure in the obscurity of the hedge. Although there was no moon the sky was clear and the stars shed sufficient light for Jimmy's purpose. He was wearing a pair of rubber-soled shoes and his training had taught him to move silently. A minute or so after the departure of the last of the strangers he heard a crunching of feet upon the gravel. A dim form emerged through the shadows and he recognised this as that of a man wheeling a bicycle.

This was undoubtedly Lavis. Jimmy strained his eyes to see what the man would do. He came straight towards him until he reached the centre of the road, and then he stopped, leaning upon his bicycle and apparently listening.

The night was very still and, except for the dwindling voices of the departing revellers in the distance, no sound could be heard. Lavis peered about him searchingly as though to assure himself that he was unobserved. Then apparently satisfied, he mounted his bicycle. Jimmy noticed that he did not observe the formality of lighting his lamp. Then he proceeded slowly up the road, steering a perfectly straight course. If he had been drunk when he came out of the Chequers he must have become sober again with extraordinary rapidity.

Jimmy let him get a few yards ahead, then started in pursuit. He ran easily and noiselessly, keeping himself as far as possible under the shadow of the hedge. Lavis seemed to have no suspicion that he was being followed. But as he passed the cottage by the roadside his pace slackened and he began to wobble along alarmingly. Anybody who might have seen him from the cottage would have thought he was exceedingly drunk. Once clear of possible observation, his progress became normal again.

As Lavis neared the point where the path to Hobb's Corner turned off from the road, Jimmy felt a thrill of excitement. Would Lavis keep straight on towards Park Gate, or would he take to the path? He was going straight on -- no, by Jove, he wasn't. Jimmy pulled himself up abruptly as Lavis dismounted from his bicycle and pushed it through the narrow space between the posts which guarded the end of the path; once safely through he mounted again and rode on.

The path ran straight across the open meadow without fence or hedge on either side. It seemed to Jimmy, perhaps because his eyes were getting accustomed to the night, that it was lighter here than it had been on the road. It would never do to risk being seen now. He waited at the end of the path until Lavis was out of sight. Then once again he resumed the pursuit. He had not gone far before he caught sight of a few scattered lights coming from the open doors of the hopper huts. He reached Hobb's Corner without catching any further glimpse of Lavis. And here again he found himself in comparative darkness. A row of trees by the cross-roads cast an almost impenetrable shadow. Jimmy sought the shelter of these and stood still and listened. If he could not see Lavis at least he might be fortunate enough to hear him.

As he stopped, Jimmy became aware that he was not alone in the shadow of the trees. He could hear a shuffling of feet close at hand and a murmur of whispering voices. And then some one spoke softly but distinctly. "There he is!"

For an instant Jimmy imagined that his presence had been discovered. His hand went to his sleeve where lay concealed a short but serviceable truncheon. But there was no movement towards him. His ear caught the sound of footsteps, and the unmistakable clicking of a bicycle being wheeled. Then the footsteps stopped and a second voice which Jimmy recognised as Lavis's spoke softly. "Hallo, mates, here you are then! Did you think I was never coming?"

"We guessed you'd turn up right enough," the first voice replied. "We'd best move on behind the huts, though. There's a bloke keeps coming in and out of the oast here, and if he sees us he'll wonder what we're hanging about for."

"In and out of the oast," said Lavis scornfully. "Why, that'll be Fred Adcorn, the drier. He won't take any heed of what we're up to. Still, we'll move on a bit if you like."

The voices and footsteps made off in the direction of the huts. Jimmy followed them at a safe distance. And then as a bright light shone out ahead of him, he came to a stand. He perceived that it was an electric torch held by Lavis. As its beams wavered Jimmy could see a group of men, strangers from London by their appearance, grouped round the bicycle from which Lavis was unstrapping the bag.

So intent were they all upon the proceedings that Jimmy judged it safe to approach a little closer. He fell upon his hands and knees and crawled up until he reached the corner of the huts. There he lay prone, eyes and ears keyed to the highest pitch of their alertness. He saw Lavis lay the bag upon the ground and unlock it. From it he extracted a number of small packages wrapped in newspaper, which he handed to those standing round him, receiving money in exchange.

A rough voice demanded the price. "A bob," Lavis replied. "And dirt cheap at that. There's a full noggin in each of these 'ere bottles, and perhaps a bit more. You won't get stuff like this in London at a bob a noggin, no, nor nowhere else. You'll have a couple, will you? You know how to lay hold of a good thing when you see it, any way."

The commerce did not last longer than a few minutes. By the time that the last purchaser had strolled away Lavis had apparently disposed of his stock. He relocked the bag and strapped it once more to the bicycle. Then he mounted and rode off, this time in the direction of Park Gate. Jimmy, perfectly satisfied with his evening's adventure, followed him. But Lavis's activities were at an end for this night at least. He entered the house with the same furtiveness that he had displayed throughout, and Jimmy heard him lock the door behind him.

Jimmy started at a smart pace towards Culverden. All this was very satisfactory so far as it went. Lavis's little game was now perfectly plain. He was, if nothing worse, a dealer in illicit liquor. There was no doubt that the packages he had sold for a shilling each contained the medicine bottles full of spirit which Wragge had discovered under the floor of the attic. Jimmy made a rapid calculation. A noggin was a quarter of a pint. A shilling a noggin was four shillings a pint, or thirty-two shillings a gallon. Allowing six bottles to the gallon, that worked out at five and fourpence a bottle. No spirit which had paid excise duty could possibly be sold at that price. And yet it showed a handsome margin of profit upon a crude spirit which had somehow escaped duty. Where Lavis procured this spirit hardly mattered for the moment. No doubt that would come out later. The point was that he had already broken the law by selling spirit without a licence and out of hours. That would be sufficient to justify a summons against him. Jimmy decided that he and Wragge would serve that summons together not later than the following morning.

Lavis, once in the hands of the police, might be persuaded to make interesting revelations. At all events Jimmy profoundly hoped so. For, on the face of it, the incident only served to make his inquiry the more obscure. The conversation which Jimmy had overheard made it plain that Lavis's visit to Hobb's Corner that evening had been expected. And if this evening, why not the previous Saturday as well? In which case Lavis's business at Hobb's Corner on the evening of the burglary was explained. He had gone there in order to dispose of his wares.

Had he by chance met Elver as he rode along the path? If so, what had passed between them? Had they appointed some rendezvous, to be kept when Lavis had left his customers? It seemed quite possible. Perhaps they had quarrelled at that rendezvous. Elver might have become aware of his old associate's activities and threatened blackmail. Lavis, in a sudden fit of rage, had taken a knife from his bag and stabbed him. But then again came the insoluble question. What had become of the body?

When Jimmy reached Culverden he found Wragge sitting up for him. "Well, Sergeant," he said cheerfully, "we've got Lavis laid by the heels, if that's any consolation to you. I caught him out properly. Listen while I tell you what became of those bottles of spirit you found."

Wragge listened to Jimmy's story with growing amazement. "Well, I'm blessed!" he exclaimed. "To think that a thing like that should have been going on in my district and me knowing nothing about it. Well, it's your show and it's for you to decide what we're going to do about it."

"We're going to hire a car to-morrow morning and we're going to drive out to Park Gate," said Jimmy. "We'll bring Lavis back here with us and we'll charge him. We've plenty to charge him with, and I expect that you can arrange that he won't be granted bail before he's brought before the magistrates on Monday morning. It's wonderful how a few hours in a detention cell will loosen a man's tongue. If he doesn't tell us a lot that we want to know I shall be very much surprised."

Wragge readily agreed to this course. "I'll see that he doesn't get bail, easily enough," he said. "It's only a matter of ringing up the Superintendent. And once we get him here we have a question or two to put to him. That was a pretty smart piece of work of yours, if you don't mind my saying so, Inspector."

So, early on the following morning, they hired a car and drove to Park Gate. They were admitted to the house by Mrs. Creach who informed them that her brother was still in bed. She was bidden to go and tell him to get up. Meanwhile Jimmy looked round until he had found the leather bag. This he impounded and put in the car. A little later Lavis, loudly protesting against the indignity, came downstairs, unshaved but fully dressed. He was escorted to the car, which was immediately driven back to Culverden.

Adjoining Wragge's house was a second building locally known as the Station. It accommodated the two constables who were under the sergeant's jurisdiction, and also contained a charge room and a detention cell. Under escort of the two constables Lavis was taken to the charge room. Wragge sat down at the desk, dipped a pen into the inkpot and looked at him severely. He demanded his name and age and made a note of these particulars.

"You are charged with unlawfully selling liquor without a licence," he said sharply. "Other charges will be preferred against you in due course. You will be brought before the bench at the earliest opportunity. Meanwhile you will be detained in custody."

"Who says I've been selling liquor?" demanded Lavis truculently. "You can't detain me on a charge like that with no one to back up your story."

Jimmy, who had been standing at the far end of the room, came forward. "I say so," he replied quietly. "I know exactly what you did after you left the Chequers at ten o'clock yesterday evening. You bicycled to Hobb's Corner, where you met a group of people who were obviously expecting you. In your bag you had a number of medicine bottles full of spirit. These you retailed at the price of a shilling a gill. And, as you said yourself, you can't buy spirit at that price in London or anywhere else."

Lavis looked utterly dumbfounded. It was obvious that the idea that his proceedings had been observed had never entered his head. But he made one more attempt to bluff it out.

"And who might you be?" he asked. "The Sergeant here knows me well enough. Why should he take your word against me?"

"I am Inspector Waghorn of Scotland Yard," Jimmy replied. "I think it probable that the magistrates will accept my word."

"You have heard the charge preferred against you," said Wragge. "Do you wish to make any statement?"

"What I've got to say I'll say before the magistrates to-morrow," replied Lavis sullenly.

"Very well," said Wragge. And then to the constables. "Take him away to the detention room."

Jimmy waited until the accused had been removed. "He'll come round all right," he said as the sound of footsteps died away in the distance. "Too cunning to say anything without thinking it over first. I'll bet you that he'll think of some sort of yarn to spin before the evening. Meanwhile I'd better get on the telephone to the Yard. They may have something to tell us by this time about that stuff we sent them."

On communicating with Scotland Yard, Jimmy learned that the ashes from the bungalow had been subjected to complete examination, microscopic and otherwise. For the most part the ashes were derived from wood, cloth, leather and paper. This is what might have been expected from the articles which had been consumed. There was also a certain portion of lime derived from the plaster of the ceiling which had fallen in. Among the ashes were small portions of metal so distorted by heat as to be unrecognisable. They might once have formed part of the movement of the grandfather clock. Chemical analysis had revealed that the ashes contained at least a trace of sulphate. This suggested that the old dodge of employing sulphuric acid, chlorate of potash and sugar to cause a flame had been employed in this case.

"You didn't find anything else in any way suspicious?" Jimmy asked.

"What do you mean suspicious?" replied the expert at the other end.

"Why, traces of human remains, or anything like that."

The expert laughed. "You never said anything about human remains when you told us the stuff was coming," he replied. "However, if there had been anything of that kind we would have found it. We could tell from the state of the ashes that the fire, though it must have been pretty brisk, was not really intense. That being so, if any human bones had been burnt we should certainly have detected bone ash, if not charred pieces of the bones themselves. You can set your mind at rest on that point."

"Thanks very much," Jimmy said. "Have you had time to look at the knife I sent up yesterday?"

"We haven't quite finished with it yet. We have established the stains on it as human blood, but we haven't had time to determine the class. If you care to ring us up later in the day I dare say we shall be able to tell you."

Jimmy considered this information with mixed feelings. It seemed to prove pretty conclusively that Elver's body, if he had been murdered, had not been consumed in the fire at Mr. Pershore's bungalow. In his heart of hearts Jimmy had never believed in this possibility and was glad that he could now lay it aside. On the other hand, the expert's report carried things no further. Unless indeed, the bloodstains on the knife had any significance.

The trouble about the knife was that Wragge had found it in the wrong place. He had picked it up between the Chequers and Paddock Croft, where it had lain on the grass at the edge of the main road. Now, if it had been found on the path leading to Hobb's Corner, or at Hobb's Corner itself, it would have been a very different matter. One might then work on the theory that Lavis had used it to stab Elver. It was impossible to imagine that the murder had taken place on the spot where the knife had been found. That was only a few yards from the cottage -- a most unlikely place for the murderer to select, even on the darkest night. And if the murder had taken place elsewhere, how had the knife been conveyed to the spot where it had been found? Certainly not by the murderer. If he had wished to dispose of the weapon, he would not have thrown it down carelessly by the wayside. Nor would any one else, for the matter of that. The knife was new, and of a certain value to whoever might have found it. The only remaining alternative was that the knife had been deposited there for some definite reason.

Jimmy was sufficiently experienced to know that criminals often have a habit of laying false clues. The knife might have been intended as a false clue, designed to lead the investigator astray. But in that case, what was it meant to suggest? That a murder had been committed by its aid, when as a matter of fact nothing of the sort had taken place?

The riddle puzzled Jimmy till one o'clock, when he was summoned to dinner by Mrs. Wragge. The three of them sat down to a round of roast beef with Yorkshire pudding, potatoes and horseradish. This was followed by a boiled jam roll, and some excellent cheese. As they lingered over the remains of this most satisfying meal, one of the constables appeared at the kitchen door.

"Sorry, sir, but I thought you might have finished your dinner," he said. "I wouldn't have disturbed you, but Lavis says that he wants to see the gentleman from Scotland Yard. I think he'd like to make a statement, sir."

The Sergeant chuckled. "Oh, he's thought better of it, has he?" he replied. "Well, I'm glad he didn't ask to see me. I always try and get a bit of a nap after dinner on Sundays. You'll see him, I dare say, inspector."

"Yes, I'll see him," said Jimmy. "He'll be in an expansive mood if he's dined as well as I have."

CHAPTER XV

BUT Lavis's mid-day meal had been anything but sumptuous. It had consisted of a small plate of lukewarm stew prepared by the wife of one of the constables, and a piece of remarkably stale bread. Nor was the detention room anything like so cheerful a place as the Sergeant's kitchen. It was bare, and since it had not been occupied for many weeks, smelt damp and unwholesome. The general atmosphere of depression seemed to have affected Lavis's spirit. When Jimmy came in he was sitting on the edge of the wooden bed, chewing the end of a burnt-out match and staring dejectedly at the blank wall opposite.

Jimmy nodded to the constable that he should leave them alone. He waited until the door had been closed and then sat down on a hard chair opposite the prisoner. "You asked to see me?" he said cheerfully. "Feeling lonely, perhaps?"

Lavis shifted his glance round slowly and surveyed his visitor furtively yet keenly. "The Sergeant said just now that a further charge would be preferred against me," he replied. "I've a right to know what that charge is, haven't I?"

"You haven't any right to know," said Jimmy. "But I don't mind telling you that the charge will be a very serious one indeed."

This was not calculated to raise Lavis's spirits. It was quite obvious that he was thoroughly frightened at finding himself in the hands of the police. His former truculence had evaporated and his voice assumed a whining tone.

"It's very hard on a chap to threaten him like that," he said. "You might just as well tell me right out what the charge will be, Inspector."

"Well, you'll have to know sooner or later," Jimmy replied. "In all probability you'll be charged with murder."

Lavis leapt from the bed in a sudden access of terror. "What?" he exclaimed. "Murder! Me! I'll swear I'm innocent of that, anyway."

"Sit down," said Jimmy sternly. "We don't want any heroics here. If you can tell me where to find Christopher Elver, I'll believe in your innocence. But not unless."

Lavis's eyes widened in amazement. "Sea Joe!" he exclaimed. And then with sudden eagerness he added, "Why, has somebody done him in then?"

"You should know that better than I do," Jimmy replied.

"I don't know a thing about it, I'll take my oath on that. Why, as I've told you over and over again, I haven't set eyes on the chap since he was arrested years ago."

Jimmy shook his head reprovingly. "That won't do, you know," he replied. "We know too much for you to be able to get away with that story. Now, let's get down to facts. To begin with, Elver called at your house last Saturday. There's not a shadow of doubt about that. Your sister told you of his visit when you came home that evening, I suppose."

"She told me that somebody had been to see me, but that he hadn't given his name. I took it to be one of my customers and never gave the matter another thought. How was I to guess that Sea Joe would turn up again after all these years? And it beats me how he found out where I was living."

"We know how he found that out. You'd have been pleased to see your old friend again, no doubt."

Lavis's eyes shifted uneasily. "I don't want convicts coming to my place," he replied virtuously.

"On the principle that evil communications corrupt good manners, I suppose? Of course, as a thoroughly law-abiding citizen you wouldn't wish to associate with anybody who had been in gaol. Oh, come off it, man, for goodness' sake! We're not children to be taken in by that sort of yarn. You and Elver were associated in some mischief together before he was arrested. You helped him to get rid of the dope, I dare say."

No, no, it wasn't that. I'll swear I never knew until I saw it in the papers that he'd been doing anything in the dope line."

"Then what was it?" persisted Jimmy relentlessly. "Look here, Lavis, you're in a fix. You say that Elver is still alive."

"If he was alive a week ago I don't see why he shouldn't be now."

"Well, then, sooner or later we shall find him. And when we do we shall only have to ask him what it was that you two were up to between you. He'll tell us right enough, as it won't make any difference to him. So you may just as well give me your own version of the story."

Lavis considered this for a moment. Apparently he decided that it would be better to confess than to be confronted with a possibly hostile witness.

"It wasn't anything much," he muttered. "Sea Joe used to bring a few things over, and I'd get rid of them for him, that's all."

"Not forgetting to take a commission for your trouble. What sort of things did he bring over?"

"Oh, just spirits, eau de Cologne, cigars and things like that. I never knew he brought dope as well. He never breathed a word of that to me. He wouldn't have been able to get the stuff ashore but for me. The customs men are too wide-awake for that. If he'd tried to leave the ship with a bag they'd have searched it at once. But they knew me as the ship chandler's man, and didn't take any notice. I always had a bag to put my samples in and what not. And they got so used to seeing it that they never asked what I brought ashore in it."

"Oh, so that was it, was it? I rather suspected that it might have been something of the kind. You and Sea Joe did a bit of smuggling between you and shared the proceeds. By the way, did he leave any money with you before he was arrested?"

Lavis suddenly went white, and Jimmy saw that the shot had told. "Money!" exclaimed the former. "What should he leave any money with me for?"

Jimmy shrugged his shoulders. "Oh, just because he couldn't think of anybody else to leave it with, I suppose," he replied. "I certainly can't think of any other reason. You haven't got the sort of face that inspires confidence, you know."

"Well, he didn't leave any money with me," said Lavis stubbornly.

"Oh, think again! He must have made a good bit out of that dope smuggling business of his. You know best what he made out of his other little ventures. He didn't carry it all with him on the ship and he wouldn't care to deposit it in a bank. They might ask too many questions. So why not leave it with a confidential friend to be called upon as required? And you know perfectly well, Lavis, that's what Sea Joe called to see you about the other day. I'll ask him as soon as I come across him. Just a simple question. 'How much of your money was in Lavis's possession when you were arrested?'"

Lavis's anxiety was unmistakable. "You wouldn't take the word of a chap like that?" he asked almost piteously.

"He might be able to prove the truth of what he told me," said Jimmy quietly.

"Well, there may have been a few pounds, nothing more," said Lavis reluctantly. "But if the money hadn't been honestly come by he wouldn't have any right to it, would he?"

"That's a matter I'm not prepared to discuss. The point is that in his eyes you certainly had no right to it. You were merely taking care of it for him. He'd say that you ought to have got in touch with him as soon as he was released. Then naturally as soon as he found out where you were he came to ask you what about it. And you weren't very pleased to see him. You didn't like the idea of handing over money. None of us do."

"I never did see him," exclaimed Lavis earnestly. "That I'll swear."

"I'm not altogether impressed by your oath, I'm afraid. By the way, you lost a knife that Saturday evening, didn't you?"

Lavis's eyes flickered. "That's so," he replied. "It must have tumbled out of my bag when I fell off my bicycle after leaving the Chequers. I'd had a drop more than was good for me that night, I'll admit."

"Oh, surely not! No more than you had last night, I expect, and that didn't affect you much. You didn't guess that I was following you all the way from the Chequers to Hobb's Corner, did you? But let's get back to that knife. You say it must have tumbled out of your bag. But since you're very careful always to keep that bag locked I don't think it's likely. Why did you tumble off your bicycle to begin with? Come on, out with it."

"Because I thought I saw Jack Wright watching me over his garden gate," replied Lavis sulkily.

"I see. You wanted him to think you were drunk. Well, you certainly succeeded. But how did you come to leave that knife behind you?"

Lavis shook his head helplessly. "You've been one too many for me. Inspector," he replied. "True, I wasn't drunk. I only shammed so that folks shouldn't guess what I was up to. But that knife wasn't in my bag at all. It was shoved down the left leg of my trousers where I could get it when I wanted it."

"Oh, so you thought you might want it, did you?" remarked Jimmy significantly.

"I had a pretty rough lot of customers to deal with down at Hobb's Corner. I always managed to show them that I had a knife about me if they turned nasty."

"How do you account for the knife having human bloodstains upon it?"

"Easily enough. I meant to fall off the bicycle lightly when I must have stumbled somehow. Anyhow, I came down pretty heavy on my left side and cut my leg with the knife. The mark's there yet. I'll show you if you don't believe me."

He pulled up his trousers, exhibiting his leg for Jimmy's inspection. There was certainly the mark of a long cut apparently recently inflicted. And Lavis's furtiveness had left him. Jimmy decided that in this respect at least he was telling the truth.

"Well," he said, "I'll accept that part of your story for the moment. You got on your bicycle again and rode on towards Hobb's Corner. But why did you leave the knife behind?"

"It had fallen out of my trousers and I didn't like to stop and look for it. Jack Wright was still there watching me. So I left it where it was, thinking I'd look for it in the morning. But when I came along it had gone. I guessed that somebody else must have picked it up."

"So you told Sergeant Wragge that it had been stolen. Not a bad idea in its way. You went on to Hobb's Corner. There you served your customers as I saw you doing last night. What did you do after that?"

"Why, I just went home to bed."

"Who did you meet on your way home, Lavis?"

"Why, only Tom Adcorn, the weigher up at Hobb's Farm. He came upon me suddenly just as I was past the crossroads. I was on my bicycle and I began to wobble about so that if he recognised me he'd think I was drunk. But he didn't seem to notice me and I saw him going to the oast where his brother Fred was working."

"And you met nobody else?"

"Not another soul, I'll swear. It isn't often one meets any one along there at that time of night."

Jimmy suddenly changed the subject. "You get the spirit from Sea Joe," he asked lightly.

Lavis shook his head in violent denial. "I tell you I haven't seen or heard of Sea Joe these last nine years," he replied. "I used to do a bit of trading with him. I've admitted that already." Then the old look of cunning returned to his eyes. "Will it do me any good if I tell you where I got the spirit from?" he asked.

"It certainly won't do you any harm," Jimmy replied. "But you may just as well tell the truth while you're about it. We can find out for ourselves easily enough."

"Well, you see, it's like this," said Lavis eagerly. "Sea Joe wasn't the only one of those chaps who used to do a bit on their own. There were half a dozen of them that I used to deal with. I could always get rid of the stuff for them one way or another. And after Sea Joe was put away I still kept in with the rest of them."

"Even after you lost your job with the ship's chandlers?" Jimmy suggested.

"I didn't lose my job. I chucked it up because they didn't treat me right. I knew the man that followed me, and I put him up to the trick. And at hop-picking time I get hold of some of the stuff and sell it to the pickers' friends. They'll take any amount of it. It doesn't seem to do them any harm, I'm bound to say that."

"Good brandy wouldn't do anybody any harm," said Jimmy.

"It isn't rightly brandy at all," Lavis replied in a sudden burst of confidence. "It's potato spirit flavoured to make it taste like brandy. And those steward chaps buy it abroad at something like a bob a bottle."

"Quite a paying game as long as it isn't found out. You'll have plenty of time before to-morrow morning to write me out a list of those chaps you deal with. I can't say so officially, but any evidence you may be able to give is pretty sure to be reckoned in your favour. And you'll want as much in your favour as you can get, it seems to me."

Lavis once more became apprehensive. "Why, selling brandy, even if it's been smuggled, isn't so bad as all that," he exclaimed.

"It's bad enough to get you a pretty stiff sentence. But as you've already been warned, that isn't all we've got against you. What time was it that you met Tom Adcorn that night?"

The now familiar symptoms of uneasiness reappeared in Lavis's demeanour. He hesitated for a moment or two and then: "I couldn't say," he replied faintly.

"Oh, well, it doesn't matter. You say that Tom Adcorn went into the oast house immediately after you met him. I've only got to ask him what time that was. He's sure to remember within a little."

"I was longer than usual serving the chaps down at the hopper huts," Lavis muttered uncomfortably.

"It took you about ten minutes to sell the stuff last night. How long did it take you the week before?"

"Maybe an hour, maybe not quite so long."

"In other words it must have been well after eleven o'clock when you met Tom Adcorn. It isn't a bit of good your lying to me, for I can check all your statements. I can find out to whom you sold brandy that night, and they'll be able to tell me when you packed up and left them. Last night you had finished by half-past ten, for I was there and took a note of the time. I refuse to believe that you were very much later the previous week. If Adcorn tells me that you didn't meet him until after eleven I shall begin to wonder how you put in your time. I've got my suspicions about that already."

Lavis averted his eyes and made no reply.

"I may as well tell you what those suspicions are," continued Jimmy. "You met Elver before or after he did that spot of burglary at Paddock Croft. He had something to say to you that you didn't like. Something about that money of his that you hadn't handed over, I expect. By way of shutting his mouth you stabbed him with one of those knives you carry about the countryside with you. What did you do with the body, Lavis? It didn't by any chance occur to you to hide it in Mr. Pershore's bungalow, did it?"

Lavis gasped in sheer terror. "I never set eyes on Elver, I swear I didn't," he almost shrieked. "It wasn't for that --" He stopped abruptly but not before Jimmy had fathomed his feelings.

"It wasn't for that that you went to Mr. Pershore's bungalow, you were going to say," he countered easily.

"I never said a word about the bungalow," Lavis assured him hastily.

"I know you didn't. But if you could prove that you were at the bungalow during that particular period I should think it less likely that you had met Elver and had murdered him. That ought to be plain enough to you, surely?"

"Well, I had just a look round there before I met Tom Adcorn. I wanted to find out whether Mr. Pershore was down for the week-end by any chance. If he had been I was going to ask him if he could help me like he did before once."

Jimmy shook his head impatiently. "You know perfectly well that there was no chance of Mr. Pershore being there," he replied. "You'll get yourself into very serious trouble if you keep on lying like this. A charge of murder is a pretty nasty thing to be up against, I can tell you. You've already admitted that you went round to the bungalow. What was your business there? Come on, out with it."

"I've told you the truth, strike me dead if I haven't," replied Lavis stubbornly.

"It seems to me that you're likely to be struck dead before you're many months older," Jimmy replied equably. "You've got a wireless set at home, I notice. Do you ever buy sulphuric acid to put in the battery?"

By this time Lavis's teeth began chattering with fright. "I did buy a little drop not so very long ago," he stammered.

"And I expect you're apt to get a sore throat, hanging round the hopper huts at night. Have you ever tried chlorate of potash for it? They tell me it's the best thing in the world, especially if you mix it with a little sugar."

Lavis's jaw dropped in utter consternation. He was about to make some sort of reply, but Jimmy forestalled him. "I expect you learnt the dodge while you were working in London," he continued. "Anyhow, this is what you did. You got into Mr. Pershore's bungalow somehow and made an infernal machine out of his grandfather clock. You arranged it so that the descent of the weights would tip a saucer full of sulphuric acid on to a mixture of chlorate and sugar. And you filled the base of the clock with oily rags, or paper or something. What did you do it for, Lavis?"

"I never did it, Inspector, that I didn't. I only went to the bungalow to have a look round."

Jimmy took no notice of this denial. "You admit that you looked round the bungalow then? How did you get in?"

"I've got a key that will unlock the back door. Mrs. Adcorn goes out by the back door when she leaves the house, so she can't bolt it behind her."

"If you knew that your key fitted the lock you must have tried it before. It wasn't the first time that you'd been into the bungalow in Mr. Pershore's absence."

"Well, there's no sense in denying it now, I suppose," Lavis replied reluctantly.

"And I dare say you picked up one or two trifles while you were there. But the point is that last Saturday night you entered the house with the deliberate intention of setting fire to it. You must have had all the necessary materials packed away in that bag of yours. Arson is a pretty serious crime, you know, Lavis."

"You've got no proof that I did it," said Lavis sulkily.

"I've got evidence enough to put before a jury. You've admitted that you entered the bungalow on Saturday night. Of course, you can withdraw that admission if you like."

Lavis looked up sharply. "And what if I do?" he asked.

"Why, I shall take it that you told me a false story to put me off the scent. And then I shall be fully convinced that you met Elver that night and murdered him. You know what action I shall take accordingly. Now, you sit down for a bit and think it over."

Jimmy left the detention room and returned to the sergeant's house. He found Wragge fast asleep in his favourite chair and made no effort to disturb his slumbers. He lighted a cigarette and began to pace softly up and down the room.

He felt distinctly elated by his interview with Lavis. The man was an obvious liar, and under ordinary circumstances no statement made by him could be relied upon. But he had penetrated his defences and reached the kernel of truth within the hard shell of subterfuge. Lavis had fired Mr. Pershore's bungalow. This was certain, though he had not actually admitted it. He had confessed in some detail to dealing in illicit liquor. A confession so full that there would be a clear case to put before the magistrates. All this was for the good. But, unfortunately, it threw no light upon the fate of Elver. It would be perfectly futile to charge Lavis with Elver's murder. There was not a shred of evidence to prove that Elver had been murdered, that he was not at that very moment alive and well.

When Wragge awoke from his nap Jimmy repeated to him the substance of his interview with Lavis. "It was all highly irregular, I know that," he said. "But the man is a self-confessed scoundrel and a little interrogation was justified. I think I frightened him into telling the truth. And I'm inclined to believe his statement that he never met Elver at all during his visit here."

"I think you did very well, if I may take the liberty of saying so," said Wragge. "But, whatever put it into your head to accuse him of having murdered Elver? That's quite a new idea to me."

Jimmy shrugged his shoulders. "We can't find Elver alive," he replied. "He's been missing for over a week now. It is not impossible that he may have been killed and his body concealed somewhere."

Wragge looked incredulous. "But whoever would have killed him if not Lavis?" he asked. "And you say you think that Lavis didn't. Besides who could hide a body with the countryside over-run as it is just now?"

"I don't know," Jimmy replied. "Those are the very questions I've been asking myself for the last two or three days. Hallo, that's the telephone bell."

Wragge went to answer the call. He came back a few moments later. "It's for you, Inspector," he said. "A gentleman from London. Says his name's Merefield. Will you go?"

Jimmy leapt up eagerly. A call from Harold Merefield must mean that Dr. Priestley had something to say to him.

"Yes, I'll go," he replied. He went to the telephone and announced himself.

"Hallo, is that you, Jimmy?" came Harold's voice at the other end of the wire. "I've got a message for you from my old man. He's been spending the morning reading through the notes I made about that case of yours. And just now he told me to try and get on to you."

"Well, you've succeeded," Jimmy replied. "I'm sure I'm very much obliged to Dr. Priestley. What's the message?"

"If you can make sense of it, it's more than I can," said Harold. "He told me to tell you that since you were in a hop growing district it might pay you to investigate the method of drying hops. You know what he's like by this time. I didn't dare ask him if he couldn't be a little more explicit. He told me to give you that message and I've done so. It's up to you to make what you can out of it."

"Thanks, I'll do my best," Jimmy replied. "If you have any more crumbs of wisdom to transmit you'll find me here or hereabouts. So long."

Jimmy rang off and returned to the Sergeant's front room. "Message from a friend of mine," he said. "Nothing to do with what we were speaking of. He talked about drying hops. Do you dry hops? I always thought you wetted them by putting them in beer."

Wragge chuckled. "So you do," he replied. "But you've got to dry them first. What do you suppose all the oast houses you see about here are for?"

"I hadn't thought much about them, I'm afraid," said Jimmy. "What's the idea? How do you dry the things, and why?"

"They wouldn't keep if you didn't dry them. You saw the pickers at work up at Hobbs' Farm. And you saw the measurer empty their bins into the poke. Well, as soon as the pokes are full they are taken to the oast houses and the hops are dried there. Then when they are dried they're pressed into pockets and sent off to market."

"Hold on," said Jimmy. "These technical terms are so much Greek to a Londoner. What's a pocket?"

"A big sack holding a couple of hundredweight of dried hops. You must have seen dozens of them stacked on lorries on their way up to London. The farmers for the most part get them off as soon as they're ready."

"I see," said Jimmy. "Now tell me how the drying's done. Do you wipe the jolly little hops over with a towel, or something?"

"Ha, ha! that's a good one," exclaimed Wragge. "No, you dry them by heat. There are two ways of doing it. The new-fangled way is to blow hot air through them. It's quicker and cheaper, they say. But most of the farmers about here believe that the old-fashioned way is best. It gives a better quality hop, though it's a bit more trouble."

"And what's the old-fashioned way?" Jimmy asked.

"Why, put 'em in the oast house and light a fire under them. You've only got to drop into the first oast house you come to and have a look. That would show you much better than I can explain to you. Get hold of a good drier, like Fred Adcorn at Hobb's Farm, and he'll put you in the way of it in no time. There are good driers and bad. It's a knack, I suppose."

"That's a good idea. I thought of riding over to Hobb's Corner this afternoon to have a look round, in any case. But the oast houses aren't working on Sundays, I suppose?"

"It all depends. If they haven't finished drying the hops they've picked during the week, they'll be working all right. You'll be back in time for tea, I dare say."

"Unless anything detains me I certainly shall," Jimmy replied. He got out his hired bicycle and took the now familiar route to Hobb's Corner. That was an excellent suggestion of the Sergeant's. He wanted to see Fred Adcorn, who might be able to confirm a detail in Lavis's story. And if he found him at the oast house he'd ask him to show him over. And when he had learnt the intricacies of hop drying he might be able to unravel the mystery of Dr. Priestley's suggestion.

As soon as Jimmy came in sight of Hobbs' Corner the thin haze of vapour issuing from the cowl of the oast houses showed him that they were working. As he approached them a perspiring figure emerged. Jimmy accosted him.

"You're Fred Adcorn, aren't you?" he asked.

"That's right, sir," the man replied. "I've seen you afore round these parts, the last day or two."

"Yes, I've been sent down from Scotland Yard to look into this burglary at Paddock Croft. We're looking for the chap who did it. Have you got time for a word or two with me?"

"Well, I've just made up my fire," Fred replied. "There won't be nothing for me to attend to for the next few minutes."

"That's good. You've heard that we've arrested Lavis, I dare say?"

Fred spat contemptuously. "Yes, I heard it when I popped into the Chequers for a moment at dinner time," he replied. "And a good job too, I say. The sort of chap that's never up to any good. What's he been doing of now?"

"We've caught him out breaking the law," replied Jimmy evasively. "I've been having a talk with him this afternoon. He told me a lot of things which I don't know whether to believe or not."

"All a pack of lies, I make no doubt," said Fred pessimistically.

"I shouldn't wonder. Now, I was questioning him about his movements on the night of the burglary. That was a week ago last night, as I dare say you remember. I know that he was here or hereabouts sometime between ten and midnight. He told me that as he was going home he saw your brother go into the oast house. Is that right?"

Fred stared at Jimmy as though he had been accused of some heinous crime. "Saw my brother Tom go into the oast house," he repeated slowly. "Well, and what harm would there be in that? Tom often comes along here and gives me a hand after he's finished measuring."

Jimmy smiled. He knew very well the countryman's distrust of the police and their questioning. "No harm at all," he replied. "You don't quite see my point. I'm trying to find out what time Lavis went home that night. If your brother did come to the oast house perhaps you or he could tell me what time it was. That would give me some idea when Lavis went home."

Fred's countenance brightened at once. "Oh, I see your meaning now," he exclaimed. "Let me see. Tom and I had been to the Chequers that evening. We weren't there long, for I can't get away from the oast house for more than a few minutes. We came out at closing time and Tom and I walked down along the path."

"Just a minute," said Jimmy. "Do you remember what happened as you came out of the Chequers? There was a bit of a row going on outside, wasn't there?"

Fred glanced at Jimmy suspiciously. "Nothing out of the ordinary," he replied. "One or two of the Londoners had a drop too much, that's all. One of them gave Tom some lip and he turned round and told him to mind his manners."

"Was Lavis mixed up in this?"

"Oh, yes, he was there all right. He was as drunk as a lord and I dare say he might have turned nasty. But he went off on his bicycle as soon as Mr. Raymond hollered out."

"I see. I only wanted to check Lavis's stories. You went back to the oast house, you say. What became of your brother?"

Another suspicious glance from Fred. Evidently he did not approve of Jimmy's passion for detail.

"What business has the police poking into people's affairs like this?" he replied shortly. "Went home for a bite of supper, most like." And then, grudgingly, as though he doubted the wisdom of volunteering any information at all, he added, "He told me he'd come and give me a hand with the fires later."

"And did he?" Jimmy asked. "That's what I'm trying to get hold of."

"If Tom says he'll do a thing he does it. He came along all right."

"Have you any idea what time he arrived?"

Fred considered this question for a moment or two. "I wouldn't like to say within a few minutes either way," he replied. "But it was after eleven, because I looked at my watch then, and that was before Tom came along. Maybe it was a quarter after, or perhaps twenty minutes."

Jimmy nodded. "Thanks, that's all I wanted to know," he said. "That gives me a very valuable check upon Lavis's statement." He held out his cigarette case. "Have one of these."

"Thank you kindly, sir," said Fred. "I've left my fags up home and I don't want to leave the oast yet awhile. There's a batch of hops nigh on ready to draw and I don't want to take my eyes off them too long."

This seemed to give Jimmy his opportunity. "I'd very much like to look inside the oast and see how you manage things."

"Look inside the oast?" exclaimed Fred, as though the expression of such a desire on the part of an officer from Scotland Yard was beyond his comprehension. "Why, whatever would you be wanting to see there?"

"Well, you see, I've never seen hops dried and I'd like to know how it was done."

This explanation seemed to remove Fred's scruples. "There's nothing to it," he replied. "You've got to know how to keep your fires, right, of course, and just when to draw the hops. Experience would tell you more than anything else. If you like to come along I'll show you."

He led the way up a short flight of steps outside the nearest oast house and opened a small iron door. The scent of drying hops was so strong that Jimmy caught his breath. In front of him was what appeared to be a circular floor many feet across. The air above it was warm and pungent.

"Them's the hops drying," said Fred at his elbow. "We put them in just as they come from the gardens and lay them on a horse-hair cloth. You have to lay them in just the right thickness or they won't dry properly. And you've got to spread them over properly, of course."

"How long do they take to dry?" Jimmy asked.

"It all depends on the state they're in. In nice dry weather like this they don't take so long. But if it's been raining and they come in all wet it's often the very devil of a job to get them to dry properly. Even then sometimes they won't make a good sample however much trouble we take with them. That lot you see there will be ready within the next half-hour or so."

"How do you know when they're ready?" Jimmy asked.

"By the smell of them, mostly. And then you can pick up a few and see what they feel like. You soon get to know once you're used to the job. Let's shut this door now. It doesn't do to keep it open too long."

Fred shut the door and they descended the steps. "You've got a fire of some kind below here, I suppose," said Jimmy when they reached the bottom.

"That's right. We start it with charcoal, then coal, and throw brimstone on it from time to time. Come winter Mr. Velley will get in wood from the coppices. Then later on one of those charcoal burner chaps will come round and burn it. Wonderful how they manage to do it without burning the wood all away. You couldn't tell it was any different when they've finished with it, except that it's much lighter and black all through. That's how we get charcoal. The brimstone and coal comes from the merchants, of course."

"You keep the fire going all the time?" Jimmy asked.

"It's alight from the time we start drying until we've finished. You'd like to see it, maybe? Well, there you are." Fred threw open the furnace door and Jimmy looked in.

He saw a red mass of glowing fuel with faint blue flames dancing upon the surface of it. High above the bars was a wooden framework supporting the hair-cloth upon which the hops rested.

"It doesn't do to leave the fire to itself too long," said Fred. "You've got to watch the draught with every shift of the wind and weather. You mustn't let the fire get too hot or you'll burn the hops and spoil the whole batch, and you mustn't let it get too low or the hops won't dry. It's a matter of watching the draught, keeping the fire fed, and seeing that you put on just enough brimstone."

As Fred closed the furnace door they heard approaching footsteps. Fred turned round. "Hallo, Tom," he said. "I thought you'd be along. This batch will be ready for drawing in a few minutes now."

Tom Adcorn appeared to recognise Jimmy, for he touched his cap awkwardly. "Good-afternoon, sir," he said. "My brother showing you round the oast?"

"He's been satisfying my curiosity," Jimmy replied. "By the way, now you're here you may be able to tell me something. You remember the night of the burglary at Paddock Croft?"

Tom started guiltily and looked at his brother. Once more Jimmy felt that these men regarded questions by the police as a veiled accusation. "Saturday night of last week," he continued hastily, "you came along to the oast house sometime before midnight to help your brother, didn't you?"

It was Fred who replied. "That's right, Tom, you did. Don't you remember?" he said. "Sometime after eleven it was we went round the fires. This gentleman here has been talking to Lavis what's up at the station. Lavis told him that he saw you come along."

"So I did," said Tom slowly. "I often come along before I go to bed and see how Fred's getting on."

"That's all right, then," said Jimmy cheerfully. "Lavis wasn't lying when he said he saw you. I wonder if you happened to see him, by any chance?"

The question seemed to puzzle Tom, who scratched his head in some perplexity. "Lavis now," he replied. "I remember seeing him when Fred and I left the Chequers, and properly sowed up he was, too."

"Yes, but did you see him again when you came here to help your brother?"

"Can't say that I did," replied Tom guardedly. "But then I didn't take any particular notice. I was rather later than I meant to be, and I was in a bit of a hurry."

Fred turned hastily towards the oast house. Perhaps some subtle inflection in the odour warned him that the hops were ready for drawing. "If you'll excuse me, sir, my brother and I must be getting busy," he said. "It won't do to leave that batch much longer. Come along, Tom, and bear a hand."

Jimmy hesitated. Should he remain and watch the hops being drawn? There seemed no particular point in doing so since he had obtained the information he required. Besides, tea-time was approaching and he had promised the Sergeant to be back in time for that meal. Also Lavis might have made up his mind to further revelations.

These considerations decided him. He mounted his bicycle and rode off. But he was uncomfortably aware that his investigations had not revealed to him the inner meaning of Dr. Priestley's message.

CHAPTER XVI

HIS failure to read the riddle preyed upon Jimmy's mind. He knew Dr. Priestley well enough by now to be certain that he would not have sent him such a message without some very good purpose. He had offered a hint, and Jimmy had failed to understand it. There was only one thing to do. He must confess his failure and ask for further enlightenment.

So, soon after nine o'clock that evening, when he knew that Dr. Priestley would have finished his dinner, he rang up. Harold answered the phone. "Hallo, is that you. Jimmy?" he asked. "What's your trouble?"

"My trouble is that I've investigated the mysteries of hop drying and I don't in the least see what the Professor was driving at. I'd like you to tell him so, if you don't mind. And, if you could get him to expand a little, I'd be grateful."

"All right, hold on," said Harold. "He's in a pretty good mood to-night. I'll tell him and see what he says."

Jimmy held on, half expecting some reprimand for his obtuseness. Then, after a couple of minutes or so, he heard Harold's voice again. "I rather fancy that the old man thinks you've been pretty dense. He hasn't told me what he meant even now, so I can't enlighten you. But he wants me to drive him down to Hobb's Corner again to-morrow morning. If you've nothing better to do, you're to meet us there at half-past eleven."

"I'll be there, whatever else I have to do," replied Jimmy eagerly. "So long till then."

It was now time, Jimmy thought, to pay a second visit to Lavis. He found him disconsolate, as well he might be. His one anxiety was how far any information he might give would mitigate his sentence. He was by now thoroughly frightened, and it was perfectly obvious to Jimmy that he would cheerfully sacrifice all his friends and acquaintances if thereby he could secure lenient treatment for himself. He gave Jimmy a complete list of the various people who were associated with him in the illicit spirit trade. And in the end he confessed to having fired Mr. Pershore's bungalow. He had long meditated doing him some evil turn and the conversation he had overheard between some of his associates had given him the idea. In his anxiety to appear contrite he offered to answer any questions Jimmy cared to ask. But in the face of the most skilful cross-questioning, he persisted in his statement that he had not seen Elver since the latter's arrest ten years before.

Directly after breakfast the next morning Jimmy started for Hobb's Corner. The weather was still beautifully fine and he found the business of hop-picking in full swing. A generous area of hops had been taken down and the pickers, grouped about their bins, were busily at work upon these. Jimmy caught sight of Tom Adcorn steadily measuring the hops from the bins to the pokes, regardless of the showers of chaff poured upon him. His brother Fred no doubt was working at the oast house. Their mother, Mrs. Adcorn, was fluttering round the bungalow, the roof and windows of which were by Mr. Pershore's orders being temporarily repaired with boards and sacking.

Jimmy walked through the gardens until he found the group of which Kate was a member. She gave him a scared glance as he beckoned her aside.

"Chris? He hasn't turned up, has he?" she whispered.

Jimmy shook his head. "I've had no word of him," he replied. "I was going to ask you if you'd heard anything of him during the week-end."

"No, though I've been dreading it all the time. I haven't seen or heard anything of him. He must have got away from here and I hope he'll never come back."

At this moment Tom Adcorn came with his basket to empty the bin at which Kate had been working. It seemed to Jimmy that Tom frowned when he saw him. There was something defiant, almost malevolent, in his glance. Jimmy remembered what Mr. Velley had said about him and Kate. The man was obviously jealous of this apparent intimacy between Kate and the officer from Scotland Yard. Clearly he regarded Kate as his particular property.

Jimmy was seized with a sudden curiosity. Kate was still standing beside him searching his face anxiously. "Does anybody down here know that you're married?" he asked.

"Nobody knows it," she replied earnestly. "Nobody but you and Chris, and he won't say anything about it until it suits him."

Jimmy strolled away and Kate returned to her work. He was intrigued by the triangular situation between Elver, Kate and Tom Adcorn. Tom's sentiments could be perceived at a glance. Kate was by no means so transparent. She might or might not reciprocate Tom's affection. But even if she did, she couldn't marry him. Elver's mysterious disappearance did not release her. Even his death, without the production of some identifiable part of his body, would not help her. After all, Mr. Velley need have no fear that she would settle down in Matling as Tom Adcorn's wife. It was rather hard on Tom, though. Jimmy wondered what explanation Kate would give for the refusal of the offer which he must eventually make.

But as the time of his appointment approached, Jimmy forgot all about Kate and Tom. Dr. Priestley's visit could only mean that he had some revelation to unfold. What that revelation might be Jimmy could not guess, but surely it must concern Elver. Jimmy had the greatest respect for Dr. Priestley's powers, but how he, sitting in his study in London, could have perceived something that careful examination on the spot had failed to reveal, Jimmy could not imagine.

It was exactly half-past eleven when he saw a car advancing towards him. He hurried to the crossroads to meet it, expecting to greet Dr. Priestley and Harold, but to his amazement he found that the car contained a third occupant, no less a person than Superintendent Hanslet. Jimmy glanced at him inquiringly, but the Superintendent merely shook his head. They had no time to exchange even a word, for Dr. Priestley beckoned to Jimmy mysteriously.

"I have very little time to waste, Inspector," he said. "Get into the car. There is room on the seat beside Harold."

The car was a large saloon. Harold had been driving, and Dr. Priestley and Hanslet were seated in the back. Jimmy obeyed Dr. Priestley's instructions, expecting that Harold would be bidden to drive on elsewhere, perhaps to Park Gate. But, instead of this, Dr. Priestley's next words were addressed to him.

"We can talk conveniently in the car without being overheard," he said. "Yesterday afternoon you adopted my suggestion that you should investigate the methods of hop drying?"

"Yes, I did, sir," Jimmy replied. "I paid a visit to these very oast houses, and Fred Adcorn, the drier, showed me round."

"Indeed! Have there been any further developments in the matter of Elver's disappearance?"

"Well, not exactly, sir. We arrested Lavis yesterday and he is appearing before the magistrate this morning."

Hanslet grunted. "Arrested Lavis, did you?" he said. "What's the charge?"

"Dealing in illicit liquor at the moment. But we shall prefer a charge of arson later. He confessed to me that he fired Mr. Pershore's bungalow in revenge for his dismissal, Sergeant Wragge is attending the court and will ask for a remand in custody."

Dr. Priestley made an impatient movement. "All this is beside the point," he said testily. "You appear to have questioned Lavis since his arrest? Did he throw any light upon the disappearance of Elver?"

"He sticks to his declaration that he has never seen him since his arrest nine years ago, sir."

"He may possibly be telling the truth. You say that yesterday afternoon you interviewed Fred Adcorn, the drier?"

"Yes, I made the excuse of a small point in Lavis's statement to me."

"Will you repeat as exactly as possible your conversation with Fred Adcorn?"

Jimmy complied with this demand, and Dr. Priestley listened attentively. "This is even more interesting than I had hoped," he said when Jimmy had finished. "Now will you explain to me the process of hop drying as you have observed it?"

Jimmy described his visit to the oast house and Dr. Priestley nodded approvingly. "Most instructive," he remarked. "There is, however, one point which is not quite clear to me. I understand that the fires of the oast houses are not allowed to go out during the whole period of hop-picking. Is only one drier responsible for this during the period, or are there two or more working in relief?"

"I'm afraid it didn't occur to me to ask, sir," Jimmy replied. "Fred Adcorn didn't mention any other drier."

"It is nevertheless a point of some considerable interest," said Dr. Priestley. "I should be glad if you could procure the information without delay."

Jimmy, accustomed to these strange whims of Dr. Priestley, made no objection. "I saw Mr. Velley going across to the hop gardens just now, sir," he replied. "It wouldn't take me more than a few minutes to find him and ask him."

"I should prefer to hear his statement at first hand," said Dr. Priestley. "Perhaps you will find Mr. Velley and ask him to be good enough to join us here."

Jimmy got out of the car and went off in the direction of the hop gardens. He had no difficulty in finding Mr. Velley, who was in conversation with Tom Adcorn.

"I'm sorry to trouble you, Mr. Velley," he said. "My Superintendent has come down from London in connection with this Paddock Croft business and he's brought an expert with him. They want to ask you a few questions. I wonder if you'd mind very much coming across and talking to them?"

"I'll come like a shot," replied Mr. Velley readily. He and Jimmy walked back to the crossroads, where they found that Dr. Priestley and Hanslet had descended from the car and were apparently engaged in earnest consultation. They separated as Jimmy and Mr. Velley approached and Hanslet came forward. Having been introduced to Mr. Velley he put the question which Dr. Priestley had suggested.

"Some farmers employ a relief drier and others don't," Mr. Velley replied. "I'm one of those who don't. I've suggested it to Fred Adcorn before now, but he always says he'd rather I didn't. Fred's a thoroughly trustworthy chap, and I know that so long as he's about the hops will be all right."

"But surely a man can't be on duty for three weeks without getting some rest?"

"It's like this, you see. He's not actually working all the time. He can always manage to slip home for a meal or over to the Chequers for a drink. And as for sleeping he rigs up a camp bed in the lodge against the oast. It's nice and warm there."

"Is the oast house left unattended whilst he's having his meals?"

"Never. Fred always arranged for somebody to keep an eye on the place while he's away, which he never is for more than half an hour at a time. Usually it's his brother Tom, but if he's otherwise engaged one of the other men on the farm keep an eye on the place. You can't leave hops to dry themselves, you know. It's rather a delicate process."

Dr. Priestley, who had been standing within earshot, at this point approached. "Do I understand that it would be impossible for any stranger to enter the oast house without the drier's knowledge?" he asked.

Mr. Velley glanced at this new questioner. "I think I've seen you before," he said. "You were down here looking over the bungalow the other morning, weren't you? Yes, you can take it as a fact that no stranger could get into the oast house. Fred's very jealous of his hops. Doesn't like strangers poking round them. But you know, I haven't the least idea what all this is about."

"It will I fear become plain enough to you in due course," Dr. Priestley replied. "I wonder if we might ask a favour of you, Mr. Velley? Would you very kindly conduct us over the oast house yourself?"

Mr. Velley laughed. "You police folk are pretty mysterious," he replied. "All right, I'll take you round. But there isn't very much to see, really."

He led the way to the oast house. On hearing their footsteps, Fred Adcorn, who had been tending his fire, looked up. He touched his cap to his employer, then shot a glance full of suspicion in Jimmy's direction.

"I'm just going to show these gentlemen round, Fred," said Mr. Velley briskly. "You needn't take any notice of us. Just get on with your job."

The drier growled something in reply. He did not appear to relish this unceremonious invasion of his province. Mr. Velley first showed his visitors the bed of hops, then flung open the furnace doors so that they might inspect the fire. The glowing mass of fuel with the blue flames dancing about it seemed to fascinate Dr. Priestley. He gazed at it until his eyes watered and then he turned to Mr. Velley.

"You do not employ a pyrometer, I suppose?" he asked.

"I beg your pardon?" replied Mr, Velley in a puzzled tone. "A what?"

"Pyrometer -- an instrument for determining the heat of the fire."

"Oh, a sort of thermometer, I suppose. No, we aren't quite so scientific as that, though some of the farmers who employ the hot air method are always buying new gadgets. We depend upon the drier's judgment and experience. We may be old-fashioned, but we turn out as good or better hops than the newfangled folks."

"Scientific methods are more infallible than human judgment," said Dr. Priestley oracularly. "May I ask when the batch of hops you have just shown us will be ready for drawing?"

"Pretty soon now, by the smell and look of them," Mr. Velley replied. "Fred will tell us." He raised his voice. "Fred!" But there was no reply. "Confound the fellow, where's he got to?" Mr. Velley exclaimed. "We'll soon find him, he can't be far off. These chaps are funny, sometimes. Fred takes a pride in his oast houses, he didn't like me showing you round, I expect. I can almost hear what he'll be saying in the Chequers this evening. 'If the boss like to show blokes round my oast houses he can take on the drying himself, that's all.'"

"Perhaps he has gone to speak to his brother," said Dr. Priestley quietly. "Would you be good enough to go and see, Inspector?"

Jimmy hurried off. He had no sooner entered the hop gardens when he saw the two Adcorn brothers standing apart from the pickers and apparently engaged in earnest conversation. It seemed to him that Fred was urging something upon Tom, which the latter was loth to accede. More than once he shook his head stubbornly and at last, as though his mind were made up, he parted from his brother and walked slowly back towards the pickers.

Jimmy went back to the oast house where he found a violent conversation going on between Mr. Velley and Hanslet. He caught Dr. Priestley's inquiring glance and replied to it.

"You were quite right, sir. He's on his way back now." Then he turned his attention to the other two.

The normally good-tempered Mr. Velley was clearly annoyed. "But I never heard of such a thing, Superintendent," he was saying, "in the middle of hop-picking like this, with the pokes coming in every moment almost? What am I to do until they're started again? Stack the pokes in the lodge for the hops to sweat and spoil? Why, the damage it could do might run into hundreds of pounds."

Hanslet shrugged his shoulders. "Well, I've asked you, and I can't do any more," he replied. Then he turned to Dr. Priestley. "You hear what Mr. Velley says about it, Professor?"

"I fully sympathise with Mr. Velley's objection," said Dr. Priestley. "But I believe that if he were to realise that this may be a matter of life and death he would accede to your request."

Mr. Velley turned upon him angrily. "A matter of life and death!" he exclaimed. "Why can't people talk plainly instead of in riddles? What's any man's life or death got to do with my raking out my fires, as the Superintendent wants me to do?"

"I should not like Fred Adcorn to overhear my answer to that question," Dr. Priestley replied gravely. "He will be back here any moment now. Suppose we return to the car, where we can discuss the matter without being overheard."

175

Mr. Velley accompanied them rather sulkily. He was obviously very much upset by the suggestion which had been made to him. "Now then, perhaps you'll give me an explanation of all this," he said as soon as they were out of earshot of the oast house.

"I will endeavour to do so, though I fear the explanation may come as a shock to you," Dr. Priestley replied. "There is reason to believe that a murder had been committed in this neighbourhood and that the Adcorn brothers are implicated in the crime."

Mr. Velley's amazement was so complete that for a moment or two he could find no words in which to express it. "That's sheer damned nonsense!" he exclaimed at last. "I've known the Adcorns since they were little chaps, and I'd as soon suspect them of murder as I would myself. You clever folks from London are on the wrong track, let me tell you that."

"There is only one way in which the innocence of the Adcorns can be proved," said Dr. Priestley quietly. "That is to draw the fires in your oast house."

"Then by gad, I'll do it!" shouted Mr. Velley impulsively. "I'll prove you're wrong whatever it may cost me." He turned his back and started rapidly towards the oast house. "Fred!" he shouted as he went. "Fred! Are you there? I want you."

Fred appeared, shovel in hand. As soon as he appeared, Mr. Velley began shouting instructions. "Get that batch of hops out as soon as you can, Fred. See that you don't put any more in. We're going to rake the fires out."

The shovel fell from Fred's hand with a prodigious clatter. He stood rigid, as if turned into stone, staring at his employer.

"Rake the fires out?" he stammered. "Why --"

"Yes, rake the fires out," replied Mr. Velley bitterly. "The world's been turned upside down this morning, though we didn't notice it, living buried here in the country as we do. Look sharp and see to it, and don't be too long about it. We don't want to waste more time than we can help over this tomfoolery. Better run and get a couple of chaps to bear you a hand."

At last Fred seemed to understand what was required of him. He turned away, leaving the shovel where it was. And then he shambled off, not towards the barn but in the direction of the hop fields.

"Thinks I've gone off my head," was Mr. Velley's comment. "Well, perhaps I have, though I never heard before that madness was catching. I suppose you gentlemen will have the patience to wait while this batch of hops is drawn?"

Dr. Priestley nodded, and they waited in awkward silence beside the oast house. It was five or ten minutes before a couple of farm hands arrived and looked inquiringly at their employer.

"Where's Fred?" asked Mr. Velley impatiently.

"Don't know, sir," replied one of them. "Came up to us just now and said you wanted a couple of hands down here. Then he went off."

"Damn the man!" exclaimed Mr. Velley impatiently. "Everybody seems to be going potty this morning. Never mind, you two will do. I want this lot of hops drawn. They'll be ready by now. Get to it now, and look lively."

Under the interested eyes of Dr. Priestley and his companions, the hops were drawn and laid upon the platform to cool. Mr. Velley watched the process with an experienced eye. "They'll do," he said shortly. "Now then, turn to and rake out the fire."

The two men looked up and stared at him stupidly. "Rake out the fire, sir?" exclaimed one of them. "Why?"

"Oh, for heaven's sake don't argue with me," Mr. Velley replied. "I've had enough to try my patience this morning without that. You heard what I said, get on with it."

The man who had spoken shook his head forebodingly. The boss must have been drinking, though he'd never known such a thing before. Well, they were his hops and his fires. He could give what orders he liked, but this was clean against reason. He opened the furnace door with a clang and then picked up a long rake. "Come on, Dick," he said. "We'll draw the fire out on to the floor here."

They set to work raking out the charcoal embers on to the floor in front of the furnace. A suffocating smell of brimstone rewarded their efforts, but Dr. Priestley did not flinch. He found for himself a smaller rake and with this began to turn over the embers as they came from the furnace. Mr. Velley watched him scornfully but made no comment.

The two men continued their work until the furnace was nearly empty, but Dr. Priestley made no sign. And then as one of them drew out his rake something fell with a curious tinkling sound upon the brick floor. Dr. Priestley bent down eagerly and drew it towards him. It appeared to be a ring of metal, blackened by the heat but otherwise undamaged. Dr. Priestley picked it up on the prongs of his fork.

"Is there any water handy?" he asked.

"You'll find a butt outside the oast," replied Mr. Velley surlily.

Dr. Priestley carried the ring of metal to the butt and immersed it beneath the surface of the water. There was a puff of steam and a loud hissing. He held the metal under the water for a full minute, then let it drain and touched it gingerly. It was now cool. He took it off the rake and handed it to Hanslet, who had followed him. "What's that?" he asked.

Hanslet took it from him and rubbed it in his fingers. "An iron ring by the look of it," he said. "What about it, Professor?"

"It's certainly not iron," Dr. Priestley replied. "An iron ring taken from the fire would certainly show a film of oxide, and this does not. Besides, if you weigh it in your hand you will find that it is far too heavy to be iron."

"Well, what is it then?" Hanslet asked without any great interest.

"Platinum, unless I am very much mistaken," Dr. Priestley replied.

"Platinum!" Hanslet exclaimed. "Why, where the dickens can it have come from?"

"From Paddock Croft, I imagine," said Dr. Priestley. "You will remember that among the jewellery stolen from there was a pair of platinum bangles. But let us return to the fire. It may have other secrets to reveal."

A minute or two after they had re-entered the oast house a second ring similar to the first had made its appearance. Dr. Priestley had just hooked it on to his rake when a shadow fell across the entrance.

Mr. Velley turned swiftly. "Hallo, Fred's turned up at last, has he?" he exclaimed. "No, he hasn't, it's you, Tom. What the devil are you doing here?"

Tom Adcorn made no reply. He came forward like a blind man groping for some invisible object which had eluded him. He came to a sudden stop and seemed to scan the faces before him. Mr. Velley uncomprehending, puzzled, somehow not quite sure of his ground. Jimmy, half comprehending, wondering where his acumen had failed. Hanslet, menacing like a beast of prey ready to pounce but not yet sure of his victim. And Dr. Priestley, detached, wearied of the play of which the end he had long since foreseen.

Tom Adcorn looked from face to face. It seemed to those who watched him that his decision was infinitely delayed. Then suddenly Jimmy saw that he had been chosen. He stepped forward, conscious of the responsibility that rested upon him.

"Well, Tom, what is it?" he asked.

With a sudden gesture Tom stretched his arms before him, as though he anticipated the click of the handcuffs.

"I've come to give myself up," he replied in a clear voice which rang through the low vaults of the oast house.

Jimmy dared not glance round him. He knew without doubt that the other three were watching him intent upon the move which he would make. He laid his hand lightly upon Tom Adcorn's arm. "Tell me!" he said quietly.

"I killed the chap you're looking for," Tom replied in a loud voice which held scarcely a tremor.

CHAPTER XVII

THE spectators of this scene received Tom's statement in many different ways. Mr. Velley staggered backwards a pace as though he had been shot. His expression of incredulity was almost ludicrous. Hanslet uttered a brief exclamation, but he gave no other sign of emotion. Dr. Priestley nodded, as though Tom had merely confirmed something which he already knew. It seemed that the subsequent proceedings had no interest for him, for he turned aside and began to rake among the now fast cooling embers.

Jimmy let his hand fall slowly from Tom's shoulder. "Do you mean that?" he asked. And then, automatically aware of Hanslet's eye upon him, he added the traditional formula. "Do you wish to make a statement? If so, I must warn you in advance that anything you say may be used subsequently in evidence."

Tom's face strayed from Jimmy to the horrified face of Mr. Velley. "I'd like to tell you how it happened," he replied.

Jimmy glanced at Hanslet, who nodded approvingly. In the Superintendent's eyes the more witnesses there were to hear the statement the better. "All right then, Adcorn, tell us all about it," said Jimmy quietly.

"It's hard to know where to begin," said Adcorn painfully. "There's others concerned whose names I wouldn't like to bring in."

"That's all right, Adcorn," said Jimmy. "We know all about Kate Rivers."

Tom started as though Jimmy had struck him. "You know?" he growled angrily. "And who told you, I'd like to know?"

"She told me herself," Jimmy replied. "But I'm sure that she doesn't know that you share her secret."

Tom looked vastly relieved. "Oh, if she told you herself, that's all right," he said. "But she doesn't know that I overheard what that chap said to her that afternoon. And I wouldn't never have told her. It was her business and no one else's. I'm fond of that girl and I thought once -- but never mind, that's all over now."

In spite of Tom's inarticulateness his audience could feel the depth of his emotion. He continued brokenly, "I would have asked her long before this. But somehow I couldn't bring myself to it. And something told me I had better wait until I didn't know what. And I think she guessed, for whenever I said anything to her out of the ordinary she managed to get talking about something else. It seemed somehow that she knew what was at the back of my mind and didn't want to give me the chance of saying it.

"Well, it's no use talking like that. It was on the Saturday afternoon of last week that I made up my mind to speak to her. I knew I'd find her alone at the hut, for I met Molly Sheares and she told me Kate had stopped behind to tidy up. So I went along, knowing that there wouldn't be many folk about. And when I got there I saw a stranger go across to her hut and speak to her.

"I thought this a bit queer, for I'd never known Kate to have men folk from London come to visit her before. This chap was a Londoner, I knew that at once. He had on a town suit and one of them silly paper caps on his head. I thought he might be wanting one of the other pickers and seeing Kate had stopped to ask her after them. But just then he stepped into the hut familiar like, and I knew he must be a friend of Kate's.

"I got a sort of shock, for she hadn't told me anything about having a friend. And then something told me that things weren't altogether as they should be, I had a sort of feeling that Kate might want help, though I didn't know how or why. So I did a thing I've never done before. I went round to the back of the hut and listened. They're only a plank thick at the back, and you can overhear every word that's spoken."

"You overheard the entire conversation between those two?" Jimmy asked.

"No, I didn't do that. They had started talking before I got round to the back of the hut. But I heard enough to put an end to what I'd been hoping for. I learnt that Kate was married and that this man was her husband. I didn't wait to hear any more. I just cleared off by myself."

"You overheard no mention of Lavis?" Jimmy asked.

"Lavis!" exclaimed Tom suspiciously. "No. What had Lavis to do with it?"

"Nothing apparently. Go on. You say you went off by yourself. Where did you go to?"

"I couldn't rightly say. I just walked away along the first road that came. I didn't want to meet any one I knew in case they spoke to me. If any one had spoken to me just then I won't say what I mightn't have done. I felt I sort of couldn't understand what it all meant and I wanted to think it over. And it wasn't until it was getting dark that I remembered that I had promised Fred to come and give him a hand with his fires round about nine o'clock.

"I'd sort of pulled myself together by then. I saw that it wasn't any good saying anything to anybody. I'd just have to put up with it and make-believe that nothing had happened. I came along here and helped Fred with his fires. He may have noticed that something had upset me but he didn't say anything about it. And when we'd finished Fred said there was just time to go along to the Chequers for a quick one. I didn't much care where I went, the Chequers seemed as good a place as any other. Well, we went along and had a drink and at ten o'clock we came out. There, standing outside the gas-lamp, I saw Kate's husband."

"Did you?" said Jimmy quickly. "You're quite sure of that?"

"I wasn't likely to be mistaken. I didn't know his name except that I'd heard Kate call him Chris. But I'd had a good look at him while he was standing outside the hut that afternoon. Besides, he'd still got the same paper cap on his head. He was out there standing all by himself, just as if he were expecting some one. As he saw Fred and me come out he came up to us. 'Have either of you chaps seen Lavis about?' he said, sort of insolent like.

"It was the same voice I'd heard that afternoon mocking Kate, and all at once I came over black angry. I answered him, but I can't tell you now what I said to him. I know I told him that if I found him hanging about the place again I'd punch his head for him. And if Fred hadn't taken me by the arm and pretty near dragged me away I'd have done it then."

"Did Lavis come up while this was going on?" Jimmy asked.

"Lavis? Likely he might have done. He was in the other room at the Chequers when Fred and I went in, I know that. But I wasn't in a state to see anybody but the man whom Kate had called Chris. It wasn't that I'd had too much to drink, Fred'll tell you that. I had no more than my usual pint. But the sight of that chap had fair driven me into a fury. Wait a minute, though. Now you speak of it, I do remember seeing Lavis come out and get on his bicycle. But Mr. Raymond had put the light out by then and you couldn't recognise anybody for certain."

"All right," said Jimmy. "It's of no particular importance. Where did you go when you left the Chequers?"

"Why, Fred still had hold of my arm. He sort of dragged me a few yards down the road towards Culverden. I didn't know where he meant to go and I didn't care. He's told me since that he saw that chap go off the other way, and he didn't want me to meet him again. Then, since I didn't say anything to him, he asked me what had come over me. He'd never seen me go off the deep-end like that before. He said that I must have a fever coming on or something and the best thing I could do was to get home and go to bed straight away. I didn't tell him anything, not then. It wasn't my secret to tell. And after a bit we walked back to Hobb's Corner. Fred had to see to his fires. I told him I was going home, but I didn't, not then."

"Where did you go?" Jimmy queried.

"Round to the meadow where the huts are. I had it in my mind that chap was after Kate again to worry the life out of her. But he wasn't there, though there were a few chaps about and I thought I saw Lavis on his bicycle. If it was him he'd got wonderful sober all of a sudden, for he was dead drunk when he left the Chequers. Then, seeing the other chap wasn't there, I began to wander about Hobb's Corner. I knew it was no good going home, for I shouldn't have slept if I had. I mooched round for maybe an hour or so, thinking of Kate and that chap until I went near crazy. And then all at once I saw somebody coming up the road towards me. There was a bit of a moon that night, as you may remember, and it was light enough, except under the trees. I knew the chap at once by the shape of him, though he'd lost that paper cap of his. I dodged into the hedge before he caught sight of me."

"One moment, Adcorn," Jimmy interrupted. "Where were you exactly when this happened?"

"Maybe a hundred yards from Hobb's Corner on the road leading to Park Gate. The chap was coming from Hobb's Corner way and I made sure that he'd been to the hut to see Kate. I was that savage I didn't know what I was doing or what I meant to do. But as he came up to where I was I stepped out of the hedge in front of him.

"Lord he was frightened if ever a man was! He gave a sort of gasp, and then let out at me with something he was carrying in his hand. But I was too quick for him. I ducked, then gave him one under the jaw with the whole of my weight behind it. He went down as if he'd been felled. I waited for a second or two for him to get up and then I bent over him. 'Get up, you swine,' I said. 'Get up and I'll give you such a hammering that you won't dare to show your dirty carcase again within ten miles of here.'

"But he didn't move. And then in the moonlight I could see something dark coming out from under his head. I put my hand down to see what it was and it was warm and wet. I'd seen blood before, plenty of it, but somehow this gave me a nasty turn. But then I saw that there were two or three big stones lying in the grass, left there by the roadmen after they'd mended the road. The chap's head had come down on one of these, and when I felt the back of it the bone sort of gave way under my fingers and I knew he was dead.

"That brought me to my senses quick enough. I saw what I'd done, and I turned suddenly cold all over. I hadn't meant to kill the man, but who'd believe that? I'd threatened him outside the Chequers only an hour or so before. And besides, there was Kate to be thought of. It was bound to come out, since the chap was her husband. Then folk would say I had killed him on purpose to put him out of the way. I stood there wondering what I'd best do, and all the time his blood was running over the ground. It turned me fair sick, I couldn't bear to see it.

"Then I thought of Fred and his fire. If I could only get the chap into the furnace under the oast nobody would ever know. But I couldn't do that without Fred's help.

And what Fred would say when I told him I couldn't guess. Well, I just had to chance it. If Fred wouldn't help me, then it would all have to come out and I should have to stand the racket. So I came along here to this very oast, and there was Fred lying asleep in the lodge. He started up as soon as he heard me come in. 'Who's there?' he called out. And I answered him: 'It's me, Tom, and I've just killed a man way up the road there.'

"Fred had a torch lying beside him. He switched it on and pointed it at me. 'Whatever's amiss with you to-night, Tom?' he said. 'You're going daft, I do believe. Now go home to bed and don't have any more dreams like that.'

"To tell the truth I was beginning to wonder myself if I hadn't been dreaming. 'Well, come and look for yourself,' I said. 'You know a bit about doctoring as you've been through a first-aid course. And if he's not dead then you'll know what to do with him.'

"Fred got up. 'All right, I'll come,' he said. But it was only to humour me. He didn't believe that we'd find anybody. I let him go ahead with the torch, and sure enough he came upon the man lying there just as I'd left him. And there was the blood spreading all about the place where he lay.

"'Hold the torch,' said Fred sharp-like, so that I can see what I'm doing.' He bent over the chap and turned him on his face. Then he began fingering the back of his head. Then he stood up straight and looked at me. 'This will break mother's heart,' he said.

"'There's no need for it to do that,' I said, 'not if you help me to get rid of him.' And then I told him the whole story, the same as I've just told you gentlemen. About Kate and what I'd overheard that afternoon, I mean. Then I told him how I'd met the man unexpected like and what had happened. 'And now,' I said, 'if anybody learns about this I'll be hanged for murder as sure as my name's Tom Adcorn.'

"And then I told him how easy it would be for the two of us to pick him up and carry him to the oast. Fred didn't like it at first. He said that somebody would be bound to find out, and then I should be worse off than I was already. But I told him that nobody ever could find out, for the oast would burn up every trace of him. And at last he said that he'd do it.

"Well, we picked him up and put him right into the heart of the fire, just as he was. We shut the door quick, for we knew it would give us the horrors if we saw him burn. And when we opened it a couple of hours or so later we couldn't see anything of him."

"You didn't happen to look into his pockets, I suppose?" Jimmy asked.

"His pockets!" Tom exclaimed. "We had other things to do than that. I do remember they were all bulgy like as if they were full of things, but we didn't stop to see what it was. We wanted to see the last of him before anybody might happen along. And then I kept on drawing buckets of water from the butt yonder, carrying them to the place and throwing them over the grass by the roadside. I didn't stop until the blood was pretty-nigh washed away, so that no one would notice it.

"For a day or two Fred and I were in mortal terror that somebody would find us out. But as nothing happened we began to think that it was all right. Then you came along here yesterday and said you wanted to look over the oast. Fred was afraid then that you'd guess what we'd done, but I said that no one could guess a thing like that. And then Fred came to me just now and told me that you and these other gentlemen had come to look over the oast again. Said it was all up, and that the best thing that I could do was to clear out while there was still time. But I wouldn't do that. I told him that if the worst came to the worst I'd stop and face it out. Then he came a second time and told me that Mr. Velley had said that the fires were to be drawn. I knew what that meant, right enough. So I just went and emptied Kate's bin. I felt somehow that I had to see her before I was put away. And then I came along here and gave myself up."

"In its way a most instructive case," said Dr. Priestley that evening. "It furnishes an example of an investigation being injured by the very simplicity of the facts. Our young friend Inspector Waghorn did very well up to a point, but in the end his imagination failed him."

Dr. Priestley was sitting in his study at Westbourne Terrace. He had invited Oldland to dine with him and after dinner he had, with the help of Harold's notes, unfolded the whole story to his guest. "The facts were so simple that in nearly every case only one deduction could be drawn from them," he continued. "The first incident was the burglary at Paddock Croft. The burglar most obligingly left his fingerprints upon the silver box. It so happened that a record of those prints was in the possession of Scotland Yard, and they were immediately identified. There was, from the first, no doubt that the crime had been committed by Christopher Elver.

"The second incident was the immediate recognition of Elver's photograph by Lavis and his sister. Having recognised it they were called upon to explain where they had seen the original. It then transpired, firstly, that Elver and Lavis had been acquainted before the former's arrest and, secondly, that Elver had called at Lavis's house on the afternoon preceding the burglary. This second point was of great importance as confirming Elver's presence in the neighbourhood of Matling at the time.

"The third incident was the fire at Mr. Pershore's bungalow and the discovery that it was of malicious origin. Lavis's former association with Elver and his local reputation had already made him an object of suspicion to the police. Circumstances seemed to point to him as an originator of the fire. The approximation of the scenes of these crimes and of the time when they were committed suggested very strongly that there must be some connection between them.

"To me the most puzzling feature of the case was the failure of the police to arrest Elver. It was established almost beyond a doubt that he could not have left the neighbourhood. I could not understand how he could remain concealed there if still alive. I was logically forced to the conclusion that he was dead. Considerations of motive showed me the likelihood that he had been murdered.

"I did not, at the time, deal fully with these motives as I had no wish to confuse the Inspector's mind. Two obvious motives existed, those of his wife and of Lavis, and it was upon these that I concentrated. But other possibilities had suggested themselves to me. Elver had in his possession the proceeds of the burglary. Some unknown person might have discovered this and murdered him for the sake of robbery. From what was already known of Lavis he seemed the most likely criminal. I contrived to impress this upon the Inspector, not because I was certain of the fact but because I thought that Lavis, when taxed with the murder, might confess to other crimes. As it turned out, I was justified. The Inspector, by somewhat irregular methods, I must admit, managed to extract from Lavis a confession that he had originated the fire at the bungalow. I had from the first believed in the possibility that Lavis was the culprit, and a possible connection between the two crimes suggested itself to me. The bungalow might have been set on fire in order to provide the means of destruction for Elver's body. This was a natural deduction from the simple facts that had been ascertained."

"And yet it proved to be false," said Oldland.

"It proved to be false, and yet it led me to the right conclusion. The disposal of the body was the chief obstacle to my theory that Elver was dead. The fire at the bungalow suggested to me burning as the means of disposal. And burnt the body was, as events proved."

Oldland nodded. "All the same, there's one thing I don't quite understand," he said. "You told me just now that when you sent that message to Jimmy on Sunday you were pretty certain in your own mind that the Adcorn brothers had murdered Elver between them. How did you arrive at that conclusion?"

"By a perfectly logical process of reasoning. Elver's body had not been concealed in the fire at the bungalow. Were there any other fires in the neighbourhood of sufficient intensity to consume a human body? I had already visited Hobb's Corner, you must remember, and there seemed to me no indication of any such fire having existed. I reviewed the neighbourhood very carefully in my mind, and then I remembered the oast house that stood at the crossroads.

"Now I had not at that time seen the interior of an oast house. I looked up such information as was available. I discovered that an oast house was used for the purpose of drying hops, and that a large fire was kindled in it for that purpose. A large fire was the very thing I was looking for. Was it possible that Elver's body had been consumed in the oast house?

"I decided that it was possible, with one reservation. The body could not have been placed in the oast house without the connivance of the person who attended to the fires. This person I knew from Harold's notes to be Fred Adcorn.

"You will remember that I had already suggested that the girl known as Kate Rivers had a motive for desiring Elver's death. It had already been suggested by Mr. Velley in the course of his conversation with the Inspector that Tom Adcorn was in love with her. Then had he become aware that Elver was her husband he would share this motive. Now, on the face of it, it was unlikely that Fred Adcorn had been the murderer. So far as was known he had no motive for such an act. But if the body had been taken to the oast house he must have been an accomplice in its destruction."

"People don't as a rule go so far to oblige a stranger," Oldland remarked. "The natural inference was that Tom Adcorn had murdered Elver and that his brother Fred had assisted him to dispose of the body."

"Exactly," Dr. Priestley replied. "Having come to this conclusion I sent my somewhat cryptic message to the Inspector. It was purposely inexplicit, for I wished him to arrive at the same conclusion for himself and to reap the credit for having done so. However, when he telephoned to me yesterday evening I realised that his imagination had failed him. I thereupon determined to visit the spot and investigate my theory for myself. I asked Superintendent Hanslet to accompany me, for I thought that his authority might be useful. But I did not tell him what I had in mind. I had very little hope of discovering recognisable human remains, for a week might have elapsed since the body was thrown into the fire. But it occurred to me that Elver might have had the proceeds of the burglary still in his possession when he was killed. And I remembered that among the articles stolen were a pair of platinum bangles. If these bangles had been thrown into the fire they would almost certainly be recovered intact, for platinum would not be affected by any fire which could be kindled in an oast house."

"A very neat piece of deduction," said Oldland approvingly. "How do you suppose that Elver really employed himself that Saturday afternoon in Matling?"

That we shall never know with any certainty. But I think we can reconstruct his movements from the various statements which have been made. Undoubtedly he went to Matling to visit his wife. He had neglected her since his release from prison, for he had no wish to renew their association. But under the conditions which he then found himself he decided to appeal to her for support.

"He did so, and in the course of conversation with her he discovered for the first time that Lavis resided in the neighbourhood. No doubt he realised that Lavis was a far more promising source of revenue than his wife. He went to see him, found him away from home, but learnt that he would be at the Chequers that evening. And, during the hours of daylight, he noticed Paddock Croft and the possibilities of entering the house unobserved. At some time after six o'clock he went to the

Chequers to find Lavis. But owing to the dispositions made by Mr. Raymond during hop-picking time he was unable to obtain access to the room in which Lavis was sitting. He was forced to remain outside the house and wait for Lavis to leave it.

"At ten o'clock Tom Adcorn emerged and he immediately fell foul of him. In the course of their dispute Lavis came out, mounted his bicycle and rode away. Elver had not seen him for nine years and in the darkness failed to recognise him. But he had another string to his bow, for he almost certainly took the path towards Hobb's Corner and reconnoitred Paddock Croft. Finding conditions favourable to his attempt, he entered the house and took the jewellery. He had already decided what he should do with it. His old accomplice, Lavis, was an expert in the disposal of such things. He would take the jewellery to him, sure that Lavis would not betray him if he threatened to reveal their former association.

"Undoubtedly he was on his way to Lavis's house when Tom Adcorn saw him. Accosted thus suddenly, with the stolen goods in his possession, Elver lost his head. I think it extremely improbable that he recognised Adcorn. He struck out blindly and Adcorn retaliated with the fatal blow. Once again the facts are capable of a very simple explanation."

"Yes, when you know what that explanation is," Oldland remarked. "But if it hadn't been for you, Priestley, the police would have gone on looking for Christopher Elver till the end of time."

The arrest of the Adcorn brothers made a tremendous sensation in Matling. Even the all-absorbing matter of hop-picking was forced into second place. Tom repeated his statement before the magistrate and Fred confirmed such parts of it as concerned him almost word for word. Nobody in the neighbourhood doubted for a moment that they were telling the strict truth.

Examination of the ashes in the oast house revealed no human remains whatever. The most that the experts could say was that there were indications of bone ash, but the platinum bangles remained and also fragments of metal identified as gold. No inquest could be held and, and as was pointed out at the time, Adcorn could not very well be tried for murder on his own confession alone and in the absence of any indication of his victim.

The judge obviously believed the story told by the brothers and the jury brought in a verdict in accordance with his summing up. The Adcorns received short sentences, more on account of their having destroyed the body than for the death of Elver, which, if their story was accepted, had been purely accidental.

Lavis was not so leniently dealt with. He got seven years and local opinion was unanimous in declaring that it served him right.

Mr. Raymond is still the landlord of the Chequers, though he swears that he won't stay there for another hop-picking -- no, not if you were to offer him a thousand pounds.

After the trial Kate Rivers returned to London, but before she went she confided in Jimmy that she had made up her mind. If on his release Tom Adcorn asked her to marry him she would accept, whatever people might say.

It is to be hoped that Mr. Velley's gloomy prognostications will not be fulfilled.

THE END

CPSIA information can be obtained
at www.ICGtesting.com
Printed in the USA
BVHW031301030919
557447BV00001B/43/P